Shirts and Skins

A remarkable debut novel from Jeffrey Luscombe—a compelling series of linked stories of a young man's coming-out, coming-of-age, and coming-to-terms with his family and fate.

Josh Moore lives with his family on the 'wrong side' of Hamilton, a gritty industrial city in southwestern Ontario. As a young boy, Josh plots an escape for a better life far from the steel mills that lined the bay. But fate has other plans and Josh discovers his adult life in Toronto is just as fraught with as many insecurities and missteps as his youth, and he soon learns that no matter how far away he might run, he will never be able to leave his hometown behind.

"*Shirts and Skins* is an assured and compassionate novel. Jeffrey Luscombe understands the power of what isn't said and has created a work that sizzles with repressed sexuality and family tension. The characters are utterly believable. A satisfying and compelling work."
—Lauren B. Davis, author of *Our Daily Bread*, *The Radiant City*, and *The Stubborn Season*

"Tightly written and keenly observed, *Shirts and Skins* is an impressive debut from a writer we're sure to hear more from."
—Nino Ricci, author of *Lives of the Saints*, *Testament*, and *The Origin of Species*

"*Shirts and Skins* is a novel that will speak to anyone who has ever felt the inextricable bonds of the past, or felt the long shadow of family and home places as they strive towards the light of wholeness of identity and self-ownership. A first novel deeply felt and skillfully told, by a writer with insight, compassion, and talent to burn."
—Michael Rowe, author of *Enter, Night* and *Other Men's Sons*

Jeffrey Luscombe was born in Hamilton, Ontario Canada. He holds a BA and MA in English from the University of Toronto and attended The Humber College School for Writers. He lives in Toronto with his husband Sean. *Shirts and Skins* is his first novel.

For Sean

Shirts and Skins

a novel

Jeffrey Luscombe

Chelsea Station Editions

New York

Shirts and Skins by Jeffrey Luscombe
copyright © 2012 by Jeffrey Luscombe

Book design by Peachboy Distillery & Design
Cover art by Seth Ruggles Hiler
Author photo by John Burridge Photography

Published by Chelsea Station Editions
362 West 36th Street, Suite 2R
New York, NY 10018
www.chelseastationeditions.com
info@chelseastationeditions.com

ISBN: 978-1-937627-00-3
Library of Congress Control Number: 2012935635
First U.S. edition, 2012

Portions of this work were originally published, some in different versions, in the following: "Just a Taste" first appeared in *filling Station Magazine*. "A Mere Matter of Marching" first appeared in *Chelsea Station*.

This book was written with the support of the City of Toronto through the Toronto Arts Council.

C

Little Pictures

"The doctor said the baby was dripping with syphilis," Josh's mother said. "And it died before it was six-months old."

"Oh yeah?" his Aunt Doris replied vaguely. She gripped the steering wheel with both hands, her eyes darting between the road in front of her and the rearview mirror.

Behind them, alone in the middle of the long vinyl bench-seat, six year old Josh sat quietly trying to put together the story his mother was telling. It was about Grandma Moore, his father's mother, who once had a baby girl who got sick and died. That was way before I was born, Josh thought. It was way before Dad was born too.

Most of the words Josh's mother used were familiar to him, but some he had never heard before. These strange long words left big white holes in the story. To fill in these gaps, Josh looked for clues in the way his mother spoke. She had spat out the word "syphilis" like a fly that had found its way into her first sip of morning tea and Josh understood that syphilis was something bad, something you did not want to get on you. Maybe, Josh thought, it's like the bleach beside the washing machine—with the creepy boney white hand on the label.

Aunt Doris stopped her car at a yellow light, bouncing Josh and his mother in their seats.

"Jesus, Doris!" Josh's mother said. "Be careful."

Aunt Doris looked left and squinted. Her cigarette shook slightly between her bright red lips as she waited to turn. Aunt Doris always waited for a really big space in traffic before she'd turn right on a red light.

Josh studied his aunt's profile from the back seat. Aunt Doris looked a lot like his mother. They both had the same oval face with high cheekbones, the same long black shiny hair and the same smooth brown skin. But they were different too.

Today his aunt wore a yellow top and a red miniskirt that matched her lipstick. She had a bright lavender satin scarf tied around her hair and below, huge gold hoop earrings hung down to her shoulders. Sitting beside her in the passenger seat, Josh's mother, already dressed for work, wore black slacks and a white cotton blouse. Josh thought his Aunt Doris looked like his Mom—all colored in.

"Ted's mother didn't even know she had syphilis until the baby was born," Josh's mother continued.

Aunt Doris sighed.

"And after the baby died she had a nervous breakdown. And a year later when she gave birth to Ted's older brother, Jack..."

Josh's mother's voice became softer and Josh had to lean forward to hear her over the wind that blew through the open car windows.

"Ted's mother dressed Jack up in that dead baby's clothes," his mother said.

"In girl's clothes?" Aunt Doris asked. For a second, she took her eyes off the road and looked over at Josh's mother with her mouth wide open, making a bright scarlet circle with her lips.

"She kept Jack in dresses and refused to cut his hair until he was almost two years old."

"She's lucky Jack didn't grow up funny," said Aunt Doris.

His mother nodded.

Josh thought of his big uncle Jack in a dress and giggled. His mother looked back over her left shoulder at him and frowned.

"I have to take you to the barber this week," she said.

Josh crossed his arms and threw himself back into the cracked vinyl seat. He liked his hair just the way it was. His mother turned back around and rolled up the passenger window, leaving only a small gap between the glass and the dusty cracked rubber strip that fit along the top. Josh felt the wild cool air that blew through his light blond hair die down to only the tiniest breeze that tickled the top of his head.

As Aunt Doris's car sailed past the steel mills that lined the polluted dark bay along the city's north end, Josh looked out toward the brown curls of smoke that rose from the smokestacks. He hummed quietly to himself and tried to compose the sort of music a puff of smoke would make as it twirled high into the sky.

The vertical line between his mother's brows became darker and a frown on her face grew as the car traveled farther west through town and the stench of the steel mills grew stronger. In her lap, she held a folded newspaper open to the "Homes for Rent" section. At the bottom of the page was a small grainy black and white photo of a house with an incomplete circle drawn lightly around it in pencil, as if someone had second thoughts before finishing.

The car turned south down Carrick Avenue and both his aunt and mother craned their necks examining the black numbers on the houses.

"It's number one-two-four," his mother said. "Just look for the smallest and ugliest house on the street."

"Well, you need the extra room, Gloria," said Aunt Doris. "And it won't be for long. Now that Ted's working again you could save for a down payment on your own house in a nicer area."

"I guess," Josh's mother said.

Aunt Doris pulled up in front of number one-two-four and shifted the car into park.

"So what did they do for syphilis back then anyway? Before penicillin, I mean," Aunt Doris asked.

"Ted said that they took arsenic."

"Arsenic? But wouldn't arsenic have killed them?"

"I guess the doctors gave them just enough to kill the syphilis without killing the person," said his mother.

"Oh," his aunt replied. "And if they gave them too much arsenic and they died, then the doctors could always blame it on the syphilis."

They both laughed.

"How do you think she got syphilis?" Aunt Doris asked.

"I guess Ted's father gave it to her," his mother said.

Aunt Doris turned off the car and Josh's mother stepped out onto the curb. As Josh hopped out after his mother, his aunt held onto the doorframe and pulled herself out of the driver's seat with a grunt.

"So that's it, eh," Aunt Doris said as she walked around the front of the car, pulling down the short red skirt that had ridden up on her wide hips.

"So what do you think?" Josh's mother said, looking at the house.

"I think it looked better in the picture," Aunt Doris said.

◈

In the kitchen of his family's small basement apartment, Josh sat playing at his desk while his mother made dinner. Josh's father worked "days" and his mother worked "afternoons" so soon his father would be home—and then his mother would leave for her job at the factory.

Josh wasn't quite sure what his father did at his new job, but Josh knew his mother worked on a machine that cut grooves in long steel rods. She had once told him that her rods were put in cement to help hold up tall new buildings being built thirty miles down the highway in Toronto. When other kids in his first-grade class asked Josh what his parents did, he told them that his mother made skyscrapers.

Now as he waited for his dinner, Josh sorted through a bundle of colorful plastic letters at his desk. The small children's desk had been a birthday present. It had shiny red aluminum legs that supported a small olive-green bucket seat and a blackboard desktop that flipped up to reveal a glossy metal whiteboard on the other side. It was on this whiteboard that Josh's plastic magnetic letters would stick like magic. For Josh, his desk was the only space in the house that was truly his, since no one else in the family was small enough to fit in the seat.

While his mother laid out fish sticks onto an oven pan, Josh wrote out his full name *JOSHUA MOORE* using as many different colors as he could on the whiteboard, starting with a bright yellow *J*. He smiled. Sometimes, when he grew bored at his desk, he would spell out his name and then carefully place the desktop down so, after a few hours or the next day when he lifted it up again, (if none of the letters fell or slid apart) he would be greeted by his own name. It was like being turned magically into a rainbow.

Now Josh looked at the red *O* from his first name on the whiteboard. It reminded him of his Aunt Doris's lips.

He reached out, took the bright red *O* off the whiteboard and put it to his own mouth.

"In girl's clothes?" Josh said in a high lady-voice. And although his aunt didn't say it, he added, "That's awful!"

Josh was carefully spelling out *SONG*, *FISH*, and *EGG* in magnetic letters when his father came in the door. His father shuffled into the kitchen and took a stubby brown bottle of beer out of the refrigerator.

"So, how was the house?" his dad asked. He sat down at the kitchen table and kicked off his work boots onto the white linoleum floor.

"Your feet smell," Josh said.

"That's because I work hard," his father said. "And hard work smells."

"I work hard too, but I don't smell" Josh said, not taking his eyes of the whiteboard.

He was now putting together some words he knew into whole sentences: *JOSH OVER MAN* and *RED APPLE TREE*.

"And men are supposed to smell," his dad said, chuckling. He pulled off one of his woolly gray work socks and, rolling it up in a ball, tossed it across the kitchen. It soared through the air and landed in front of Josh's desk.

"Ewwww," Josh said. He pinched his nose with his fingers.

"I think that house is too close to the steel mills," his mother said. "Who knows what those smokestacks are spewing out?" She scraped a spoon through a pot of mixed peas and carrots she was heating up on the front burner of the stove.

Josh's father laid his head back on the kitchen chair and closed his eyes.

"And it's such a small house," Josh's mother continued. "There's no basement. It's what my mother used to call a *wartime house*. You know, a small cheap thing thrown up during the war."

Josh's father lifted his head, stretched out his long legs and ran his fingers through his thick light-brown hair. He took a sip of his beer and exhaled like he had been holding his breath all day.

"Well, it's all we can afford," his father finally said.

Josh's mother opened her mouth as if to speak and stopped.

"Besides, you grew up in a *wartime* house, Gloria. And your mother had seven kids in a *wartime* house and she survived alright without a basement—or a husband."

"And I really didn't want to live in one again. And you know my mother did have a husband—she was just married in the old Indian way that wasn't recognized by the government."

"Yeah, right," his father said. He lit a cigarette, took a long drag, and leaned back in the chair. "So the worst thing you have to say about the house is that there's no basement?"

"It's small, it's dirty and the neighborhood smells."

"The whole damn city smells!"

At his desk Josh wiped all the letters off his whiteboard with one sweep of his left hand. They fell clacking onto the wooden bottom of the open desk.

"Jesus Christ, Gloria! If you don't want to move then let's just forget about the whole goddamn thing and stay right here."

"You know we can't stay here," his mother said. Lowering her voice she added, "There isn't enough room."

"Then dirty and smelly is all we can afford right now... at least until we get back on our feet."

His mother turned the dial on the stove to "off."

"I just wish we'd planned this better, Ted."

"Well, it's too late to worry about that now."

"Maybe."

"Maybe what?" he asked, sitting up in his chair.

"Maybe we should take Kevin and Troy over to see the house before we decide to rent it? They'll have to go to a different high school, you know."

"Why? Did your mother ever ask you for your permission before she'd haul that tribe of hers from man to man all around the city?"

Josh's mother flung around and pointed the spoon at his father. A cloudy mixture of hot carrot and pea juice dripped onto the kitchen floor.

"At least my mother took us with her when she left," she said. "She didn't leave all her kids to run off with some guy."

Josh's father rose from the kitchen table.

"She came back," he said softly. Then, leaving his work boots in the middle of the kitchen floor, he walked into the living room still wearing only one sock.

"Shit," his mother said, wiping her face now flushed to a deep burnt-red, with a tea towel.

In the corner behind his desk, Josh swiped the rainbow of magnetic letters spelling out *SIFLIS BABY* off his whiteboard and into his desk.

◆

Three weeks later, in early October, Josh's family moved into their new house on Carrick Avenue. Josh had wanted to make sure his desk wasn't left behind so he had carried it to the back of the van himself and handed it to his Uncle Jack.

"I hope it doesn't fall out on the way to the new house," Uncle Jack said.

Josh watched his uncle put the desk near the back of the moving van beside the unassembled parts of Josh's old baby crib.

Now, as Josh sat in the rented van nestled between his mother and father, the smell of the slag from the steel mills grew stronger, coating his nostrils and lungs. It was the same smell that clung to his father's jacket and shirt when he came home from work.

"You know," Josh's mother said as his father parked the van in front of their new home, "each time I see this house it looks smaller."

"Maybe it'll disappear soon," Josh said.

"I hope so," she replied.

The small house was shaped like a box with a sloped roof of gray asphalt tiles. Sea green aluminum siding had been installed only to the front of the house while the back and sides were the original wood siding, now covered with chipping dark green paint. It reminded Josh of Kevin's aquarium when he forgot to clean it. The only window visible from the street was a small picture window to the right of the front door. Just above the door hung a small brown and white striped metal awning barely the width of the door and projecting out a few feet from the house below the gutter. Between the window and the front door, the two big screws that fastened the black mailbox to the house had rusted in the rain and left two dark lines of rust dripping down the wall all the way to the grass.

Josh and his parents stood for a moment in the front yard of their new home beside two young maple trees that had been planted too close to one another.

"It's not so bad," his father said.

Josh darted up the pathway of cracked patio stones that ran from the sidewalk up to the one shaky step in front of the landing. He swung open the aluminum storm door a step up from the square cement landing and tried to open the brown front door.

"It's locked," he said looking back at his father.

"Then we better open it," his father said. He walked up the path leaving Josh's mother still staring at the house, still holding her purse across her chest.

Once inside, Josh ran through the small house. On the ground floor were four rooms: the master bedroom, a living room, kitchen and bathroom. Up a steep flight of stairs were two more small bedrooms. Every room was painted dark smoky blue.

While his mother began cleaning the kitchen, Josh carried his desk to the small space between the back door and the refrigerator.

"I'm going to put my desk right here," Josh said.

"Fine," said his mother without looking at him.

Josh opened the desktop to make sure that nothing was lost on the way over. He was happy to see his plastic letters, his chalk, his eraser, and his worn copy of *Alligator Pie* still there. This morning it had all been at their old apartment and now it's all here. Moving is easy, he thought. Suddenly the back door swung open and hit Josh's desktop, causing plastic letters to fly across the kitchen floor.

"Get out of the way," Troy said, slamming the door behind him. He ran past Josh and up the stairs.

"Go find someplace in the living room for your desk, Josh" his mother said.

Over the afternoon, Josh's father, his Uncle Jack, and Josh's brothers carried in furniture and boxes. Upstairs his brothers put their beds into one bedroom while Josh's bed was carried across the hall to the other.

"I'm almost sixteen and the fucking oldest," Kevin said to Troy as they dragged the dresser up the stairs. "I should have my own room."

"We should both have our own fucking room," Troy said.

"We would if it wasn't for *him*," Kevin said.

Josh wondered who Kevin was talking about and for a second he even considered telling his father that his brothers had used the word *fuck* but decided he'd better not. Instead he watched his uncle and father carry the sofa through the front door and drop it down against the wall opposite the picture window in the living room.

"Let's take a break," Uncle Jack said.

The two men walked outside and sat on the front step. Josh followed them out the door and stood beside his father. He rested his head on his father's thigh.

"I'm sure she lived on this street somewhere," Uncle Jack said.

"I thought that was over on Rosslyn Avenue," his father answered.

"No, that's where her old man and the mother lived. She lived on Carrick with John… it was on Carrick that they found the baby."

"Are you sure?" Josh's father peered down the street.

"Pretty sure."

"Well for God's sake don't tell Gloria."

A few houses down the street an old man with white hair was out in his front yard raking leaves into a pile.

"I'll go ask that old guy," Uncle Jack said. "Looks like he'd know."

Uncle Jack grinned and strolled toward the man. The old man stopped raking and leaned on his rake as Uncle Jack spoke to him. The man nodded and then pointed at a big white house down the street.

Josh's father stood and looked down at Josh.

"It does kinda smell here doesn't it?" his father said.

Josh followed his father around the house to the back door and entered the kitchen. At the far end of the room, Josh's mother was standing on a chair with her head in a kitchen cabinet while Troy and Kevin were both leaning on the countertop drinking tap water from blue plastic cups.

Josh's father looked at Tory and Kevin.

"Have you two finished unloading the boxes yet?"

"Not yet," Kevin said. "We were just having a break—like you."

"Well when you boys are done bringing in the boxes, I'll let you both have a beer."

"I think we've earned three a piece," Kevin said. He tossed his black hair out of his eyes.

"One is enough," his mother said.

"Alright, we'll settle for two each," Kevin said.

"How about you settle for my boot up your ass," his father said. He sat at the kitchen table. "I said you could each have one."

"She lived in number thirty-two Carrick!" Uncle Jack yelled as he stormed in the front door.

"Who did?" Josh's mother asked. She looked up from battling the shelf paper that kept sticking in the wrong places.

"Evelyn Dick," Uncle Jack answered, grinning.

"Jesus," his father said under his breath.

"You're not serious?" his mother said. She stepped down from the chair.

"Who's Evelyn Dick?" Josh asked.

"Your new neighbor Ed told me all about it," said Uncle Jack. "She lived in that big white house down the street—number thirty-two." He laughed. "And now you're living just a few houses down from *that* attic."

"Oh my God," his mother said. She sat down on the kitchen chair and covered her mouth with her hand.

"And just a few houses down from *that* furnace," continued Uncle Jack.

"What furnace?" Josh asked.

Kevin and Troy looked at each other, smiled and then ran out of the front door toward number thirty-two.

"Hey, I don't want the two of you standing there in front of that house staring," Josh's father yelled after them. "I don't want the whole neighborhood to think we're a bunch of goddamn gore freaks."

"Ed told me he lived here back in the forties when it happened," Uncle Jack said. "He said that the week John Dick disappeared there was a disgusting smell all around Carrick Avenue that was turning everyone's stomach. He watched them bring out that beige suitcase too."

"I can't believe this," Josh's mother said.

"You know, if it was me," Uncle Jack said, "I would have thrown that suitcase into the bay. Then they never would have found it. Do you know how many bodies are lying at the bottom of the bay in this city?"

"All wearing cement loafers," his father said.

Uncle Jack sat down at the kitchen table and turned to Josh's mother. "You know our father knew her, don't you?"

"No he didn't!" his mother said.

"He did so—didn't he, Ted?"

"Yeah he really did," Josh's father said. "The old man and John Dick were both streetcar conductors with the Hamilton Street Railway when Evelyn worked in the office."

"Your father's never said anything before about knowing Evelyn Dick," Josh's mother said.

Uncle Jack grinned.

"You're making that up," his mother said.

"Let's have one more beer before we bring in the television," his father said.

That night Josh lay alone in his own room for the first time. His bedroom door was left open and a dim light from the television downstairs shone into the corner of his room, lighting up the five wooden pieces of his old unassembled crib that his uncle and father had carried up the stairs and placed neatly against his bedroom wall.

◈

As October passed, and friends and family dropped by to see his parents' new house on Carrick Avenue, there was always someone who wanted to talk about Evelyn Dick.

"Is it true?" they would ask.

"Was this really the street where it all happened?"

"Is that the house where they found the suitcase?"

At night, as Josh lay in bed listening to the grown-ups talk downstairs, he slowly put together the story of Evelyn Dick.

She had been a goodtime girl (at least that was what Uncle Jack had called her) who, after marrying poor John Dick, had killed him (or had one of her many boyfriends kill him), hacked off his head, arms and legs, (which she burnt in her furnace), and then tossed what was left of him off Hamilton mountain. Later, when the police searched Evelyn's house at thirty-two Carrick and discovered human bones and teeth in her furnace, they arrested her for murder.

But that wasn't the worst part of Evelyn's story.

The police continued their search through the house and in the attic found a lady's beige suitcase. They opened it and found it had been filled with cement. But there was something else. Hanging out of the cement was piece of a baby's sweater. Once the cement had been chipped away, they discovered the body of a baby boy. He still had the rope he was strangled with wrapped around his little neck.

Now Josh threw his blue bedspread over his face and covered his ears when people downstairs talked about Evelyn. He didn't want to hear any more about her or John Dick or her baby in the suitcase. But even though he would lie in bed and try not to think about her, being under the blankets would always remind him of being covered with cement.

On Saturday morning while Josh was watching cartoons in the living room, Aunt Doris walked through the front door. She wore a purple miniskirt, a white halter-top and carried a paperback in her hand.

"Your skirt's too short, Doris" Josh's mother said. "Thirty-eight year old women with four kids shouldn't wear miniskirts."

"Why not?" Aunt Doris said. She sat down at the kitchen table, threw the book on the table and took her cigarettes out of her white leather purse.

"They only make you look older." Josh's mother filled the kettle with water from the tap and plugged it into the wall.

"Well I'm not gonna take fashion advice from a woman who still has crinolines in her closet," Aunt Doris said.

Josh tried to guess what crinolines were. The word sounded orange. I'll go look through Mom's closet sometime and find out, he thought.

Josh's mother chuckled and sat at the kitchen table. "Remember when we could just raise the waist of our dresses when we got pregnant? I hid both Kevin and Troy under crinolines."

"We weren't fooling anybody, you know." Aunt Doris giggled and then coughed into her fist.

"I know. I just wish it were that easy now."

"It was never easy, Gloria."

"What's that there?" Josh's mother asked as she pointed at the book in the middle of the kitchen table.

"It's the Evelyn Dick story—there are pictures in it too."

"Take it away, Doris. I don't want to see it."

"Kevin asked me to lend it to him."

Josh's mother stood and poured the hot water out of the kettle into the teapot.

"I can still remember that day she was sentenced to hang. And I remember, a little while later, when she was acquitted on some technicality, too," Aunt Doris said.

"I can't remember much about it at all," Josh's mother said.

"Evelyn did go to jail for killing the baby, though. But she didn't spend much time in jail. That book I brought you says that all she got was a few years for manslaughter... not even murder! Like the baby accidentally fell into a suitcase full of cement. And after she got out of jail she changed her name and moved out west someplace... but I think I saw her drinking a cup of coffee at a Tim Horton's Donut shop on Ottawa Street a few years back."

What kind of donut would Evelyn Dick eat? Josh wondered. *Something chocolate, I bet.*

"I'm getting so sick of hearing about Evelyn Dick," Josh's mother said. "It's like my house is stained with blood just for being on the same street as hers. Did you know that Ted's mother won't even step foot in our house?"

"Well, the rent's cheap and you need the extra room," said Aunt Doris. "And that's that."

"That's that," his mother repeated.

After Aunt Doris left and his mother went to her bedroom to take a nap, Josh picked up the paperback that was lying on the kitchen table. Just like Aunt Doris had said, right in the middle of the book were six or seven pages of glossy black and white photos.

In the first photo, a woman stood outside a courtroom. She was wearing a fur-trimmed coat, dark gloves and a beret that sat sideways on her head like a pancake. She was holding a box of *Sweet Corporal* cigarettes and looking up smiling at a man standing beside her.

That's Evelyn.

Josh wished the picture was in color. He wanted to know what color her dress was. In this black and white photo, Evelyn's eyes, hair, lips and dress were all the same shade of dark black as the tiny round mole on her right cheek. Josh tried to imagine what Evelyn would look like in a green dress, then a red dress, then a blue dress. This was the woman who poured cement over her own baby and cut her husband up into pieces. *Evelyn Dick should be in color.*

Josh continued to stare at Evelyn's face. She was beautiful, with dark black hair like his mother and Aunt Doris have. *I wonder if she was part Indian too.* As the minutes passed and Josh continued to stare at the photo, Evelyn's lovely face slowly became more and more grotesque. Her lips began to look like two huge leeches attached to her face, growing fatter as they filled with blood. Her eyes became cold and deadly. Her hair grew unruly, trying to burst from under the pancake beret and her gloved hands, crossed so delicately over one another, became claw-like and Josh could almost see them holding a cord tight around her baby's tiny neck.

"Sweet Corporal," Josh said slowly under his breath, sounding out each syllable of the second word the way his teacher had taught him.

He turned the page.

The next photograph showed the front of the house at thirty-two Carrick Avenue. *That's the house.* And although the veranda that ran the full width of the house was no longer white, the house looked exactly the same today as it did in the picture. He turned another page.

For a second, Josh was not sure what he was looking at. Then his mouth fell open. It was John Dick without his head or legs displayed on a chipped white metal table. Disoriented, Josh did not know which wound was the remnants of a leg and which was the stump of an arm.

In the middle of the white smooth skin of the torso, across the stomach, someone had tried to further cut down the body but seemed unable to cut through with the tools that they had. The enormous gash in the belly made Josh lightheaded and a tickling feeling in his groin began to grow and slither down Josh's legs to his feet.

This is what I look like on the inside? It looked like a roast that his mother would defrost on the kitchen counter Saturday nights.

He looked down the glossy page to another photo. It was John Dick's torso from a different angle. A bright white circle was in the middle of the exposed wound in the arm just below the shoulder. *Bone.* Josh wrapped his thumb and index finger around his slim arm and felt the hard bone that ran through the middle of his small mushy bicep. He closed the book and put it back on the kitchen table.

Josh crept past his mother's bedroom to the living room and sat at his desk. He opened the flip top and saw his name, *JOSHUA MOORE*, on the whiteboard but it didn't seem magical anymore. It just looked like a silly jumble of used toy letters.

All he wanted was his mother to wake up and tell him that he wasn't just meat inside.

◈

The following week Aunt Doris pulled her station wagon up to Josh's house with his mother beside her. His aunt helped his mother out of the car, across the lawn and up the one small step into the house. His mother's brown skin had turned strangely pale like a cup of tea with too much milk and she looked tired and sick. Josh's father stood in the middle of the living room, but Aunt Doris pushed past him, walking Josh's mother to the bedroom.

"Did Mom lose her job too?" Josh asked.

"Your mother doesn't lose jobs," Aunt Doris snapped, "just your father."

For three days his mother did not go to work. She stayed in bed and slept while his father slept on the couch. Josh knew that the wartime house was making everyone sick and angry. It was on a bad street where bad things happened. He wanted to tell his mother that the family had to pack up and leave the house on Carrick and return to their old basement apartment.

"Leave your mother alone," his father said. "And go to bed. It's getting late."

Josh walked slowly up the narrow stairs to his small bedroom. He flipped the light switch and began to undress. The room looked bigger now that the crib was gone. That morning his father had carried all five wooden pieces down the stairs and tossed them beside a pile of green garbage bags on the curbside.

Josh smiled.

Now I have a place for my desk.

The Good Luck Charm

"Don't tell your mother."

"I won't tell anybody."

Josh was only seven but this was not the first secret that he and his father had shared. Adults liked to tell Josh secrets. He had secrets with his mother too.

Josh and his father were driving out of Hamilton, east along Lake Ontario toward Toronto. That afternoon, just after lunch, Josh had been doing math problems in his second grade class when the school secretary called over the PA system.

"Please have Josh Moore collect his things and come to the principal's office."

At first Josh had been scared that he had done something wrong and as he put on his red windbreaker he wondered what offense he may have committed in the playground over lunch. The secretary usually sounded happy but over the PA system today she had sounded annoyed.

When Josh had reached the principal's office his father was waiting in front of the secretary's desk twirling the ring of his keys around his index finger. He was wearing his green workpants, a pair of scuffed up black leather shoes and a white T-shirt with small holes around the collar that he usually only wore to bed. His long light-brown hair was messy like he had just woken up and his eyes, though bloodshot, were wide open and staring out the window at the playground.

"I came to this school when it first opened," he said to the secretary.

The first thing Josh thought of was that something bad had happened to Reefer, the golden retriever puppy his father had bought a few weeks earlier. Why else would his father be up in the middle of the day when he was on night shift.

"Is Reefer okay?" Josh asked.

The secretary raised one eyebrow and looked over her glasses.

"Sure he is," his father said. "Why wouldn't he be?" He twirled his keys once more and they flew off his index finger onto the floor with a clink. He scratched his beard under his chin and grinning, picked up the keys from the tiled floor.

"Then how come you're not sleeping now?" Josh asked.

"We've got things to do," his father said. "Places to go and people to see."

"What people?"

His father turned his head to the secretary. "Thanks."

The secretary nodded without smiling and Josh's father took him by the hand and pulled him quickly out of the office, down the hall and out the big wooden front doors of the school. The doors slammed behind them with a thud. Not letting go of Josh's hand, his father fell into a slow run as he made his way toward the car at the bottom of the driveway near the road, making Josh run too. His sneakers slapped on the asphalt as he ran.

"Where are we going?"

"To the track," his father said. "And I needed my good luck charm."

Josh's belly swirled with excitement as he hopped in the passenger seat and swung the heavy door of his father's car shut. The car smelled like the tree shaped air freshener hanging on the rearview mirror.

His father had put on a pair of scratched yellow-tinted sunglasses, lit a cigarette and drove away from the school. Although his father had taken him to Toronto to bet on horses before, this was the first time that he had taken him out of school to go to the racetrack.

"But we gotta hurry," his father had said.

Now their burgundy Chevy Impala traveled down the highway

out of the city toward the drab green Skyway Bridge that straddled the harbor and would take them toward Toronto, the biggest city Josh had ever seen. The autumn air was cool but the sun was still hot, warming Josh's face through the windshield.

Josh's father grabbed an 8-track tape off the dashboard. The tape had been white when his father had got it for Christmas a few years back, but it had turned gray from his handling it with dirty hands after his shift at work. Glued to the front of the 8-track tape was a picture of Kris Kristofferson smiling and leaning on his guitar. Josh thought that Kristofferson looked like his father—they both had beards and scraggly long hair. *When I grow up, I'm gonna grow a beard like that too.*

Josh's father shoved the tape into the tape player under the dashboard and *Jesus Was a Capricorn* began to loudly play from the car speakers. His father began to sing along. He liked to play that song over and over so the tape warbled a bit from being rewound so many times. His father's voice was higher and softer than the voice on the tape: *Long hair, beard and sandals and a funky bunch of friends. Reckon they'd just nail him up if He come down again.*

His father drove quickly along the highway to the Skyway Bridge, passing other cars. Weaving in and out of traffic, his father would occasionally swear at other drivers as he maneuvered around them. Beside them, the black water of the bay was smooth and shiny like the skin on chocolate pudding after it cools. It looked like Josh could walk on it straight to the mills.

"Show me where you work, Dad."

"Let's see," his father said as he looked across the bay. "Right abouts there."

He pointed toward the far end of the lineup of smokestacks. Josh's eyes followed his father's arm over the bay.

"I'm gonna work there too."

"Oh, no you won't," his father said. "You'll do something better than waste your life in the steel mills."

Josh continued to stare at his father's factory across the bay, craning his neck until it moved behind him.

Oh yes I will work there.

As the car reached the highest point of the bridge, Josh turned around in the vinyl chair, squatting on his knees with his chin on the leather headrest. It smelled like his mother. He looked back over the city they had just left. He wondered what else he could do if he didn't work in the mills like his father, mother and older brother Kevin did. Once he had seen a man on television making a pot out of clay by spinning it on a big wheel. His hands were wet and muddy as he molded the clay into any shape he wanted. Maybe I could do that, Josh thought.

"You could be a doctor like Che Guevera," his father said.

"Who's that?"

"Che was a very smart man who tried to look after the working man." Josh bit his nail. The reverent way his father said the word *Che* instinctually made Josh nervous. It was the same way Josh's Aunt Wilma said the word *Jesus.*

"I *think* I've heard of him." Maybe he had heard of Che from one of his father's union friends who came over to their house, got drunk with his father, and talked all night about the newspapers his father bought, *The Militant* and *The Socialist Worker.* Josh didn't like his father's newspapers. They didn't have pictures of the movies that were playing in Hamilton or the theatres they were in.

"Was Che with you when you took the day off to picket at City Hall?" Josh asked.

"No, Che's dead. And he lived in another country."

Josh wondered if his father had been drinking today. He moved closer to him in the front seat, trying to smell his breath. It smelled like cigarettes.

"Tell me again what you were picketing for. I forget."

"We were picketing against wage control. The government has stopped working people from getting raises... so we all decided to strike for one day."

"Oh right."

"Maybe they should try profit control. Goddamn bastards."

The 8-track clicked to another track in the middle of *The Best of*

All Possible Worlds and then started again. Josh had never heard that Kristofferson song without the hard click in the middle. Even when he sang the song quietly to himself, Josh always stopped, made the click noise with his tongue and then finished the song. *Cause there's still a lot of wine and lonely girls—CLICK—in this best of all possible worlds.*

At the top of the bridge, Josh tried to look down to the cottages along the Beach Strip. Below the middle of the bridge there was a small amusement park with a haunted house that his father had taken him to.

"What would happen if you fell from here into the water?"

"I guess you'd probably get killed," his father said.

"Even if you hit the water?" He thought about cartoons where people would jump into a bucket of water from a platform.

"From this height, hitting water is just like hitting cement."

"Huh?"

"Did you know people fell off the top when they were building the Skyway Bridge? Your Uncle Carl picked one up when he was driving an ambulance. He had to scoop them up off the road below with a shovel after they splattered all over the place."

"Yuck!" Josh covered his ears. His father looked at him through his round yellow glasses and smiled.

"Wanna push the lighter in for me?"

Josh pushed the car lighter into the dashboard. "What's that horse's name we're betting on?"

"Step In Time."

"I like that name. If it wins will we be rich?"

"For a minute," his father said.

The car lighter made a popping sound that meant it was hot and red. His father pulled the lighter out of the dashboard and lit another cigarette. As smoked filled the car, he tapped the triangular window vent on the driver's door with his fist and it whistled as they drove down the highway.

They descended the bridge and in the distance the skyscrapers of Toronto grew larger as they approached. Josh liked looking at big buildings. The biggest was the CN Tower. One day his father promised to take him up to the top.

"What if we kept on going down this highway? Where would we end up?" Josh asked.

"In five or six hours we'd be in Montreal," his father answered. "Then if we kept on driving, we'd hit Quebec City and then... if we still kept on going we'd drive straight into the Atlantic Ocean. *Splash!*"

"Can we go to those places sometime?"

"I don't know? Can you speak French?" his father asked.

"No."

"Then what would we do when we got to Montreal? We couldn't ask anybody for directions or even buy dinner. No one there speaks English."

"I'll learn to talk French and then we could go."

◆

Less than an hour later they arrived at Woodbine Racetrack. Josh's father paid at the entrance booth and Josh pushed his way through the turnstile. They walked to a booth where his father bought a racing form. For Josh, he paid fifty cents for a thin glossy program with a photograph of a horse running on the front page. Josh's father stopped for a beer and an Orange Crush at the snack bar and then the two of them walked to the seating area where hundreds of blue plastic chairs sat in rows below a protruding roof. The track always smelled of freshly dug dirt and manure.

The second race had just been run and the oval track was empty. Peppered between the plastic chairs like confetti were colored cardboard tickets from the losing bets of the first two races. There weren't as many people there as when Josh came on weekends. And today they were almost all men, hardly any women and no other kids.

"Is your horse running now?"

"Not until the sixth race."

"Can I have money to bet too?"

"Sure. How about I give you two dollars to bet with for each race?"

As they sat in two blue chairs in the stands, his father, hovering over the racing form, studied it from behind his yellow sunglasses, making circles and lines on the paper with a black Bic pen.

"Which one are you going to pick this race?" Josh asked.

"I don't know yet," his father said. He put a lock of his long hair that had fallen in his face behind one ear. "I'm handicapping. Remember I showed you how to do that?"

Josh shook his head. The only thing he could remember about handicapping was that the horse you pick had to have lost the last time it raced.

"See this number here?" His father pointed at one of the tiny columns on the racing form. "That's the number of days the horse rested since his last race. That number has to be more than fourteen." His father moved his finger across the paper. "This here is the number of days it rested between the last race and the one before. That number has to be less than nine."

Josh looked at the paper.

"And this number here shows you where the horse came in the last time. When you handicap, you try and find a horse that lost the last time it ran. That means the odds would be higher. And that means that you'll win more money. See?"

Josh didn't understand but nodded anyway. He looked at the paper and tried to find a number in the column more than fourteen. Since his father and mother fought about betting on horses, Josh decided he would not tell her that he almost knew how to handicap horses.

"And this number is the claiming number... the dollar amount. It has to be smaller than this number... that's the last time it raced. That means it's falling in class and is running with crummier horses than it did last time." His father was now talking to himself. He took off his yellow sunglasses and rubbed his red eyes. They didn't look as open and wide as they had before.

Josh studied the racing form. "This one?" he said pointing at it.

"No." His father shook his head. "What did I just say? That one won the last time... see?" He pointed to a number in the racing form. "He's the favorite."

Josh grew bored and began to pick up the losing betting slips around them that people had thrown on the ground. The trumpet sounded. Josh had been to the racetrack enough times to know that the bugle meant that there were only a few minutes left before the race started. Josh sat beside his father and made the trumpet song again as best he could.

"Da da da da da dump da dee da da da."

"Okay, hurry up and make your pick," his father said.

Josh looked at the list of horse's names in the third race. "I'll read them out to you," his father said. "Just pick the one you want. It'll be faster, eh." His father stretched out his legs and read over the names in the racing form. Josh liked the names Gold Rush and Dolly's Dream but finally chose number seven, Carnival Game.

"Win, place or show?" his father asked.

"Show!" Josh liked having three chances to win.

They walked to one of the betting windows and stood in line. Josh was worried that they would run out of time before his father could bet but a few minutes later his father had two betting slips, two dollars on Carnival Game to show and ten dollars on Amigo to win.

They both lost.

Carnival Game didn't even show. He finished fifth. Josh wished he had known that the jockey for Carnival Game would be wearing a blue and white checkered shirt. He wouldn't have bet on him if he'd known. Josh didn't like blue and especially blue checkers and stripes.

"Shit," his father said as he ripped up his ticket. Amigo had come in second. "Ah hell, it's just for fun, right?"

"You should have bet it to place or show," Josh said.

After three races, neither of them had won.

"Want something to eat?" his father asked.

They walked inside the stands. Josh looked up at the pictures of food on the walls at the snack bar. Both the hotdog and hamburger looked good in the pictures but he had had the hot dog before and knew it didn't look anywhere near as good in real life.

"What do you want?" his father asked.

"A hamburger."

Sitting at a picnic table near the men's room, his father drank another beer from a white plastic cup and studied the racing form. While Josh ate his hamburger and sipped on a root beer, a man with long sideburns and black pants and the final stub of a cigarette hanging out of his mouth walked past them into the men's room.

"I have to go to the washroom," Josh said.

"Do you need me to go with you?" His father folded the racing form.

"No, I can do it myself," Josh said.

He walked to the urinal. It was higher than the ones in the boy's room at his school. Josh unbuttoned his pants and pulled out his penis. Beside him, the tall man with sideburns stood pissing. Josh looked over and saw a large bluish cock-head and a thick stream of pale-yellow urine. The man continued to read from his racing form and did not seem to notice Josh watching him. After he emptied his bladder, the man tossed his cigarette butt into the urinal, shoved his penis back in his pants, zipped up, and walked out the door. Josh looked down at his small penis shrinking back into his white underpants. *I'll grow a big penis one day too.*

Back at the picnic table, Josh looked over his father's shoulder at all the scratches, arrows, and circles his father had drawn on the racing form.

"I got this tip from your Uncle Jack. He told me Step In Time was going to win."

"For sure?"

"Well there's no such thing as a sure thing, but I think he will."

"Because Step In Time's the best?" Josh asked.

"That's what they say." His father took a last swallow of his beer. "And his grandsire was Northern Dancer."

"His what?"

"His horse grandfather." His father grinned.

"What color shirt is the jockey wearing?"

"Let's see," his father said. Josh was surprised that his father didn't tell him that it was a stupid question. Instead he looked over the racing form like he was searching for any other important handicapping information. "White and yellow."

"I wanna bet on Step In Time too… but to show not to win."

"Okay, I'll put two dollars on Step In Time to show for you and… a little more on Step In Time to win for me."

He watched his father at the window laying their bets. He put down light brown and red bills. Josh didn't often see bills that color. The pretty bright red ones with the Mounties on the back were fifties and the light brown ones were hundred dollar bills. The hamburger Josh had just eaten turned in his stomach.

They walked down toward the track and sat at one of the empty picnic tables by the fence so they could watch Step In Time walk past them on his way to the starting gate. Josh waited for a horse with the jockey wearing yellow and white.

"There he is," Josh said. "Number three, right?"

"Yep, that's him."

The number three horse was a dark brown horse with a line of white from the middle of his ears to his nose. His mane, a lighter brown, matched a tail that swayed nonchalantly as he trotted past Josh toward the starting gate. The jockey wore a bright yellow shirt with a matching yellow cap. He had on white pants and shiny black boots and stared forward through his amber goggles with intense concentration. "Yellow is lucky," Josh said.

The race began. Step In Time shot out fast and moved to the front of the ten horse field. Josh's father stood with the rolled up racing form in his hand as the horses ran past with a thundering roar. Josh saw a swoosh of yellow and brown run past first. They were going to win. Josh turned and saw his father jump up on the seat of the picnic table.

"Yes! Yes! Yes! You beautiful son-of-a-bitch!" his father yelled.

Josh climbed up onto the picnic table beside his father. Mimicking him, Josh waved his glossy program at the horses as they rounded the final turn. We're going to win, Josh thought.

Then, in the final stretch, Step In Time began to fall back. A jockey in a blue shirt and another in a green and gold shirt were coming up beside him. Losing his lead, Step In Time was now neck and neck with the horse with the blue shirt jockey while the horse with the green and gold shirt jockey was right behind.

"Move you son-of-a-bitch!" his father yelled. "Move!"

"Move!" Josh yelled, jumping up and down on the table, leaving out the *son-of-a-bitch*.

Josh's father was waving his hands, as if trying to push the horse along with the air current he was making. But it didn't work. Step In Time finished third.

"You dirty filthy cunt!" his father spat. He stepped down from the picnic table and sat down on the wooden bench looking at his orange cardboard betting slip. Josh sat down on the bench beside him.

"I won and you lost," Josh said. He laughed and held out his own orange slip of cardboard. "You should have picked him to show like me."

His father looked at him through yellow-tinted sunglasses. "I guess I should have."

His father picked up Josh's winnings and handed him $6.75. Josh wondered what he was going to do with all his money.

"We'd better start back," his father said.

"But there are three more races," said Josh. He held out the $6.75 in his hand. "And I have my own money to bet now."

"We have to get back home before your mother gets home from work."

"Okay. But I have to pee again before we go," Josh said.

Ten minutes later they were on their way. Josh's father had bought another beer and drank it as they walked to their Impala in the parking lot. Josh wondered if he was still a good luck charm. Step In Time did come in third, he thought.

His father started the car and Kris Kristofferson began to sing.

Josh jumped. It sounded much louder than it was when they arrived. His father pushed the eject button and the tape popped out of the slot in the 8-track. As they waited for the light to change at the onramp to the highway, his father hesitated. He stared up at the two green signs over the road. He looked left toward the EAST—MONTREAL sign, and then tilted his head and looked at the WEST—HAMILTON sign to the right.

"You sure you don't speak French, Josh?" The left side of his mouth rose in a smile but his eyes remained sad.

"No I don't," Josh said.

The Impala did not move after the light turned green.

"We have to go home that way, Dad" Josh pointed his finger toward the Hamilton sign. "That way!"

The car still didn't move.

The light changed from green to red and then to green again.

Splash, Josh thought.

"Right," his father said. He turned the car westward and they headed back toward home.

"I can be a doctor like Che if you want me to," Josh said. "And help working men."

"That would be nice," his father said.

His father was quiet all the way home. With no music, only the whistling of the triangular window vent was heard.

◈

A month later, Josh's family was packing to move again.

"I swear to God it will never happen again," his father had pleaded when Josh's mother threatened to leave "for good this time".

"And now we can save up five hundred or so for a down payment on our own place while we're at Lydia's," his father said.

Josh was excited about trying a new school and meeting new people. Besides, he had done it a couple of times before when his father had lost their rent money. They would be staying with Josh's Aunt Lydia, his mother's sister, until his mom and dad were able to get the money together for another place to live. His older brother Kevin had decided that he wouldn't be moving with them this time. He said it was time for him to get his own place. Josh thought that was a good idea. And that way Josh would have more room to himself when they finally get their own house again. Maybe he'd even be able to share a room with his other brother, Troy.

At least until Dad does it again, he thought.

Now, in the kitchen his mother was wrapping their dishes in the pages of *The Young Socialist* newspaper for the move while Josh sat alone in the living room singing quietly to himself.

"Cause there's still a lot of wine and lonely girls—CLICK—in this best of all possible worlds."

All That Was in Jericho

"Are you still here, Mom?" Josh yelled as he tossed his schoolbooks on the kitchen table. "Did you go see Dad today? Did they say he could come home?" Josh moved into the hallway toward the living room. He sniffed the air. There was a strange odor. It smelled like late spring, when the tiny flowers on the lilac bush beside his house turn from purple to brown.

Josh entered the living room cautiously. He knew that scent.

Looking grim on the sofa was his Grandmother Moore and two of his father's older sisters, Aunt Sue and Aunt Peggy. Full cups of tea sat on the coffee table. His aunts would never have come just to visit his mother. Beside the television, Josh's mother sat somberly on a wooden chair with her arms folded over her chest. She didn't like people dropping in while she dressed for her afternoon shift at the mill, especially women like Aunt Sue and Aunt Peggy, who didn't have to work and could wear dresses during the week. Josh's mother awkwardly lifted a hand to her head and smoothed the grimy blue handkerchief that she always tied around her hair before heading to the factory. Reefer, their golden retriever, lay at his mother's feet like her protector. He looked up, saw Josh, and laid his head back down on the carpet.

"Hello, Joshua," someone purred in a voice dripping of black molasses. Turning his head, Josh saw his Aunt Wilma sitting in his father's burgundy chair by the window. Josh cringed at the sound of his full name. Aunt Wilma always called people by their full names.

Aunt Wilma only made the trip up from her home in Georgia when she smelled trouble. She never came up for Christmases or weddings or even for Josh's grandmother's seventieth birthday. Josh had only seen his Aunt Wilma a few times, always when someone was sick or going through some horrible problem. Then, like a bird of prey catching the scent of a battleground from miles away, she would swoop down from the south with a yellow and orange canvas suitcase bulging by her side. The last time Aunt Wilma had come up to Canada was when Josh's grandfather was dying. But that trip had not ended the way Aunt Wilma had hoped, and she flew home without getting what she wanted from her dying father. "I was so close," Josh heard her say to his Aunt Peggy at the funeral, "I spent three days at his bedside, but he wouldn't give in."

Now Aunt Wilma was back. Someone must have told her Dad was in trouble. Josh glanced sideways at his aunts on the sofa.

"Hi," Josh said. He gravitated toward his mother who had reached out to him. His mother was only thirty-five but already had the hands of an old lady, wrinkled, thin, and covered with greenish veins. Working for years on a big machine that cut steel rods had damaged her hands and now they trembled slightly. Sometimes she dropped knives and plates on the kitchen floor.

"How old are you now, Joshua?" Aunt Wilma asked as she brought a teacup up to her pink lips.

"Almost nine."

"You're really big for eight." She stretching out the word really until Josh thought it would snap and sting his ear.

Aunt Wilma was tall and thin with a long pointed nose. Around her lips and eyes she had deep wrinkles that she tried to fill up with greasy makeup that gave her face an orange tint. She wore a light pink dress with tiny white buttons down the front and a wide black shiny belt with a big silver buckle around her waist. The dress covered her knees, even when she sat, and had a large flappy collar and long sleeves. Aunt Wilma's dresses were always pale solid colors like Easter candy. Josh had never seen her wear polka dots, stripes, or flowers. Unlike everyone else in the living room, Aunt Wilma had not taken off her shoes, which were polished glossy black and had short thick square heels. Her hair looked unnaturally dark and was combed up and off her forehead like a brown pumpkin, with a small flip on each side near her ears. *She is trying hard to look like Betty Ford,* Josh thought.

Aunt Wilma was the second oldest of Josh's father's twelve brothers and sisters. Josh's dad had told him that Aunt Wilma had married a traveling salesman from Indiana and moved to America when Josh's father was just a little boy. Later she moved to Georgia. Josh knew that Aunt Wilma had a husband, Uncle Greg, and two grown sons who had moved away to other parts of the States, but Josh had never met any of them.

Aunt Wilma did not talk like anyone else in the family. She had a funny way of stretching out her words. Josh's father said she spoke this way because she had spent most of her life deep in the southern part of America. In conversations with the rest of the family, Josh's aunts and uncles fell into Aunt Wilma's rhythm. The normal sound of family exchanges, as quick and invigorating as a game of tag on the playground, suddenly became frustratingly slow and exhausting.

Aunt Wilma picked a few strands of Reefer's fur off her dress.

"Tell me, Joshua, do you know who Joshua in the Bible was?" Aunt Wilma asked, not smiling, not even looking at Josh but at his mother, as if Aunt Wilma was testing her instead of Josh.

"Nope," he answered.

Aunt Wilma looked at Aunt Sue and Aunt Peggy on the sofa, raised her eyebrows and pursed her lips as if to say, "Well, what can you expect?" Josh wondered if Aunt Wilma sent Aunt Sue and Aunt Peggy her old dresses, since his aunts were dressed so similarly in the same pastel colors.

"He knows who Joshua was," his mother announced. "Don't you." She glanced down at the watch on her wrist even though there was a clock on the wall over the sofa.

"Joshua took over for Moses when Moses died," Aunt Wilma said. "He blew the trumpets that made the walls of Jericho come tumbling down."

"How many trumpets did he have to blow to do that?" Josh asked.

"He didn't blow them himself. He had his army do it all at once." Aunt Wilma put down her teacup with a loud knock. "Joshua was a very brave man who did what God told him to do. That's why your parents named you Joshua."

"I was named after my mother's brother who died when he was little," Josh stated, each word clipped and hard, determined not to fall into Aunt Wilma's drippy American drawl.

Aunt Wilma waved her hand as if Josh had told her a lie. His ears burned. From the basement, music began to beat. Troy must be home, Josh thought. An annoyed look crept across Aunt Wilma's face as the sounds of his older brother's *Roxy Music* album vibrated under her thick black heels. Josh smiled.

"I came up, all the way from Georgia, so I could speak to your father," Aunt Wilma said, shifting in the chair. On the sofa, Josh's grandmother and the others said nothing, only nodding when Aunt Wilma looked over toward them.

"You know that your father has been sick," Aunt Wilma said.

"He's sick in the head," Josh said. He gazed over Aunt Wilma's shoulder at the tree outside the window and sank deeper into his mother's side.

"He's sick in the heart," Aunt Wilma said. She touched her own heart with the fingertips of her right hand. She looked like she was about to cry, though there were no tears in her eyes. Josh studied her strange gesture and decided that she was play-acting.

"There's nothing at all wrong with Ted's heart," Josh's mother said.

"But do you know who can fix his heart?" Aunt Wilma asked.

"A heart doctor?" he answered. He felt his mother hold him tighter around the waist.

"No. *Jesus* can, Joshua." Aunt Wilma grinned and showed her big stained teeth. All his aunts and uncles looked like horses when they smiled. Josh imagined her chewing on a carrot. "And that's why I flew all the way up here to see him," Aunt Wilma continued. "I was up at the hospital this morning and I think he's almost ready to have Jesus fix his heart. Wouldn't that be wonderful?" Josh's mother looked as if she was trying hard not to say something. A sound, part-sigh and part-growl, slipped from between her lips.

Jesus rarely slipped into Josh's house. Once, one Sunday morning when he was around seven years old, Josh had turned on a television show on one of the Buffalo TV stations. There were ten ladies; all wearing ruffled lime-green dresses that hung down to their white shoes. Six stood together with their arms at their sides in a beautiful white gazebo in the middle of a rose garden while the other four sat in pairs on white benches on each side of the gazebo with their hands folded neatly in their laps and their ankles crossed to one side. The symmetry of the scene had made Josh uneasy. The smiling ladies sang: *Turn your eyes upon Jesus, look full in his wonderful face, and the things of earth will grow strangely dim, in the light of his glory and grace...*

"Christ, what are you watching?" Josh's father had asked as he entered the living room in his old dark blue terrycloth bathrobe. He carried a folded newspaper under his arm and his morning cup of instant coffee in a huge white mug with "Pop" written in black old-time writing on the side. Wool work socks had slipped off his father's naked calves into a rumpled lump around his ankles. He's hung-over, Josh thought with a twinge of amusement at his father's pain. Behind Josh's father, Reefer followed wagging his tail.

"I don't know," Josh had answered.

"Turn that shit off," his father had said as he playfully hit Josh over the head with the sports section of the *Hamilton Spectator*. "It'll warp your mind."

Now, Josh thought, Aunt Wilma has flown back to mess everything up. She had done this before, hauling up Jesus in her suitcase from Georgia folded neatly somewhere between her makeup bag and pantyhose. She had come up and converted Aunt Sue to Jesus when Aunt Sue's daughter had died in a car accident and she converted Aunt Peggy a few years later when Aunt Peggy's husband left her for a woman named Roz. Josh did not remember Aunt Sue's conversion because it happened before he was born. To Josh, Aunt Sue had always been strange, but Josh remembered when

Aunt Peggy changed. After Aunt Wilma's visit, she called herself a "Baptist" and a "born again Christian." She talked about being happy but Josh thought that she had become sadder and meaner. Unlike the rest of the family, Aunt Sue and Aunt Peggy battled more with other family members—and even between themselves. Maybe neither wanted to be seen as less Baptist than the other.

When Aunt Wilma flew home after saving his aunt's souls, she had left each with a big black leather Bible with red tinted-edged pages. On the front, in the bottom right corner, Aunt Wilma had their full names, *SUSAN* and *MARGARET*, printed in gold lettering and on the inside front covers she had written: *This book will keep you from sin or sin will keep you from this book.* Josh wondered if Aunt Wilma had a personalized Bible in her bedroom closet for everyone in the family. Then whenever she heard that someone in Canada was sick, she would grab their Bible from her closet and stuff it into her orange suitcase along with her pastel dresses, pale pink lipstick and a few cans of hairspray and dash up to Hamilton. But Josh's grandfather had not caved in to Aunt Wilma—so she was not invincible. Josh imagined Aunt Wilma keeping score in her own bible, scratching two vertical marks under the heading *Saved* and one under the heading *Lost.*

Now a split as wide as the Niagara River ran down the Moore family. On one side were those who drank, laughed, and used words like *bullshit, goddamn,* and *sonofabitch* when they talked, and on the other side were the ones who never swore or drank, rarely laughed, and scattered words like Jesus, Lord, and Christ throughout their sentences. In the middle, Josh's Grandmother Moore seemed lost as she walked in a no man's land. Her attempts to straddle both sides of her family had failed, and now she nodded wearily as each side pointed fingers and complained to her of the other. And although he was not allowed to swear, Josh would shout out *SHIT* in his head as loud as he could when something made him angry, just to prove to himself what side he was on.

Fly home, you witch, Josh now thought as he held to his mother and watched Aunt Wilma's lips creep out towards the only spot left on the rim of the white teacup not smeared with pink lipstick.

Josh's mother stood. "I have to go to work now."

"We can take Joshua up now to see Edward," Aunt Wilma said, even though she wasn't the one driving. "And drop him off back here when we're done."

Josh's mother hesitated.

"I want to see Dad," Josh said. His mother looked Josh up and down, from his feet to the messy brown hair on the top of his head, as if she could see under his clothes, checking to make sure his body was healthy and strong enough to combat hospital germs.

"Okay," she said.

They walked to Aunt Sue's long blue Thunderbird and Aunt Wilma got into the front passenger side. In the back seat, Josh sat between his Aunt Peggy and his grandmother.

"I think there is something wrong with Ted's whole generation," Aunt Wilma said as they drove. "The sixties messed up a lot of people. I'm glad I'm old enough to have missed it. And now, if the drinking and drugs wasn't enough, he does this. Putting electricity in his head won't do him a bit of good. Only Jesus can save him."

Josh's grandmother raised her hand up to her mouth and cleared her throat.

"Do you know that Jesus cured me when I was sick, Joshua?" Aunt Wilma said. "One day, just after my second little boy was born, I was walking through an aisle at an A&P store in Atlanta, and just as I was about to reach up for baby formula... I found that I wasn't able to move my arms. Both of them just hung there at my sides, paralyzed."

Josh tried not to laugh. *How did she lift her teacup to her lips?*

"I was terrified. Uncle Greg took me to all kinds of doctors and none of them could find anything wrong with me. Some of them even thought I was some kind of a loony-tune. Then one day, a few weeks later, a Godly neighbor lady of mine knocked on my door and asked if she could come in and pray with me. She actually had to lift my hands and put them together, like this." She put her hands together as if to pray.

How did she wipe her bum?

"Well, right then and there, Jesus broke the chains that Satan had on my arms and I raised my hands up in the air." Aunt Wilma re-enacted the scene by lifting her palms to the roof of the car.

When they arrived at the hospital, Aunt Sue and Aunt Peggy left Josh, his Aunt Wilma, and Josh's grandmother at the front door. Aunt Wilma told Aunt Sue to pick them back up at the same place when visiting hours were over at eight o'clock. And then Aunt Wilma, waving Josh's aunts off like bugs that flew too close to her face, led Josh and his grandmother into the elevator. When they reached the eighth floor, the door opened and Aunt Wilma darted out. Josh stepped out of the elevator with his grandmother and was suddenly hit by the strong smell of bleach... with something sour hiding just underneath.

Aunt Wilma walked quickly down the white hall, clicking her black heels on the floor like Morse code announcing an advancing army and Josh thought of Patton smacking a shell-shocked soldier in that movie he had watched on television with his father a few months earlier. Aunt Wilma marched ahead so quickly that Josh's grandmother had to break into a shuffling trot to try and keep up. Finally his grandmother gave up and fell back to her normal stride. And although he could have kept up with his Aunt Wilma, even beaten her to his father's room, Josh chose to keep to his grandmother's pace. At one point, Aunt Wilma turned around and stared at her mother and Josh.

"Hurry up," she said.

When Josh and his grandmother reached his father's room, Aunt Wilma was already in front of the hospital bed. His father stood by the little table next to the bed. He wore a new pair of blue plaid flannel pajamas Josh's mother had bought at the Robinsons department store across the street and his old blue bathrobe. With one hand leaning on the table for support, Josh's father slid on a pair of slippers over thick gray and white work socks. His father's long light-brown hair appeared clean and was parted down the middle. The sides were flipped behind each ear, hanging down past his shoulders, and it looked like he had shaved that morning.

"That hair makes you look like a girl, Edward."

"Maybe I should put it in a ponytail," Josh's father responded while putting in his upper plate. He turned his head towards Josh and winked.

"Hi, Dad," Josh said as he rushed over and hugged him, pushing his face into his father's belly. His father smelled of some harsh cleanser. Then, pulling away, Josh tried to wink back.

"So how's Josh doing today?" his father asked, cheerfully but slowly. Josh's mother had told him that the doctors gave his father medicine that made him kind of dopey.

"I'm good," Josh said. When they had first let Josh come up to visit his father a couple of weeks ago, his father had not wanted to talk much. But today he seemed stronger. More like himself. Maybe someone gave him a drink. If he were old enough, Josh would have brought his dad a bottle of rye. He had even searched the house for a bottle to bring to the hospital but could not find one.

Josh's grandmother had stopped at the threshold of the door as his father tightened the belt of his bathrobe. She said something, but spoke so quietly that Josh did not hear her.

"Hi, Mom," Josh's father said.

Josh tried to think of something else to say to his father. His mother had told him not to ask his father when he was coming home. "Troy's working tonight but said he'll come tomorrow morning with mom," Josh finally said. His father nodded and ran his fingers through Josh's hair.

"I told Susan to pick us up at eight," Aunt Wilma said.

Together the four of them, with Aunt Wilma leading, traipsed to the end of the hall and through heavy metal doors into the lounge.

The lounge was painted pale yellow, like day old custard, and was divided into two unequal parts, smoking and non-smoking, separated by a glass window that ran the width of the room. The non-smoking side was more than twice the size of the smoking side and had a color television set, but whenever Josh came to visit his father, the chairs, tables, and sofas on the non-smoking side were always empty, with most people sitting or standing in their pajamas and bathrobes on the other side of the window, chain-smoking cigarettes. Sometimes Josh sat in the smoking room with his father and talked about school. The smoke, like his father's drinking, never really bothered Josh too much.

"Your father wants to go to the smoker's side," Aunt Wilma said. "You and grandma can sit on the non-smoking side and watch television while your father and I talk."

"I want to go with Dad," Josh said.

"No," Aunt Wilma said. Josh waited for his father to say he could come along with them, but he didn't. Even though there was no one on the non-smoking side of the lounge, Josh was afraid to change the television channel. Josh's grandmother sat on the end of a fake leather sofa and Josh sat in the matching chair to her right. It smells like a dirty toilet in here, he thought, and he wondered if someone had peed on the chair. Josh placed his elbow on the arm of the chair and then rested his head on his open palm and stared across the lounge into the smoking room where his father and Aunt Wilma sat behind the glass window. They sat at a table near the back of the lounge alone, across from one another.

"Do you think my dad is crazy, grandma?" Josh asked.

"No," she answered softly. "He's just really, really sad."

"But why's he sad?"

"Sometimes grown-ups get sad for no reason."

It had all started a few months earlier when Josh's father had quit drinking. For a few weeks, everything was fine, but then his dad changed. Josh could not remember exactly when this change occurred; there was no red velvet curtain that opened like at the movies. Josh woke up one day and found that he was in the middle of it. His father had become depressed. Usually loud and outgoing, Josh's father was now quiet and sullen. He complained of being tired and not being able to sleep. Once Josh woke up in the middle of the night to go to the bathroom and found his father sitting in the living room, all alone, in the dark.

"What are you doing, Dad?" he asked.

"Go back to bed," his father murmured.

Soon he stopped going to work at the mill and spent most of the day in his bedroom with the lights out and curtains closed, often locking the door. Men from the union called asking Josh where his father was. "Tell them he's sick," his mother had whispered to him across the room, not wanting them to know she was home.

Alone in the dark bedroom, Josh's father became worse. He stopped showering and changing his clothes. Josh's mother slept on the couch in the living room. The only time Josh saw his dad was when he stumbled across the hall to the washroom, his white boxer shorts, which he did not change, were slowly turning yellow in the front. His eyeballs were glossy, as if he were looking out from under a thin layer of misty water. Sometimes he did not see Josh when he stood right in front of him.

"The doctor put me on nerve pills," Josh's mother had said to her sister Doris when Doris came by one afternoon. In the living room watching television, Josh leaned toward the hall leading to the kitchen to hear better. "I can't stand this anymore, Doris. He's going to drive *me* crazy."

"It's just a nervous breakdown, Gloria," Aunt Doris said. "Everyone has one eventually."

"It seems like now that he's sober, he took a look in the mirror and found out he hates himself," his mother said. "Maybe I shouldn't have made him stop drinking."

"You had to do something. Ted was turning into a drunk, and you had three boys watching him."

"Right now I think I would rather have a drunk for a husband than *this*," his mother answered. Her voice cracked.

Me too, Josh thought.

Not long after that day, Josh woke up just after midnight. That was when his mother usually came home from her afternoon shift at the factory. From under his bedroom door, a bright red light flashed. Josh slowly opened his door and saw an ambulance parked in front of the house. His father was being carried by two large men in blue uniforms out of the front door on a stretcher while his mother stood, still wearing her navy blue work handkerchief around her head, with both her hands over her mouth. Under a blanket that went to his chin his father shivered. His eyes were closed and his long greasy hair was fanned out in a stringy mess on top of his head. Josh didn't budge from the doorway of his bedroom. His mother gave one of the men in blue an empty brown pill bottle.

"They were mine," she said with one trembling hand still over her mouth. "The doctor put me on them two weeks ago... for my nerves."

"Do you know how many were in the bottle when you left this afternoon?" the man in blue asked.

"Twenty-five or thirty," his mother answered.

The man in blue rushed out the front door and Josh dashed to the window and pulling back the heavy paisley gold curtain away from the picture window, saw a group of neighbors outside watching as Josh's father was put, shaking, into the ambulance. Josh stepped back, trying to hide his face behind the curtain.

The doors shut, the siren wailed, and the ambulance sped away. Josh let the curtain fall over the window and looked across the room blankly at his mother.

"It's going to be okay," she said. "They told me that he's going to be okay. I need to call your Aunt Doris and find your brothers."

"Why did you make him stop drinking?" Josh spat out.

Josh's mother looked like she had been slapped across the face. Josh turned around, went into his bedroom, and shut the door.

Now, over a month later, Josh peered through a glass window into the hospital smoking lounge and waited for his father and Aunt Wilma to come out. On the other side of the glass, a smoky haze hung in the air, making his father and aunt look like they were in a photograph taken out of focus.

Josh clenched his fists.

His father smoked, drank Pepsi from a can and continued to stare at his sister while she did most of the talking. As she spoke and tapped the tabletop with her index finger to emphasize each word, Josh wished he could find one of those little liquor bottles they give out on airplanes and pour it in his father's can of Pepsi. Finally Josh's father spoke back, his hands raised in the air. Aunt Wilma's face bent slightly in frustration, she shook her head but every hair stayed in place.

For two hours, Josh's grandmother had watched two game shows and then a detective program on the hospital television while Josh kept his eye on his father and aunt. Visiting hours were almost over. "Come on, hurry," Josh said looking at the big white clock on the wall over the television. In the street a car horn blew. Maybe that's Aunt Sue. In the smoker's room, Josh's father's head fell to his chest and he covered his face with his hands. His body crumpled, like the bones in his spine had come crashing down on each other. He seemed to shrink in his chair.

Josh held his breath.

Aunt Wilma straightened. She raised her head up high, higher than his father's, and reached out lovingly and caressed his father's shoulder, rubbing his neck with her thumb. Josh's father took his hands away from his face and nodded.

SHIT, Josh thought.

Three weeks later, Josh's father returned home. With him, he brought his old terrycloth bathrobe, a new short haircut, and a black leather Bible with *EDWARD* written in golden letters on the bottom right corner. In the living room, Josh watched his father, who sat quietly reading his new Bible in the burgundy chair. Not yet accustomed to his crew cut, his father gently moved an imaginary lock behind his right ear.

"Dad," Josh said, but his father didn't stir. "Dad?"

"I'm busy, Joshua."

Josh ground his molars.

"Did I ever tell you that I named you after Joshua from the Bible?" his father said, not looking up. "I'll show you." He turned to the front of his Bible and searched for the book of *Joshua*.

Josh shoved his hands deep into his pockets and walked away. Behind him, his father's voice grew weaker, *"And they utterly destroyed all that was in Jericho, both man and woman, young and old, and ox, and sheep, and ass..."*

"SHIT," Josh said. The sound hung in the air, and his cheeks flushed and his lips burned with the power of the word.

The Wrong Side

The first attack happened at night. It had seized Josh by the throat from out of the darkness, strangling him. He woke up gasping for air. *I can't breathe.* Arching his back with his stomach in the air, the boy strained to inhale and a sickening wheezing sound emerged from deep inside him. His eyes bulged. The room was dark, except for the glowing orange numbers on the clock radio beside his bed. *1:33.*

Pushing himself up on his elbows, Josh gagged and coughed something thick and wet onto the front of his flannel pajama shirt. His throat opened slightly and he sucked a small amount of air into his lungs' murky caverns. Terrified, Josh tried to call out to his parents sleeping down the hall, but could only choke out another loud wheezing gasp. His legs kicked out wildly over the faded brown horses printed on his bed sheets until one foot connected hard with the wall beside his bed. In the living room, on the other side of the wall, something fell with a thud and shattered with the tinkle of a thousand jagged shards onto the hardwood floor.

A second later Josh's dark bedroom filled with light and his father, wearing only a white T-shirt and briefs, stood over his bed. He bent down and grabbed Josh by the shoulders, shaking him until Josh's half-closed eyes were torn away from the shining numbers on the clock radio where they had been fixed on the time and focused on his father's face.

"Are you choking?" his father asked loudly but calmly. "Josh, can you breathe?"

Another whooping sound of distress bubbled from Josh's chest. He shook his head from side to side. At his bedroom door, Josh's mother stood in her yellow nightgown with one hand over her mouth. Josh flung his head back.

"Do something!" his mother yelled.

A painful blow hit Josh between his shoulder blades. *Thump.* Josh's eyes filled with tears and his mouth opened wide in a silent wail. *Thump.* The force of the second jolt pushed Josh's face forward against his knees. *Thump. Thump. THUMP.* A mouthful of thick green mucus from Josh's plugged lungs fell in slimy strings from his mouth onto the blue bedspread. He inhaled deeply, held the air in his lungs for a second, and then exhaled.

"Stop hitting me," Josh sobbed, lashing out his hand at his father's arm.

"Are you okay?" his father asked, gently rubbing Josh's back. Josh pushed his father's hand away.

"I'm thirsty," Josh cried.

"He's fine," Josh's father said. He smiled, stood up and tucked the back of his T-shirt into the waistband of his underwear. "Prop his head up with pillows when you put him back to bed so he doesn't choke again. It's probably the Swine Flu."

"I hope not," Josh's mother said.

"We'll probably all get sick now," his father said. He walked out of Josh's bedroom and down the hallway to his own bed.

Josh imagined a coughing pig with a thermometer in its snout. "I don't want Swine Flu," he said.

His mother eased herself down on the side of his bed and laid her hand on his forehead. "You scared the hell out of me, Josh," she said.

For the next hour, Josh sat on the living room couch with a box of Kleenex Boutique tissues on his lap sipping apple juice out of a highball glass. On her hands and knees, his mother carefully picked up the broken pieces of mirror off the living room floor and then swept up the smaller pieces with a broom and dustpan. Occasionally Josh coughed light-green mucus into a pink tissue and his mother glanced over.

"Still okay?" she asked.

Josh nodded and wiped another tissue over his mouth.

◈

Shirts and Skins

A few weeks later, Josh's mother sat with Aunt Doris at the kitchen table. It was a warm Saturday in June and Josh lay on the living room couch watching television with his head resting uncomfortably on the worn, carved wooden armrest. Though it was almost noon, he still wore his blue pajamas and a pair of faded black cotton socks. Josh sighed and looked up at the swirling pattern in the plaster ceiling. He was bored. Now that he was nine years old, Josh was beginning to lose interest in Saturday morning cartoons. He lifted his pajama top and jiggled his belly. *I'm getting fat.*

From the sofa, Josh could look down the hallway and see his mother and aunt drinking their tea in the kitchen. His aunt was leaning forward in her chair holding a cigarette between two fingers and hovering close to the ashtray on the table. Across from Aunt Doris, his mother sat with her back toward him. They were dressed for the mall. His aunt wore a pair of dark blue jeans and a pink T-shirt that was too tight and showed her spare tire. Josh's mother had on a pair of stretchy green nylon pants and a short-sleeve white and paisley blouse. They weren't talking about anything interesting either—something about a "white sale." Josh was wondering what a "white sale" was when he suddenly leaned forward and cocked his head toward the kitchen. Now they were talking about him.

"They did a bunch of tests on him and sure enough he has asthma," his mother said.

Aunt Doris shook her head sympathetically and then picked up one of the digestive biscuits Josh's mother had stacked on a white and pink saucer in the middle of the kitchen table. Aunt Doris bit the cookie between her front teeth, chewed slowly and then washed it down with a mouthful of tea.

"Those cookies were on sale last week at A&P," his Aunt Doris said.

"I know. I bought four packages," Josh's mother said. "I hid two in my bedroom closet so the boys wouldn't eat them all at once."

Josh laid back his head and studied the ceiling. He stuck his finger in his mouth and wiggled another bottom tooth that had become loose. He had already lost six or seven baby teeth. *I wonder how old I will be when they finally stop falling out.*

"Anyway, after the asthma test the doctor sent us to an allergist," his mother said. "And what a *goddamn* pain that was! The allergist's office was way downtown so we had to take three buses to get there."

"Couldn't Ted drive you?" Aunt Doris asked.

"Ted?" his mother's voice became lower and angrier. "No, Ted wouldn't drive us."

"Is it getting worse?" Aunt Doris asked.

Josh crossed his arms over his chest. He did not want to hear any of this. He tried to focus on the stupid cartoon playing on the television but couldn't stop himself from listening to the women in the kitchen. *Why don't you just shut up about Dad?*

"So the doctor did an allergy test on him and Josh has allergies too," his mother said.

"Do allergies cause the asthma attacks?" his aunt asked.

"They can," his mother answered. "Or that's what they think..."

"That's the pits," Aunt Doris said, finishing the last of her tea. She butted her cigarette in the ashtray. "What's he allergic to?"

"Grass, pollen and... oh, something else I forgot." She turned her head slightly toward the living room. "Josh! Come in here for a minute."

Josh thought about just yelling "dust" from where he was laying, but then they would know he had been eavesdropping. He rolled himself off the sofa with a grunt and leaped into the kitchen with his arms open.

"*Ta da!*" he sang.

"Tell Auntie Doris what you're allergic to."

Josh lifted his left hand and counted off on his fingers, "Pollen, grass, and dust." He slid over the slick mauve linoleum floor toward the kitchen table and took the last cookie off the saucer. "I hear these were on sale at the A&P last week," he said and then bit the cookie in half.

"Dust?" Aunt Doris said. Her head slid back on her shoulders, accentuating her double chin. "But your house is never dusty, Gloria." She looked sideways at Josh like his asthma was some kind of insult to his mother's housekeeping. He ran his tongue around his mouth to lick stray cookie crumbs off his lips.

"And it's not only his allergies that can trigger an asthma attack," his mother explained. She stood up and placed another handful of cookies from a package of *Peak Freens* on the counter onto the saucer. "They said that cold air, humidity, and even *strong emotions* could cause him to have an asthma attack. God knows what that means. I guess Josh shouldn't get too excited."

Josh smiled and grabbed the front of his pajama top. "Where's my smellin' salts!" he said in as good a southern accent he could muster. "Here we go," his mother said with a sigh. She stood up, walked to the counter and picked up the teapot.

"All this excitement is giving me a bad case of the vapors," Josh continued. "And I plum can't breathe." He waved his hand in front of his face like a fan and fell to his knees.

Aunt Doris laughed loudly and slapped her thigh. "You're too much, Josh. You sounded like Jimmy Carter's mother. What's her name?"

"It's not funny, Josh" his mother said. She poured more tea into Aunt Doris's cup and then her own. "Asthma attacks aren't a joke. They're horrible to see—*horrible!* And they scare me to death!" She put down the teapot on the kitchen table and shuddered.

"Just *horrible,*" Josh said in a mocking high-pitched voice. He stood up from the floor and looked through the cupboards for something to eat. It was lunchtime. Why hadn't his mother and aunt left for the mall yet? If his mother weren't around, he would have just finished the package of cookies for lunch.

Aunt Doris took another home-rolled cigarette out of her plastic cigarette case. "I don't think anyone in our family has asthma," she said. "Does it run in Ted's family?"

"Asthma? I don't think so," his mother said. "Though it seems like everything else does."

A can of tomato soup fell out of the cupboard Josh had been rummaging through and fell to the floor, denting the side of the can. Josh chased the can across the kitchen floor to where it stopped at the foot of a harvest-gold refrigerator. He picked it up with his left hand.

"What's that noise?" a hoarse voice from deep in the basement yelled.

Josh put the can on the counter and then quietly coughed a tiny bit of phlegm into his hand. Without anyone noticing, he wiped the palm of his hand on the seat of his pajama bottoms "Nothing," Josh's mother yelled back toward the stairs that lead to the basement.

Aunt Doris put her hand to her mouth as if she intended to yodel. "Hi, Ted," she yelled.

"Hi," Josh's father shouted a few seconds later.

The two sisters looked across the table at one another. They had the same dark eyes.

"I got an emergency inhaler for my asthma," Josh said to break the silence. "I use it whenever I have an attack." He opened the silverware drawer and searched for a can opener.

"The hard part is getting him to remember to take his puffer with him whenever he goes outside. I cleaned out an entire shelf in the medicine cabinet just for the inhaler so everyone knows where it is. But still he forgets to take it with him when he leaves the house— and then I start to worry... and end up having to take a pill for my nerves."

"Mom opens up the back door and screams out, *Josh, you forgot your inhaler!* You can hear her all over the bloody neighborhood." He put his hands over his face and shook his head. "It's embarrassing."

"Then you shouldn't forget your inhaler," his aunt said.

"I try not to forget it," he said.

Aunt Doris reached out and pointed to the green and red tea cozy over the teapot on the table. "You know, I knitted this tea cozy for your mother so maybe I could knit you a nice puffer cozy to match. You could hang it around your neck and always have it with you in case you have an attack."

"Don't bother," Josh said trying not to smile.

"And I could knit words into it like, *please keep away all dust and grass.*"

"And *pollen*," his mother added.

"And *strong emotions*," Josh said.

"Maybe we should just put you into one of those plastic bubbles," his aunt said.

"Or you could crochet me one," Josh said. They all laughed loudly.

"But he hasn't had an asthma attack since that night," his mother said after the laughter stopped. "Have you?"

"Nope," Josh said. "Not once."

But that was a lie. Josh had used his emergency inhaler twice last Thursday—the day his father had finally gone to the doctor.

"What did the doctor say?" his mother had asked when his father came in the door that afternoon.

"He told me to pull myself together," his father had said.

"Then why don't you?"

"I can't."

"Is there nothing they can give you for the panic? What about the kind of nerve pills I take?"

"I don't want to take nerve pills."

"Then what are you going to do, Ted?"

"I'll pray"

"Can't you take pills *and* pray?"

"Look Gloria, I just got sober... I don't want to take *anything*."

"I don't understand you. Are you just going to let this thing... box you in?" his mother shouted. "And box me in with you?"

"I said I'm not taking pills," his father repeated, his voice growing louder with frustration. He walked down into the basement with the afternoon newspaper.

"Jesus *fucking* Christ," his mother said as she stormed past Josh to her bedroom. She did not notice Josh was wheezing.

In the bathroom with the door locked, Josh took the blue emergency puffer out of the medicine cabinet and pinched it down the way the doctor showed him, using his thumb and index finger. The mist filled his lungs, but he was unable to hold it in for the ten seconds they told him to. He held the puffer to his mouth and squeezed a second time. He counted to ten quickly as his lungs screamed for air. Then, still gasping, he had sat down on the toilet and waited for his lungs to open.

Now, sitting at the kitchen table in his blue pajamas, Josh slurped his tomato soup as his mother and Aunt Doris stood by the back door putting on their shoes.

"You sure you don't want me to start that puffer cozy after your mother and I finish our shopping?" Aunt Doris said.

"I don't need it," Josh said. "I won't forget my inhaler again. Honestly."

"Yeah, I'll believe that when I see it," his mother said as she tied up the shoelace of her white canvas tennis shoe.

"Bye, Ted," his aunt yelled down the basement stairs. But Josh's father did not answer.

"Get dressed, Josh," his mother said as she and Aunt Doris walked out the back door.

Josh put his spoon down in his soup and gobbled up all five cookies remaining in the saucer. *There are two more packages in Mom's closet.*

◈

The following day, like every Sunday morning for the last six months, a long yellow school bus stopped in front of Josh's house to take him to The Good Shepherd Baptist Church.

"Sunday school won't kill him," his father had said. "It'll be good for him to finally learn some morals."

"I'm too tired to argue with you, Ted," his mother had answered.

Josh hated getting up early on weekends, but his father wanted him in Sunday school—and there was no way he could say no to his father—so now every Sunday morning Josh reluctantly climbed onto the yellow school bus.

Josh disliked almost everything about Sunday school—the other kids were creeps, the pastor was a colossal jerk-off and the songs they made him sing were ridiculous. He felt stupid the whole time he was there. The only thing Josh enjoyed about Sunday school was the storytelling. They were a lot like the tales in his big Grimm Fairytale book, but more gruesome. These weekly Bible stories were always about separation. On one side were the people God liked, they built what they were told to build, married who they were told to marry, killed who they were told to kill and so forth. This bunch usually came off pretty well—while the others, on the wrong side, were drowned or stoned or burned. There was no gray area with God; you were good or evil, clean or unclean, lamb or goat. Josh felt more goat than lamb.

As he sat in the basement of The Good Shepherd Baptist Church on Sunday mornings, Josh wondered what would have happened to him if he had lived back in biblical times. Maybe, Josh thought, he would have been one of the unlucky folks who lived in Jericho when that other Joshua came by. Then I would have been *dashed,* he thought. Given the choice between being drowned, stoned, burned or dashed, he would definitely choose being dashed. Josh liked the sound of *dashed.* It was like someone scratching a thick black horizontal line through his name. *What happened to Josh? Oh, haven't you heard? He was dashed—*

Sunday school was always in two parts. First, all the kids sat together in the church basement while the pastor preached about the need to be prepared for Jesus' return. "Like a thief in the night," the pastor said each week. Josh had considered the comparison. Would you say a thief is "like Jesus at Rapture?" Then, in the second part of Sunday school, after the pastor had left for the adult church service upstairs, the children broke into smaller groups separated by age and gender to discuss some new Bible story. Josh sat in Mr. Dunn's group with the other nine-year-old boys. Josh liked Mr. Dunn and the colorful ties he wore. Mr. Dunn was young, only around twenty years old, but he had already grown a light brown beard on his boyish face. He had deep blue eyes that would often nonchalantly stray away to the clock on the wall and seemed uncomfortable in his new whiskers, always scratching at his cheeks and under his chin with the cleanest fingernails Josh had ever seen on a man.

When Josh's father first told him that he was being sent to Sunday school, he spelled out "the plan". The plan had been simple enough: because Sunday school began earlier than the church service, The

Good Shepard Baptist Church would send their bus to pick Josh up in front of his house on Sunday morning. After Sunday school, Josh's father, who would be upstairs at the church service, would drive him home. But that arrangement did not last long. For a few weeks everything ran smoothly, but one Sunday Josh could not find his father in the church pews after Sunday school. He searched the building and finally found his father sitting in his old burgundy Chevy Impala in the church parking lot smoking a cigarette. "It was too hot in church today" his father had said. "I had to come out for some fresh air."

Then Josh's father stopped going to the church service altogether. After Sunday school, Josh would begin to walk toward his house and his father would meet him somewhere on the way. But over the last few months, Josh's father would meet him farther and farther from the church. Once Josh had to walk more than halfway home in the rain. Josh's mother had been furious when she saw his church clothes soaked. "Don't you know he has asthma!" she had shouted at his father. Josh could see his mother was growing frustrated. Josh's father had stopped picking her up from work as well, and since Josh's mother didn't drive, now she had to take the bus. Each day Josh's father traveled less and less distance from the house as an invisible and impenetrable perimeter closed in around him.

Now, on a humid Sunday in June after Mr. Dunn had dismissed the Sunday school class, Josh began the walk home. The church was only about a mile from his house, down Woodlawn Avenue. On the other side of the street on Josh's right, Edmund Park, a run-down piece of green space that had survived in the industrial area, was empty except for an overgrown baseball pitch. A warm dirty gust of wind blew across the park and fine yellow soil from the upper layer of the baseball diamond infield blew into Josh's eyes. He coughed, looked over at the park and spit in its direction.

A hundred yards in front of Josh were the Canadian National railroad tracks that cut off his blue-collar neighborhood from the rest of the city. The area where Josh lived, seemingly disowned by the rest of Hamilton, was nestled between Lake Ontario to the north and the municipal sewage plant on the south. To the east was Red

Hill Creek, now polluted from pipes continuously dumping brown stinking sludge from the sewage plant, and finally to the west, the steel mills with their black smokestacks bordered the neighborhood. On a map of Hamilton it was called Woodlawn Heights. His mother called it the wrong side of the tracks.

It was hot and Josh wanted to get home so he could put on his short pants. Sweat dripped down his back and between his legs under the brown corduroy pants his mother had bought specifically for Sunday school. From a distance, Josh heard the familiar rattle and ping of his father's car and his father's ugly old car bounced over the railroad tracks toward him.

There was a time, Josh remembered, when his father had been so relaxed behind the wheel. He would roll down the window, slip an 8-track into the tape deck and sing along as he sped down the city streets. Josh had loved the way his father's long hair had whipped around in the wind as he drove with one arm on the steering wheel and the other resting on the open car window frame, tanning his left arm and turning the light green panther tattoo on his forearm into a deep burnt-olive. But now, Josh's father drove with both hands firmly on the steering wheel.

Josh's father did a U-turn and the car clattered to a stop. "Hurry up and get in, I think there's a train coming," his father said.

"Okay," Josh said. He stepped off the curb toward the passenger car door.

"Get in. Get in," his father yelled again. For a second, Josh thought that his father would drive off before he got in and he had not even shut the passenger door before his father accelerated with a screech on the hot black asphalt.

"Damn," his father said under his breath as his foot moved to the brake. It was too late. The bells at the crossing started to ring. In front of them, red lights began to flash, the guardrails came down and the car slowed, finally stopping behind two other cars and a flatbed truck. Josh's father held the steering wheel tighter. His knuckles turned white. Silent, he looked straight ahead as his breathing quickened. Josh reached down to ensure that his emergency inhaler was in the front pocket of his church pants.

The train rolled by and the street rumbled beneath them. Josh stretched out his arm and turned on the radio. *He needs to get his mind off the train.* As Josh searched the dial for his favorite top forty AM station from Toronto, the driver's door suddenly flew open and his father jumped out of the car. The door bounced with a grating squeak on its rusty hinges and slammed shut behind him.

"Dad, come back!"

Josh slid over to the driver's side and watched his father walk quickly across Woodlawn Avenue to Edmund Park and stopped. He looked left and then right, as if he was deciding where to go. The caboose signaled the end of the train and the red crossing lights stopped blinking. The bells stopped ringing and the long line of cars and trucks jolted slightly forward as each shifted into drive.

"Dad, get back here!"

The truck and two cars in front of them drove off but Josh's father still had not moved. A couple of the vehicles behind them honked their horns. A large transport truck's whistle blew.

"Get moving, asshole!" someone yelled. Josh sunk down in his seat and covered his ears.

The door opened and Josh's father fell hard into the seat. He shifted into drive and the car lurched forward with a squeal. They bounced over the tracks with a loud crashing sound that made Josh cover his eyes and soon pulled into the driveway of their house. Josh's father leaped out of the car and rushed into the back door. Josh sat motionless. His throat closed and a low gurgle of mucus bubbled in his chest. He reached into his pocket, took out his bright blue inhaler, and put it to his lips.

⁂

On the Sunday of Labor Day weekend, Josh sat with other nine-year-old boys in the basement of The Good Shepherd Baptist Church. This was the first Labor Day weekend that Josh could remember when his family had not traveled to Toronto for the Canadian National

Exhibition to see the air show and ride the roller coaster. His father no longer even crossed the railroad tracks. His borders had shrunk to less than four blocks from their house. A month earlier he had lost his job at the mill because it was now too far for him to travel and ever since his father stayed mostly in their damp basement, smoking cigarettes, watching television and sleeping into the afternoon. On Sundays, Josh now walked all the way home from Sunday school.

As Mr. Dunn talked on, Josh's eyes wandered over the painting of a cloud with a sunbeam shining though. Was that sunbeam supposed to be God? he wondered.

"So Jacob received his brother's birthright," Mr. Dunn read from the big white picture book he held on his lap and then hesitated before adding, "But Jacob should not have lied to his father to get it... because lying is really bad." He looked up from the book and bit the inside of his cheek.

Josh squinted. *He added that part.* That book of Bible stories wouldn't say, 'really bad,' Josh thought. If it was anyone else, Josh would have asked to see the book and prove he was lying, but Josh did not want to embarrass Mr. Dunn, who looked silly enough wearing a black and red tie with a bunch of musical notes all over it. Instead, Josh looked at the way the whiskers, sparse and bare in patches below his cheeks, looked on Mr. Dunn's baby face. He wondered if a young man's whiskers were softer than an older man's, like his father. Josh imagined himself blind, like Isaac, reaching out and touching Mr. Dunn's face.

After Sunday school, on his walk home down Woodlawn Avenue, Josh looked at the railroad tracks laid out in front of him and wondered if his father would ever cross them again. If only Dad would, Josh thought, he would see that there's nothing to be afraid of. Nothing is scarier on this side than that side. If anything, it was Josh's neighborhood that was the more frightening. His father just needed a reason to go over the tracks again. Josh tried to think of things that would tempt his father over the tracks and as he crossed the junction, his sneaker became stuck briefly between the track and the cement walkway. He tripped but did not fall down. *Fucking tracks.* If Mom fell and hurt herself I bet Dad would cross the tracks to help her, he thought—or if one of his brothers was in the hospital from a car accident then his father would travel to the other side too. The day had become muggy and Josh pulled his shirttails out of his pants to cool down. His lungs burned in his chest and he reached for his inhaler stuffed in the front pocket of his brown corduroys. *Dad would cross the tracks if I were dying.* He stopped, put the inhaler back in his pocket and grinned.

That afternoon in his bedroom, Josh planned everything on one of the blank pages in the back of an old fourth-grade history notebook. He waited until his mother had climbed in Aunt Doris' car and drove off to visit Josh's older brother, Kevin, and his girlfriend at their new apartment. Then he took two dimes off his parents' dresser and checked that his emergency puffer was in its place on the middle shelf of the medicine cabinet. Before he left, he climbed down the stairs to the basement. The partially finished basement, always damper than the rest of the small bungalow, had three rooms connected by dark passages: a recreation room, laundry room and a small bedroom where Josh's brother, Troy, slept. Josh entered the rec room. It was cool and dark and smelled of mold and cigarette smoke, which made him a little queasy. The only light came from the television at the end of the room. In a black recliner, his father sat smoking a cigarette and staring at a baseball game.

"I'm going out to play," Josh said.

"Fine," his father said.

Josh walked the four blocks down his street and then turned left onto Woodlawn Avenue toward Edmund Park. He felt his front pocket out of habit. It was empty. A tremor of panic rippled through his body. He looked both ways as he crossed the railroad tracks. There were no trains as far as the eye could see. He did not want a train to mess everything up now.

He marched quickly to the park. He never went there anymore. The last time he'd been there was when his mother took him to play on the swings a few years ago. He looked around the park. It was empty. Even though there was that baseball diamond at the far end of the field, no leagues ever played there. The outline of the infield was a barren cake of crackled clay. The chain link backstop behind where home plate had been, had rusted to a dark brown and the outfield was overgrown with weeds and swaying golden rod. On the other side of the field, a large iron swing-set frame stood like a huge headless metal quadruped. No one had bothered to attach the swings this summer. Behind the swings, at the intersection of Woodlawn Avenue and Edmund Street, there stood one lone Bell telephone booth.

Josh dug in his pants and pulled out two dimes. He hiked across the field to where the grass was longest, kicking it with his sneaker along the way. And then, lying down on his side, stuck his face in the grass. He inhaled deeply. He did not know how allergic he was to grass, but hoped a reaction wouldn't take too long.

Nothing happened.

He took another deep breath and then another, never taking his eye off the phone booth. His dad would be home, he thought, that's for sure. But what if the line was busy when he called? What if he was talking to one of Josh's aunts or uncles? Josh just had to hope that the line was free. This was taking too long, he thought. *Maybe I need the juice from the grass.* He ripped the grass out of the soil and tore the blades in half. He held both hands up to his face and rubbed it under his nose.

Again, nothing happened.

Josh groaned. He stood and walked to the stems of golden rod farther back of the park. He bent over and inhaled. He wiped the yellow buds over his face. His eyes began to burn. *That's gotta be a good sign.*

As Josh stood in the field, an old man stopped his long tan town car on the street beside the phone booth and an old lady opened the passenger door and, after pulling herself out of the car, walked to the phone booth. She folded back the door and lifted the receiver to her ear. She put the receiver down immediately and walked back to the car and they drove off. *Shit*, Josh thought. The phone must be out of order. That was one thing I didn't think of.

He stood and ran toward the phone. He only took a few paces when his lungs started to close up and a whooping sound echoed from inside him. Josh held his chest and tried to run faster, but could only manage a quick hop. Near the swing set, he tripped and fell down. His palms and knees were scraped by pebbles and dry earth.

Finally Josh reached the payphone. Choking, he grabbed for the receiver with his shaking hand and brought it to his ear. He heard a click and a dial tone. Frantically, he reached his hand in his pocket and rummaged for one of the two dimes. One had fallen out of his hand when he had fallen down. He found the dime in the corner of his pocket and put it in the payphone. It got stuck in the slot. Josh pounded his bloody palm on the slot until the dime fell with a clink into the machine. Once during recess, the older boys had played "pile on the rabbit" and all jumped on Josh. Now the constriction in his chest felt the same way, like ten boys were lying on top of him. He didn't even have the air to scream out. Josh punched the buttons with his index finger quickly but carefully. He only had one dime and he had to dial the number right. It rang and rang. *Please answer.*

"Hello," his father said.

"Dad?" Josh said. "I forgot my inhaler and I'm having an asthma attack… I can't breathe… I'm at Edmund Park… bring me my inhaler… it's in the medicine cabinet… just hurry…. help me. Dad? Dad? Okay, hurry! I'll start walking now."

Josh hung up the phone and holding his chest, walked down Woodlawn Avenue toward his house. He expected to see his father's car speed down the street. He could be there in less than a minute. But his father did not come. Josh bent over and tried to cough out the mucus that was suffocating him. He couldn't. Panic rose from his belly. He looked at the cars driving up and down Woodlawn Avenue. *Would a stranger help me?*

He made his way toward the railroad tracks. His face was flushed and covered with sweat. Across the tracks, less than fifty yards away, Josh saw his father's old burgundy Chevy sitting parked on the other side. He won't come, Josh thought.

Now darkness at the edge of the horizon began to swell over the sky and seep onto the street. Josh could no longer hear the cars zooming by or his own wheezing. He tried to walk faster. He hobbled forward, stopping a few times to cough. Just before the railroad tracks,

Josh coughed so hard he gagged and, holding his stomach, threw up his breakfast of Capt'n Crunch cereal on the sidewalk. Still his father's car did not move. His lungs were closing in. *I'm going to die. This is what death is like—dark lonely silent. And he doesn't care.*

Then Josh was at his father's car. Josh had made it over the tracks. In the front seat, his father stared straight ahead at the railway crossing sign, his hands shaking on the steering wheel. On the passenger seat, Josh saw his bright blue inhaler beside his father's cigarette package.

"Are you okay?" his father asked.

Josh opened the car door. He leaned in and grabbed the inhaler. He used it once, breathed in as deeply as he could. As he counted to ten he stared at his father, searching for something in his face.

"I couldn't," his father said. "I tried... I really tried."

Josh breathed in deeply a few times more and then used his inhaler again. The scenery looked clearer and more vibrant as Josh's breathing returned to normal. The leaves were beginning to turn brown on the tops of the trees and the sun-scorched grass on the boulevard looked thirsty for the first autumn rain.

"Get in the car," his father said. "I'll take you home."

Saying nothing, Josh stepped away from the car and slammed the door. He twirled one hundred and eighty degrees around and sauntered away from his father with a wave of his hand.

"Get back here, Joshua," his father yelled. "I want to talk to you."

Josh headed south back toward Edmund Park and, crossing to the other side of the train tracks, shoved his blue plastic inhaler back into the front pocket of his pants like a gun sliding into a holster.

"*Ta da!*" Josh yelled, opening his arms wide to the afternoon sun.

Next week he would tell his father that he was never going back to Sunday school—and now his father couldn't make him. The folks at The Good Shepherd Baptist Church would just have to strike a thick beautiful black dash through Josh's name on their Sunday school class list. Josh thought of Mr. Dunn. "Well," he'd say to all the other nine-year-old lambs as he slowly scratched the light brown whiskers under his chin, "I guess Josh *was* a goat after all."

Skins

Twice a week boys and girls were separated. While one-half of Josh's fifth-grade class was in the school's gymnasium with their teacher, Mr. Tanner, the other was in the library for a weekly health lesson, learning the four basic food groups or the dangers of smoking cigarettes from the school librarian. Just why the school librarian, Miss Gaskell, should be teaching them anything at all puzzled Josh. After all, if she was any good as a teacher the principal would give her a class of kids to look after and not just a room full of books. Not that she knew much about books either. On Library Days when Mr. Tanner walked Josh's entire class over in two lines to pick out new library books, Miss Gaskell always made the same book recommendations. "Have you read *Anne of Green Gables*?" she would ask while hovering behind girls who stood too long turning the revolving metal paperback rack. Or, for boys who loitered in groups around the bookshelves, "Have you read *How to Eat Fried Worms*?" If anyone told her that they had already read her recommendation, then an annoyed look would creep onto her round face. "Just pick anything, then," she would say while stamping due-back dates on pale yellow cards with her stubby blue ink-dyed fingers.

In health class, Miss Gaskell had the boys sit 'Indian-style' on a carpeted section of the library floor that looked out over Woodlawn Avenue, the busy street in front of Laura Secord Public School. Josh didn't know why sitting on the floor with your legs crossed was called Indian style. None of his mother's brothers or sisters, all of them half-Indian, sat that way when they came over to his house to visit. They sat in chairs just like his father's white relatives.

Shirts and Skins

As dump trucks and tractor-trailers rumbled down the road outside, making the floor under them tremble slightly each time one passed, Miss Gaskell sat in front of them in a wooden chair explaining, in a halted staggered voice, the correct way to brush teeth. "Then... take the toothbrush and... um..."

She ran her blue fingers through her short black hair and tugged her skirt over her chubby knees and looked up, as if the word she wanted was typed between the florescent lights on the stained drop ceiling tiles. Then, pretending that a fat red pencil was a toothbrush, she made tiny circles in the air near her mouth. Her blue macramé sweater vest, which looked like a dozen tea cozies stitched together, slapped against the seat of her chair from the motion of her hand. Sitting apart from the other boys, Josh fidgeted as his right foot began to fall asleep under his leg. *At least it isn't Thursday.*

"Then... um... sweep away from your... um..."

Shit! Josh thought. How hard can it be to explain how to brush teeth? She only needs a handful of words: "teeth" "brush" "gums" "toothpaste." His foot ached with pins and needles as he imagined chiseling the word "gums" into a dart and throwing it into her head, like the balloon game at the carnival. Josh waited until Miss Gaskell's eyes twitched their way toward him and once she was looking at him, he rolled his eyes with a loud sigh.

❖

On a Thursday afternoon in early spring, Josh sat at his desk gloomily watching the minute hand of the classroom clock. It was the boy's gym day. At two o'clock the boys and girls queued up by the classroom door for their opposite marches down the hall. Josh took his time walking toward the line of boys. As he shuffled slowly down an aisle between desks he looked at the girls. "Take me with you" he pleaded silently. He would gladly listen to Miss Gaskell stumble through her talk on the difference between veins and arteries again rather than go to the gym for volleyball. Josh's look of earnest pleading must have instead made him look like he had to go to the toilet and three girls at the end of the line stared at him, then turned to each other and began laughing. Josh looked away, his face warming, and tried to cover the roll of fat around his stomach by crossing his arms over the top of his belly.

Josh took his place at the back of the line of boys. In the rear, no one would kick him in the butt while he walked, or try to push him down the stairs. In front of Josh, Matt Gore stood in a yellow shirt with brown stripes and faded blue jeans. Matt always stood second from the back. Although Matt was a year older, he was thin and shorter than the other boys in the class. Matt looked down at the floor with his round shoulders slouched forward and Josh examined the wonderful way Matt's light brown head of hair fell to his shoulders like a girl.

At the classroom door, Mr. Tanner, a large man with a thick brown mustache and brown eyes, was talking, but Josh was not listening. He began dissecting the time he would be gone from the classroom. One hour. That's sixty minutes or four blocks of fifteen minutes. *Stairway to Heaven* is just over seven minutes long. Sing it twice and that's fifteen minutes (or almost) and times that by four and that equals eight Stairways to Heaven. Josh imagined the spiral staircase he always saw when he closed his eyes and listened to that song. Then he doubled that image four times, putting one set of stairs on top of the other, seeing it grow, turning and turning upwards into the clouds. *Stairway to Heaven* eight times is nothing, he told himself. One afternoon he had listened to it twenty-two times in a row, carefully lifting the record needle off Troy's album each time and moving it back to the beginning of the song. Later Troy had blamed him for a scratch that appeared on the record. As the boys in front of him began to move, Josh began to hum.

Mr. Tanner, leading the line of boys, towered out in front. Josh thought his teacher was too muscular and athletic-looking for the east side of Hamilton. On gym days, Mr. Tanner wore his tracksuit in the afternoon, changing in the staff washroom after lunch. A few months earlier, one Thursday afternoon when he was running late, Mr. Tanner had changed right in the gym. Josh had watched as his teacher turned around, slipped off his gray slacks and, while he pulled his electric blue ADIDAS track pants with three bright yellow lines running down the side of the legs out of his gym bag, stood there in only a pair of light blue underwear and black socks. Josh stared. Dark brown hair covered Mr. Tanner's chest and thighs. His underwear hugged tightly to his bum and revealed a slight peek of butt-crack above the dark blue elastic waistband. Then Mr. Tanner shook out his track pants with one hand, making his right butt cheek jiggle. Suddenly his teacher was gazing at him. Josh tried to comprehend the look on Mr. Tanner's face. It wasn't just anger. There was something uglier. Now, months later, Mr. Tanner would slightly curl his lip, making his mustache grow slightly smaller, as if he smelled something unpleasant whenever Josh came near him.

Following their teacher, the line of boys entered the gymnasium through a large wooden door. Being last in, Mr. Tanner yelled "Shut the door behind you, Moore!" and Josh swung the big door closed with a slam, wondering why, once they entered the gym, they were suddenly only called by their last names. The gym was freezing, like always, and the volleyball net that had been up for the last few weeks was gone. At both ends of the gym were red hockey nets, one by the door and the other in front of the wooden stage where the Christmas pageant was performed each December. To the side by the windows sat a pile of yellow and blue plastic hockey sticks.

"Floor hockey," said Mr. Tanner, pushing his chest out and placing his fists on his hips like the Jolly Green Giant in a tracksuit.

Most of the boys cheered, but Josh held his arms closer to his chest. "Ho ho ho," he said softly. And then looking at the clock on the wall over the stage, "Fifty-four minutes left."

Mr. Tanner quickly divided the class in two with half, including Josh and Matt, on one side along the windows and the other half forming a line in front of the climbing bars. How come they never let us climb on those things, Josh wondered. That would be better than floor hockey.

"Wakey wakey, Moore," Mr. Tanner yelled. "I'm trying to explain the rules so stop staring off into space and pay attention. You're holding up the game."

Twenty boys stared angrily at him.

"Like it matters," Josh mumbled. He put his hands behind his back and leaned against the gym wall.

"Ten minute shifts!" Mr. Tanner shouted. "Five men on each team. That's four players and one goalie. The rest of you stand off to the side on the white line until I blow the whistle. Then the next five go on the court. I don't care who's in goal. Choose for yourselves."

Josh closed his eyes and began praying. "Please please *please.*" Mr. Tanner stretched out his hairy arm towards Josh's side of the gym.

"Skins," Mr. Tanner said.

"Fuck," Josh said, softly but still out loud. "He did that on purpose."

A few minutes later Josh stood shirtless at the end of the line and watched the red second hand sweep around the face of the clock. The boys were so keen they had pushed their way to the front of the line. Josh smiled. Luckily there were eleven boys on his side so he would miss the first two shifts.

Mr. Tanner dropped the puck in the middle of the gym floor to start the first shift. The sound of plastic slapping against wood filled the gymnasium.

"What a bunch of jerks," Josh said. He wished he could trigger an asthma attack before his turn.

On the ceiling, six stark lights encased in protective wire cages glowed with eyeball burning brightness. After ten minutes, Mr. Tanner blew the whistle signaling ten boys to move off the court and ten more to move on. Now in the front of the line, five eager boys stood to Josh's left deciding which unlucky one would have to sit out the next shift.

"Fine," Paul Boyarin finally said. "At least I don't have to play with him." Paul pointed at Josh and walked away from the others fuming.

The whistle blew. "Offside," Mr. Tanner yelled.

Josh looked out over the gym floor and tried to remember the rules of the game. *What the hell is "offside"?* He had played floor hockey a few times in earlier grades, but was confused by the pattern of lines and circles on the floor of the gym. The other boys seemed to be using them, knowing where to stand and how to move the orange plastic puck with their stupid looking sticks. Josh had seen the old wooden gym floor hundreds of times but had never really taken a close look at it. A bright blue circle was painted in the middle of the floor, and outside that, another larger blue circle was painted around it. On either side of the outer blue circle, cutting the floor in thirds ran two bright glossy red lines that looked as if someone had painted them with thousands of bottles of nail polish. White must fade faster than other colors, Josh thought. He scuffed his sneaker over the white line to see if he could rub any of the paint off.

The whistle blew again. Someone had hit the puck onto the stage. Claude Donner, one of the best athletes in Josh's class, jumped up on the stage, found the puck and threw it across the gym right into Mr. Tanner's hand. Josh hoped that the time they stopped to find the puck would not be counted in their ten minutes.

Mr. Tanner dropped the puck. Biting his thumbnail, Josh noticed Matt running around the floor. One of Matt's shoelaces had come undone. He's gonna trip if he's not careful, Josh thought. Matt's body and arms were thin and very white, his chest caved in slightly at the breastbone. He looked like a puppy chasing a ball, always lagging a little bit behind the rest of the boys, a mane of light-brown hair flying behind him. Whenever he stopped for a moment, he would flip any stray locks out of his face. Mr. Tanner should blow the whistle and let Matt tie his shoe before he falls flat on his face, Josh thought.

Someone scooped the puck with their hockey stick and lofted it up to the ceiling where it hit the steel cage around one of the lights. Following the puck with his eyes, Matt looked up. His mouth was wide open and his long hair reached halfway down his naked back as he watched the puck fall to the floor. In profile, Matt's overbite was—*almost sweet.* Josh's stomach quivered and his lunch of tomato soup and crackers looped the loop inside his belly with a pleasant tickle that made his legs quiver like a dump truck was bouncing down Woodlawn Avenue. Only someone standing very close could see the change in Josh's face. His eyes opened wide, and a hint of a smile grew in the corner of his mouth.

Like Josh, Matt did not have any friends in Mr. Tanner's class, having been put in their class only after the Christmas break. Matt had been in Special Education before it was cancelled and the students bused off to other schools around the city. They had said that Laura Secord Public School was too small to have its own Special Education classes. Josh had seen a few kids taken out of regular classes and put into Special Education over the years, but had never heard of anyone, except Matt, get out of it. But since coming to Mr. Tanner's class, Matt had not been doing well. The other kids, mostly the girls, called him "stupid" or "dirty" because he wore the same two shirts over and over. Girls noticed things like how often people changed their shirts.

The whistle blew and Matt walked off the floor. The last boy off, Matt handed his blue plastic hockey stick to Josh.

"Thanks," Josh muttered.

Matt smiled and shrugged his shoulders. Fascinated by Matt's overbite, Josh tried to imagine it in profile again. Matt seemed more vague than dumb. Always alone, he would walk away from the school at the end of the day towards wherever it was he lived, shoulders slumped over, his long hair draping down from under a black wool toque, not noticing, or not caring, that he had a splash of dried bird shit on the back of his brown jacket. Now, walking toward the blue bulls-eye on the gym floor, Josh decided that he would tell Matt about the stain on his coat. He would not tell Matt that it had been on his back all winter though. That might make Matt feel dumb.

On the floor, Josh never came close to the puck, only once halfheartedly reaching out his blue plastic hockey stick to where the puck had swished by a few seconds earlier. The rest of the boys played around him, yelling whenever he stumbled in their way. "Move it, fat-ass," someone spat at him.

Josh tried to run as little as possible, so his soft stomach would not jiggle over the waist of his brown *Husky* corduroy jeans while along the gym wall, Matt paced alone, away from the line of other boys, as if guarding his ratty old yellow shirt lying in a ball against the wall. The whistle blew again and Josh walked to the sidelines, handing his hockey stick to another boy like it was made of lead. Paul Boyarin snatched the stick and ran onto the floor.

"You're welcome," Josh said quietly, his face to the wall.

Ignoring the shouts and hollers echoing off the glossy white cinderblock walls, Josh hid his flabby chest and inverted nipples beneath folded arms and inched toward Matt.

"Are we winning?" Josh asked.

"Don't know." Matt's low voice sounded as if his nose was stuffed up. He shrugged his shoulders and smiled at Josh.

Claude Donner stood waiting to get back on the floor for his shift. He looked at Matt and Josh and shook his head. "They don't know who's winning!" he said to the boy beside him who then rolled his eyes and turned back to the game.

Josh moved his eyes over Matt's hair. He wondered if it was as soft as it looked.

"I want a whistle like Mr. Tanner's got." Matt said. "I'd rather be the whistle blower guy than play."

"I don't like playing either," Josh said. "Do you think we'll have time to play another shift?"

Matt looked at the clock and squinted. A confused look appeared on his face as he tried to add and subtract to figure out how much time remained. Josh looked softly into Matt's light blue eyes while Matt studied the clock.

"I hope not," Matt finally said. "Running too much hurts my leg and then I start to limp. I had an operation on it when I was a baby."

Josh struggled to think of something else to talk about in the few minutes they had left before they'd have to go onto the gym floor again. "So, do you have any brothers or sisters?" he asked.

"I got two brothers. They're both little though," Matt answered.

"I got two brothers too," Josh said, moving closer to Matt. "But they're older. A lot older."

"We don't have a dad though," Matt said. "My mom has a boyfriend who lives with us but he's not a dad. We call him Roy and not dad." Matt spoke slowly. Not much slower than normal, but like someone putting their finger down gently on a record album.

"My brothers are half-brothers," Josh said.

"What's half-brothers?" Matt asked.

"My brothers and me have different fathers and different last names. Their dad doesn't come around, though. He lives out west somewhere. But we all act like my dad is their real dad. And they call him *dad*." Josh stopped. This was the first time he had ever told anyone about him and his brothers not having the same father. It always seemed that to say such a thing out loud was like saying something bad about his mother. Josh blushed and looked around to see if anyone else had been listening.

Standing by Matt, Josh was overcome with wanting something that he could not put into words. It was not like a Christmas list where he would write *1. guitar* then underneath *2. stereo*. What Josh wanted was something that made him up, like being smart, strong or cool. What would he write beside this? In his mind he saw a big number one with a dark black period beside it, but the word meant to be beside it—that thing he longed for would not appear. Still Josh knew whatever it was it had something to do with Matt. Maybe he just wanted to have long hair like Matt, or have a body like him so everyone would see Josh's muscles move and twist just below his skin, just like how Matt's back and shoulders looked when he reached for the puck. That was not it, though it was part of it. And the harder Josh tried to name this thing, this warm soft and sweet thing, the more it seemed to come apart— like a knitted scarf, unraveling from a single pulled piece of yarn. Josh imagined Miss Gaskell standing beside him in her ugly macramé sweater with a handful of words, in thick black print like newspaper headlines, trying to throw them into his head and having them bounce off his forehead onto the floor by the rolled up shirts.

With only a few minutes left before they would head back to their classroom, Mr. Tanner blew the whistle and the final shift began. Josh reluctantly accepted a plastic hockey stick once more from one of the boys leaving the floor and, dragging his feet, walked onto the court. When Mr. Tanner dropped the puck in the blue circle, Matt took off chasing it with the other boys, a small goofy chuckle in his throat every time he neared it. Josh didn't run much. He checked the clock and waited for the whistle. Along the wall of the gym, the other boys punched their arms back into their shirts. Josh was looking toward his shirt and sweater folded neatly against the gym wall when Matt, slightly limping, ran past and accidentally brushed his naked shoulder against Josh's his side. For a second, Josh stood without moving, while the boys ran around him. Energized with a strange spark of vigor, Josh began running, following Matt as Matt followed the puck. Claude Donner shot the puck behind the net and the rest of the boys rushed toward it. Matt and Josh arrived last. As the boys dug their plastic sticks at the puck, Josh quickly gently touched the back of Matt's soft damp hair and then slid his hand down the skin of Matt's thin back to the waist of Matt's blue jeans. The whistle blew.

Matt and the other boys moved toward the blue circle for Mr. Tanner to drop the puck once more. Matt had not seemed to notice Josh's hand tenderly caress him. Giddy, Josh gasped for air and ran toward Matt. He stopped. Mr. Tanner was looking directly into Josh's face. His eyes were squinted, his eyebrows met in a frown, and his broad chest heaved. For a moment Josh thought Mr. Tanner would hit him. Suddenly Josh understood what his teacher's hateful penetrating eyes had seen in him. Blood rushed from Josh's head and stars began to burst from the caged lights over his head in the corner of his eyes. Breathless, his asthmatic lungs closed tightly. Trembling and wheezing, tears blurred Josh's vision.

Mr. Tanner shook his head and rubbed his right hand over his moustache as if holding the words that he wanted to say in his mouth. Without waiting for Josh to get into position he blew the whistle. Josh wheezed and moved slowly around the gym, dragging his plastic hockey stick. He tried to stay as far away from Matt and Mr. Tanner as he could. At any moment, Mr. Tanner would blow the whistle.

"No," Josh whispered to himself. *It can't be true.*

Near the middle of the floor, Matt ran past Josh, chuckling as he followed the others. Josh turned and ran for the group of boys. Near the net, he reached Matt and, diving, Josh's round heavy body hit Matt in the back with a loud thump, pushing Matt face first into the hard gymnasium floor with a nauseating crack.

Matt's teeth smashed against the floor. The broken and sharp remnants of his front teeth, now jagged like an animal's, ripped through his bottom lip leaving a large bloody gash. Dazed, Matt lifted himself up on his elbows and screamed. Blood bubbled and oozed from his mouth and nose onto a white line on the floor. Mr. Tanner ran to Matt, examined his mouth and then yelled for one boy to grab Matt's coat and another boy to fetch paper towels. Mr. Tanner had Matt hold a fist-full of paper towels over his mouth while he quickly put Matt's yellow shirt with the brown stripes on him and did up the buttons. Blood dripped from the soaked paper towels onto his shirt as Mr. Tanner threw Matt's brown coat with the bird shit still on the back over Matt's shoulders.

"We're going to the hospital," he said. Then, picking Matt up in his arms, he rushed toward the door. As they passed Josh near the blue bulls-eye, Josh saw Matt's torn swollen lips and cracked teeth and turned away. His stomach roiled. And as he stood shirtless, looking up at the clock above the stage unable to move, Josh's lungs finally opened, and he breathed normally again.

Just a Taste

The year that Josh started junior high school, Aunt Doris came to stay. She arrived on a Sunday morning in September in bare feet and wearing only a pair of cutoff shorts and a man's pajama top. One of her eyes was swollen shut, her bottom lip was split down the middle, and the side of her face was purple and black. Josh's mother, still in her lavender housecoat, gasped, "Oh, Doris!"

Behind her, Aunt Doris dragged two green garbage bags up the landing and dropped them beside the kitchen table. She said they were stuffed with whatever she could grab off her clothesline as she ran for her car. Luckily she had done the laundry that morning.

"Can I stay here with you and Ted for a while?" She lit a cigarette. It shook between her fingers as smoke flew out her nose, briefly obscuring her face in a gray haze. Josh's mother wrapped a handful of ice cubes in a yellow tea towel and held it to her sister's mouth. Aunt Doris' bottom dentures were missing.

"He knocked 'em out," she said. She stuck out her bottom jaw and stretched open her mouth, showing her naked pink gums.

Josh's mother's nostrils flared and she bit the inside of her cheek. Her brown face turned red and although a film of water lacquered her eyes, she did not cry. Josh suspected it was fury that held the tears in check.

Aunt Doris leaned over and opened one of the green garbage bags. She took out a brown paper bag and handed it to Josh's mother. "If you don't have any Pepsi, I'll just have it with water," she said. She crossed her legs at the knee and bounced her right leg up and down like a doctor was checking her reflexes over and over. "But put in lots of ice."

Josh's mother took the half-empty mickey out of the bag and looked at it sullenly. She placed it on the kitchen counter near the teapot and turned to Josh who had been standing in the hall by the kitchen doorway. "Either go downstairs and watch TV with your father or go outside and play." Josh sat on the landing by the back door and slowly laced up his shoes.

"Christ, Doris, I told you not to marry Ken," his mother growled as Josh stepped out the back door and closed it behind him.

For the next three months, Aunt Doris slept on the couch in their living room. In the evenings, Josh would sit with her and watch sitcoms while his mother was at work and his father occupied the basement. Whenever Josh or his aunt laughed too loudly, Josh's father would punch the wood paneling on the basement wall. Since Josh's father had retreated into the cellar, this was one in a series of knocks and bangs that served as a form of telegraph through the house: a kick on the floor after the telephone rang meant that Josh's father had a phone call, two hard knocks on the door at the top of the basement stairs let his father know that dinner was ready, and stomping three times on the living room floor told Josh's father he was wanted upstairs.

Though his father was just a floor below, Josh rarely saw him. Alone in the basement Josh's dad watched sports, read the newspaper or studied his Bible. He only pulled himself up from his recliner and away from his old black and white television to come upstairs to use the bathroom or grab a plate of food, which he would immediately take downstairs to eat alone in his chair. When Josh's father did surface, he would look at Aunt Doris and say nothing. The silence between his aunt and father was eerie. They used to talk all the time. When Josh was seven, his father and aunt had even worked together on the election campaign of one of their friends from the union, who ran as a member of Parliament for the Socialist Party. Back then lots of interesting people had come in and out of Josh's house. There were longhaired men and tough-looking women who carried hundreds of handmade fliers, smoked pot in the backyard and then mussed up Josh's hair and told him that they were going to change the world for him. Josh wondered if any of those people ever changed anything. Or had they all ended up like his father and aunt? Today Josh's father got angry whenever someone mentioned his old leftist politics. "When I was a child, I spake as a child," he would say.

Upstairs, Aunt Doris drank just like Josh's father used to. Every afternoon, when she finished her dayshift at the shoe factory, Aunt Doris brought home a bottle of Diet Pepsi and, hidden in her black leather purse, a little mickey of Five-Star rye. After dinner she would take the bottle out of her purse and mix herself a drink in a tall amber-tinted glass. But because Josh's father had banned all alcohol in the house—even mouthwash —when he quit drinking a couple of years earlier, the mickey in his aunt's purse had to remain a secret. And seeing that he was now twelve years old, he liked being in the confidence of an adult. At some point, not long after she moved in, Aunt Doris had let Josh have a sip out of her glass while they watched television. Josh did not like the taste at first, but after a few more sips, he felt his belly warm and a lightness enter his head. Now every night, Josh's aunt would make him his own small glass of rye and Diet Pepsi.

"I only put in one tiny drop of rye," she said. "Just a taste. But you can never ever tell your parents."

Now every evening, as Josh sat sipping rye and Diet Pepsi with his Aunt Doris like a grown-up, the problems that he had at Red Hill Junior High School were gently brushed from his mind, like a feather sweeping away grains of sand. And for a brief moment each night, everything was fine.

❖

Red Hill Junior High School was nestled between Red Hill Creek and Broadview Avenue in the east end of Hamilton. Like many of the buildings in the industrial city that surrounded it, the school was built with bricks made from the iron-rich red clay that lay just a few feet below ground throughout the entire county, and which gave the Red Hill Creek its name. But the school's proximity to the city's steel mills had, over the last six decades, turned its bright red brick a grimy ruddy brown, like dried blood. The school had two distinct parts. The original schoolhouse, which was now called the Castle, was a three-story square structure with two enormous green front doors. A number of long thin windows in their original wooded frames were positioned symmetrically around the building and on the roof, a black air raid siren (last having been used to announce the impending arrival of Hurricane Hazel a quarter century earlier) stood ready to notify east end Hamilton of incoming Russian bombs. In the northeast corner, the year 1908 was chiseled in the concrete cornerstone.

At the back of the Castle, a two-story extension built in the 1960s stretched out toward the steep dark red banks of the creek. With its light brown brick and aluminum, the new section of the school looked absurd beside the Castle. Together, the two chronologically opposed sections of Red Hill Junior High School resembled a grotesque sphinx, with an enormous dark red head and long slouching tan body. Every time Josh approached it, his stomach turned.

Now, at the side of the new section of the school, away from the doors where the other children were gathering, Josh sat down on the stairs that led to the gymnasium. He rested his book-bag at his feet. If he had more time, he would study for a vocabulary test he was having in French class that morning. He had trouble with irregular verbs and wondered if he could get through a holiday in France without ever using one.

From a distance, Josh saw the tiny frame of Bradley Toomes walking across the field toward the school. Bradley was small and thin for his age. He had light brown hair, big red lips and a haircut like the kid on the inside label of Josh's ugly Buster Brown shoes. From a distance Bradley looked like a girl. During gym classes, when Mr. Warren made the boys run laps around the field, it was always Josh and Bradley together bringing up the rear. Bradley was one of the few kids in Josh's class who spoke to Josh, and the closest thing that Josh had to a friend at Red Hill. Josh thought that they would eventually be good friends; they both got good grades, carried asthma inhalers, and neither of them were very good in gym class. Josh watched as Bradley cut across the field and walked right past him toward the doors. Josh's shoulders fell.

"Fag," someone yelled.

Josh knew it was Nat Danes without looking up. Nat called Josh names every day: fag, queer, fat ass, pig, blubber, fruit. He lived in the public housing complex built near the banks of the Red Hill Creek with his mother and three younger brothers. Nat had light green eyes, light blond hair that hung down to his shoulders and a long face with large protruding front teeth that made him look like a donkey. He always dressed in tight faded jeans, white canvas Nike tennis shoes, and black rock concert T-shirts that stretched over his broadening chest: *Iron Maiden, Pink Floyd, Black Sabbath*. None of which Josh believed Nat had actually seen in concert. And though he was only twelve years old, Nat towered over everyone in the sixth grade. He already had whiskers on his upper lip and chin that he proudly stroked as he sat at his desk and when he changed into his gold and maroon Trojans gym clothes, Josh noticed that Nat had patches of light hair sprouting in his armpits and a bulge in the front of his underpants almost like a grown-up man. And like a grown-up man, Nat always talked about sex and girls. A photograph of a lady in a yellow bikini was taped up in his locker.

"Hey, I'm talking to you, fag." Nat laughed once deep in his throat as he passed the gymnasium steps, as if one chuckle was all Josh was worth. Josh tried to shrink his large soft body into the concrete stairs as Nat passed. Josh's face grew hot with an almost unbearable shame. All he could think about was how Nat looked in his underwear.

Josh's first class was history. Wearing a pair of dark brown Husky corduroy pants and a white turtleneck with a navy blue velour V-neck sweater over top, he took his usual seat at the back of the classroom. The velour sweater, a men's large, was becoming tight over Josh's growing stomach.

The announcements began and, sandwiched between tryouts for the boy's junior floor hockey team and the playing of *O Canada*, the school principal, Mr. Howser, announced yet another new school contest, this time called *If I Ruled the World*. Students would write a paragraph, "in one hundred words or less," on what they would do if they were king or queen of the world. Josh grinned and gave thumbs up to Bradley who sat beside him. Bradley smiled weakly. Josh pulled out a light-green notebook from his brown book-bag and wrote on the top of a new page: *If I ruled the world, by Joshua Moore.* He made notes in point form: release the hostages in Iran, take away the world's bombs, make sure poor people have enough to eat.

"Now back to the War of 1812," Mr. Whistler said as he looked around at the room and smiled. The class exhaled a collective sigh of boredom. Mr. Whistler had been droning on about the War of 1812 for almost three months. Why didn't he just cut to the chase and tell them who won? At least it was almost over. Mr. Whistler had promised that after next week's field trip, if you could call a two mile bus ride a 'field trip', to Battlefield Park (where the British had won the Battle of Stoney Creek and stopped the American advance into Canada) the class would finally move on to some other, hopefully more exiting, piece of Canadian history.

"I'm so tired of the War of 1812," Karen Ballard, a dark haired girl sitting in front of Josh, said to the girl beside her.

"Me, too," Josh said leaning forward. He smiled.

Karen flung around. "Who asked you?" She raised her hand. "Mr. Whistler, he's bothering me again." She pointed back at Josh.

Josh sat back in his chair, looked down at his notebook and, assuming a protective position, crossed him arms over the front of his velour sweater. *Here it comes.*

"Back in your cage, Moore," Mr. Whistler said. His red moustache was yellow under his nose from cigarette smoke. "Perhaps it's Mr. Moore's feeding time?"

The class laughed and Josh's faced burned. From the other side of the room, Nat, in a black Led Zeppelin concert T-shirt, looked at Josh and curled his lip. Karen had once been Josh's friend. She had been at his seventh birthday party. She had given him a model airplane.

Josh looked down at his notebook. *If I ruled the world... I'd make Nat Danes, Karen Ballard, and Mr. Whistler eat shit.* He looked forward to his little taste of rye.

◈

That night, Aunt Doris put one of her record albums, *Knock Out Disco* from K-Tel, on the turntable in the oak console stereo that sat against the living room wall. She moved her wide hips from side to side, pointed her right hand in the air and then moved her arm down and pointed to the floor in front of her. Braless, her large breasts swung under her black and silver Bee Gees T-shirt. Josh counted in his head. Aunt Doris was two years older than his mother. That made her forty-two. But she dressed much younger than his mother did. Had he ever even *seen* his mother in a T-shirt?

"Have you ever been to a real disco, Aunt Doris?"

"Sure, lots of times."

"Did they have one of those dance floors with lights that flash like in *Saturday Night Fever*?"

"Yep, and I danced like this..." Aunt Doris grabbed Josh's hand and they did the bump, just like his aunt had taught him, in the middle of the living room. His fat rear end wobbled in his corduroy jeans each time he bumped his aunt's hip. They crouched lower and lower with each bump until Aunt Doris fell onto her backside with a thump that rattled the floor and walls. They laughed until a loud banging from the basement told them they had better be quiet. Aunt Doris, breathing heavily, turned on the television and sat down on the gold paisley couch. She lit a cigarette and put her bare feet on the coffee table. Her toenails were painted orange.

Josh, sitting in a matching chair beside her, took a sip of his small rye and Diet Pepsi, and pulled out a notebook and pencil from his brown book-bag.

"What's that?" his aunt asked. "Homework?" She tilted her head to see what Josh was writing. Josh wondered if he smelled as strongly of rye as his aunt did or if, when there was just enough rye for taste, no one could smell it. Either way, he would brush his teeth and clean out the glass with soap and hot water when he was done.

"I'm entering a contest at school. I have to write a paragraph on what I would do if I ruled the world."

"That sounds like fun. Is there a prize?"

"First prize is twenty-five dollars and they print the essay in the yearbook."

"What have you written so far? Maybe I could help."

Josh read the notes he had made in point form, "Let's see... get the hostages free from Iran, take away the world's bombs, and make sure poor people have enough to eat."

Aunt Doris raised her hand to her mouth and pretended to yawn. "Everyone and their brother will be writing that sort of stuff," she said. "Why not try and say something different to stand out."

Josh tapped his pencil on the coffee table and tried to think of something unique.

"And if you ask me," Aunt Doris continued, "you're better off not ruling the world. If you did, you'd end up just like every other rich person—screwing over hard working folks like your mom and me. Do you know what you should write? Absolute power corrupts absolutely."

"My Dad said that to me once." Josh said. "A long time ago."

"Yeah, and your dad believed it once too." Aunt Doris glared toward the basement door. "But now that God came into the picture... well a person can't believe in both. Sometimes I can't believe that he's the same man who marched alongside your Uncle Ken and me and sang the *Internationale* during the Labor Day parade a few years ago. Could you see your father singing *away with all your superstitions, servile masses, arise, arise! We'll change henceforth the old tradition, and spurn the dust to win the prize* today?"

"I can't enter *that* in the contest!"

Aunt Doris laughed. "No, I guess you can't. So what would you really do if you ruled the world?"

"I don't know," Josh said. He held his head. There was more than a taste of rye in there tonight. He lowered his voice. "I'd fix Dad so he could take me camping again. I'd give Mom enough money so she didn't have to work in the factory anymore. And I'd buy a huge house in Ancaster. And then I'd travel… to England, France and Italy too maybe. Oh, and I'd outlaw racism and war."

"How about doing something for the Indians?" his aunt said. "After all, you're one quarter Chippewa Indian yourself."

"I could give them more land."

"Did you know your grandmother couldn't even vote until the 1960s because she was Indian? And did you know that she couldn't go into a bar to have a drink? Even after cleaning white people's houses all day long they wouldn't even let her have a lousy beer?" Her voice became louder. "Gulliver's Travels Inn, right down the street there by Battlefield Park, told her to get out. They wouldn't serve her one *goddamn* beer!"

"Then I should give the Indians more land *and beer*?" he asked.

They looked at each other and burst out laughing. Aunt Doris put a finger to her lips. "Shhhh, your father will come up."

"No he won't," Josh said.

Over the next hour, as he sipped his rye and Diet Pepsi, Josh wrote a piece in ninety-five words. When he was done, he read it to his aunt.

"If I ruled the world I would hand the crown back and say, no thank-you! I believe that absolute power corrupts absolutely and, just like the bullies on the playground at Red Hill Junior High School, if I was given unlimited power, it is possible that I may wield it with an iron fist, smashing the weak. However, if I was given the opportunity to have such power for only one day, I would create a world of peace, dismantle all the bombs, and give the native Indians the land that was stolen from them." He looked up at his aunt. She stared out the window and rubbed her chin.

"That's good, Josh. For a second you reminded me of your father—when he was younger."

"But I was close to the one hundred word limit so I had to cut out the part about rescuing the hostages in Iran."

"That's okay; everyone else will be writing about the hostages, you'll be the only one talking about the Indians. But I don't think they'll let you win. It's too truthful."

The next day, Josh sat by himself at a table in the Castle's basement lunchroom. As Josh finished his usual lunch consisting of a chicken loaf sandwich and a half-pint of chocolate milk, Bradley Toomes came over and sat beside him. "Want to go down to the creek after lunch and skip rocks or something?" Bradley asked as he opened a pink can of cream soda. He pronounced creek like crick. Josh was elated. No one ever asked him to do anything.

"Okay," Josh said. He quickly shoved his Vachon vanilla half-moon cake into his mouth. Josh wondered if Bradley had cigarettes. The cool kids always went down to the creek to smoke. He would try smoking if Bradley gave him one. If not, he could steal two from his Aunt Doris and bring them tomorrow.

"Are you entering the writing contest?" Bradley asked.

"Yep," Josh answered. "Are you?"

"I might. But each time I start to write something it sounds dumb." Bradley's foot shook and his eyes jolted across the lunchroom. "Besides, these contest things always go to the Special Ed kids."

The two boys left the Castle and walked across the field toward the creek. At the top of the cliff they looked down the muddy red hill to the creek twenty feet below. The stream was barely a trickle compared to how it looked during the early spring runoff from the mountain. They could walk through the creek now and hardly get the cuffs of their pants wet.

"I don't want to get my shoes too muddy," Josh said.

"We won't," Bradley said. Josh noticed that Bradley had the same tennis shoes that Nat Danes wore. Josh wanted to get himself a pair of shoes like that too. He had seen them in the Fall *Collegiate Sport* catalog. Bradley led and Josh followed him down the steep red bank, holding onto the odd tree for support. At the bottom, Josh scowled. His leather Buster Brown shoes were covered with mud.

"Let's go this way, I gotta piss," Bradley said. He turned and walked further along the creek. Josh looked at his watch. Class started in fifteen minutes. And now he needed time to clean his shoes.

Josh followed the smaller boy toward a large silver maple tree, at least four feet wide in size, growing at an angle over the creek. "Are you going to smoke a cigarette?" Josh asked impatiently.

"Do you like looking at other guy's dicks, Josh?"

Josh's mouth fell open. He did not know what to say. Before he would answer, he first wanted to know what Bradley thought.

"Do you?" Josh asked.

Bradley walked past the big silver maple. "I asked you first. Do you like looking at other guy's dicks?" Bradley turned. He stood in front of Josh and held the top of his fly.

Josh's heart beat faster and his face felt warm. Was Bradley going to show him his dick? Josh wondered if it was small and thin like Bradley. Was it circumcised like his or did it have loose skin hanging off the end? *Would I show him mine if he showed me his?* Josh felt his own penis stir in his pants.

"I don't know," Josh said. He looked around and then whispered, "Maybe." He walked past the big tree toward where Bradley stood on the bank of the creek.

It came from the left behind the silver maple. A wet log, covered with mud, swung like a baseball bat. It hit Josh hard on the bridge of his nose. He heard a crack echo in his ears. Pain burst from the center of his face like a supernova over his head and down his back. The force of the blow knocked Josh onto his back.

"So you like dicks, eh?" Nat Danes said. He stood over Josh and smiled. Beside him Bradley bent over and laughed.

Josh lay on his back in the mud. He felt his face. He touched his nose and screamed.

"Let's piss on the queer," Nat said. He unzipped his fly and stood beside Josh's head. Nat's white canvas tennis shoes with the black swoosh on the side were covered in mud.

Josh covered his face but suddenly something rustled in the trees along the creek and Nat ran off. On his back, through the blood and mud smeared over his face, Josh watched Nat climb quickly up the hill toward the school followed at a distance by Bradley.

"Faggot," Nat yelled down.

"Fat faggot," Bradley shouted breathlessly, scurrying behind him.

Josh picked himself up and slowly limped up the hill and toward home. He wiped the tears, mud, and blood off his face with the arm of his jacket. He was careful not to touch his nose. I'll tell them I fell down the bank of the creek, he thought. As he walked along the street, he hung his swollen face toward the sidewalk. *Stop crying you faggot.*

That evening, Josh stretched out on his bed gently touching the stitches crawling out from under the metal splint over his nose with his finger. If he was going to survive Red Hill, something had to change. *He* had to change. It was time that he learned how to act like other boys. *But how?* He decided he would choose someone that he wanted to be like. Then, like a monkey, he would mimic them. For Josh, there was really only one choice of role model. He turned on his side, grabbed his light-green notebook, and rewrote his contest entry. *Let's start now.*

Two weeks later Aunt Doris packed up her clothes in a green garbage bag and returned to her husband. Josh's mother silently shook her head as Aunt Doris walked out the front door.

"Why would she go back?" Josh asked his mother.

"You tell me," she said.

⬧

Seven months later, on the June afternoon the yearbooks were handed out, Josh was sleepy. During lunch he had been down alongside the creek talking about girls, smoking cigarettes, and passing around a mickey of Five-Star rye with some boys in grade eight. When Mr. Whistler handed him his yearbook at the end of the day, Josh checked his photo first. It had been taken only a few weeks after his nose was broken and there were two dark crescents under each eye. As he sat at his desk in a black Pink Floyd T-shirt, tight blue jeans, and a pair of white canvas running shoes, Josh shuddered at the gay outfit he had worn on the day that photo had been taken. *But the black eyes look kinda cool.*

Shirts and Skins

He had changed so much since November. Starting at Christmas Josh had lost thirty pounds, grown half a foot, and began working out after school with dumbbells in his bedroom. He was proud of his new taller leaner self. Now, though he was only twelve and a half, he looked at least fourteen. He enjoyed how smaller kids in the school cowered when he walked down the halls puffing out his chest in his maroon and gold gym shirt. Sometimes, he shoved smaller kids into the lockers as he passed by.

Josh searched through the bulky yearbook until he found the right page. He smiled. He had won second prize in the *If I Ruled the World Contest*, ten dollars, and his entry was written in the yearbook. Bradley, the little queer, had been right; they had given first prize to someone in Special Education. Josh re-read his own entry. It was pretty trite. He said he would set the hostages free, feed the poor, and declare world peace. He did not mention the Indians. But he was sure it was his last sentence that won him second prize: *and as King I would make all the girls wear bikinis*. He smiled. That was a great line.

A crowd of boys gathered around Josh's desk and asked him to sign that page in their yearbook. Josh took them, one at a time, and wrote his name.

"I'd only let the girls wear the bottoms of the bikinis," Josh said as he scratched his autograph on the page like a movie star. "They'd all have to go topless in my kingdom. All except Karen Ballard— that's because her tits are too small." The other twelve-year old boys around him sniggered and nodded their heads. Even Mr. Whistler chuckled as he stood putting on his suit jacket at the front of the classroom. Karen bit her bottom lip, picked up her books, and left the room.

From his left, Josh saw Nat coming up the row of desks toward him. "That's exactly what I would have written," Nat said. He grinned, slapped Josh on the back and walked away.

Josh smirked and handed back a yearbook to one of the boys. "Who's next?" he asked.

Death in Family

Josh drove his father's Chevy west through the city toward General John Vincent High School. Though it was ten degrees below freezing that morning, the driver's side window was rolled halfway down while he smoked a cigarette. As the car accelerated down Woodlawn Avenue, Josh shoved a homemade Bruce Springsteen cassette into the dashboard tape deck and turned up the volume. An old lady standing at a bus stop turned her head toward the thumping music and frowned. Moving his head in time with the beat to *Born in the USA*, Josh blew a lungful of cigarette smoke out the car window in her direction as he passed. A few seconds later, the car bounced hard on a new pothole in the road knocking a fistful of cigarette butts out of the overflowing ashtray onto the floor. For a moment, as the car creaked with the high-pitched squeal of metal scraping against metal, Josh thought his father's burgundy Malibu would burst apart like a piñata, leaving only a trail of rusty old car parts scattered across the icy road.

He turned onto Barton Street. With the smokestacks of the steel mills now in his rearview mirror, the cityscape before him looked cleaner. He took a deep breath. It smelled cleaner too. He passed a Royal Bank branch and glanced at the large digital clock on its roof spelling out the time in bright orange light bulbs. He was late for school again. Already he had missed math class and would probably be a few minutes late for Madame O'Hara's French class as well. But today Josh did not have to come up with an excuse. He already had one—his grandmother had died the night before.

Josh covered his mouth with his right hand and yawned. He did not sleep. His mother had been on the telephone calling family and friends late into the night.

"I have some bad news," each call began. "Ted's mother passed away last night... yes, we knew it was coming, she's been sick for months... of course it's still a terrible shock when it actually happens... well, we just wanted you to know... I'll call back and let you know about funeral arrangements once they're made... just in case you want to come... thank you... yes, prayers mean so much..."

As Josh drove around his high school looking for a parking space he thought that, in some morbid way, his mother enjoyed telling people his Grandma is dead. Maybe it was the attention she got off on. He tossed his cigarette butt out of the car window and slowed down on a side street that ran along the back of the school. He pulled over to the curb. The car chugged to a stop and stalled. *You lousy piece of shit.* His father had bought the Malibu years ago after the old Impala's engine seized at a red light on Woodlawn Avenue, never to start again. For a few years his father had looked after the used Malibu, but now he had stopped doing maintenance on it completely. He didn't even wash the fucking thing. Now the car was rotting. It stalled in cold and damp weather, the driver's side door didn't open, and over the floor on the driver's side, a piece of plywood covered a large hole.

Josh grabbed his red and black canvas knapsack and struggled across the front seat and out the passenger door. As he stepped out, he groaned. His left testicle was squeezed in the crotch of his tight jeans. He shut the car door and grappled with the front of his pants until his nut found relief at one side of the middle seam.

His father had only let him borrow the car after Josh had agreed to be a pallbearer at his grandmother's funeral. He would be carrying the coffin along with most of his father's brothers. I guess I'm Dad's stand-in, Josh thought. He knew his father wouldn't be at the funeral; he had not driven more than a few kilometers from their house in over a decade. He hadn't even traveled to the hospital to see his mother when she was dying. As he walked toward the school, Josh turned his head and spit on the boulevard.

Josh entered the school through the back door, unzipped his blue bomber jacket, and after kicking the snow off from the bottom of his boots, walked down the deserted halls towards the office.

General John Vincent High School was relatively new compared to the other high schools in the city. It was built in the late nineteen-sixties to accommodate the tail end of Hamilton's baby boom but now had around eight hundred students, less than half its design capacity. Architecturally uninteresting, it was three stories and shaped like a hollow box with a concrete courtyard in the middle to maximize light in all the inner classrooms. For the three years that he had been at General John Vincent High School, Josh had never seen anyone in the courtyard; the doors leading to it were always locked with a chain.

Josh swung open the office door. A younger boy in a white Michael Jackson T-shirt sat on a chair outside the vice-principal's office. God, the grade nines are so *tiny*, Josh thought as he walked by. He stood at the counter and waited to be noticed by one of the four secretaries. The drab gray office reminded him of The Ministry of Transportation where he had recently been awarded his first driver's license. No one ever looked to be doing much work there either. Hanging on the wall beside him was a large portrait of General John Vincent, looking grim in his red British army coat with shiny gold buttons. Maybe that was painted right after he fell off his horse during the Battle of Stoney Creek, Josh thought. *What a fucking spaz.* Josh cleared his throat.

"Hello, Josh," one of the secretaries said. "Your mother called and told us you'd be late. We're sorry to hear about your grandmother." She was a short olive-skinned woman, around twenty-five years old with brown eyes and short dark hair parted at the side. On her upper lip she had fine dark fur growing like a pubescent boy. Josh tried to remember her name. *Something like Miss Penzicoli? Or Pepperzonni?* It didn't matter. She stood up from her desk and waddled toward the counter. Her brown slacks fit too snugly around her large thighs. *Quack!*

Four secretaries worked in the office, two skinny older women with gray hair and, like their mirror opposites, two chubby younger ones with black hair. Josh disliked them all, but found the younger secretaries especially officious. This chunky one in the tight brown pants had made him see the vice-principal a week earlier for being rude. Josh had told her that maybe she should keep her opinions to herself when she said to him that his chronic tardiness showed the beginnings of a "flawed moral character". He had received two days detention for rudeness. Shit! Who the hell still uses the word *tardy*, anyway?

Josh nodded his head slowly and looked down to the scuffed gray linoleum floor. "We knew she was dying. She's been sick for a few months."

"I suppose knowing it's coming can make it easier," she said.

"I guess," Josh answered. He wondered if his grandmother's demise would get him out of writing next week's mid-term exams.

"My grandmother passed away recently too," she said. Her round face fell and she glanced out the window into the snow-covered cement courtyard. She must be remembering poor Grandma Rosa from Palermo, Josh thought. Then, with her downy black moustache quivering slightly, she handed Josh a pink hall pass with *death in family* scrawled across it.

"I'll be praying for you and your grandmother," she said in a low voice.

Josh nodded. Why are you working here at all, Miss Penzipopper? he thought. You really should be spreading your Italian sunshine at some Catholic high school. He took the slip and walked out of the office. The glass door swung shut behind him with a squeak.

"Yes, prayers mean so much," he said chuckling.

As he walked back down the hall past the office window, Josh saluted the boy in the Michael Jackson T-shirt. "Don't allow chronic tardiness to flaw your moral character!"

The boy flashed a shiny grin of metal orthodontic braces.

Josh ran up to the third floor taking the stairs two at a time. Once he would have been doubled over wheezing for air after exercise like that. But now his childhood asthma, like the soft roll of blubber he used to carry around his stomach, had melted into thin air. Maybe he had never been asthmatic at all. Maybe he had willed his asthma away—mind over matter and all that crap. He put his coat in his locker. Today he wore a gray hooded sweatshirt with his Levi 501 button-fly jeans. During his years at General John Vincent, Josh had adopted the "rocker" look—tight blue jeans and either a sweatshirt (in the winter) or a T-shirt (when it was warmer). Josh bent his knees slightly and checked his hair in the mirror hanging on his locker door. He wore his hair long and parted down the middle like Bob Seger on the cover of the *Night Moves* album, but not quite so long. The part down Josh's head had made a big M with his bangs and a red pimple was hidden under the left arch. He took out his French books from the top shelf and slammed the locker door closed.

The teachers at General John Vincent either loved Josh or hated him. This division ran across eastern and western hemispheres of the brain like the Berlin Wall. The right side, Music, Art, and English teachers, thought Josh was talented. On the other side of this cerebral divide, the Calculus, Physics, and Geometry teachers thought Josh was a fool—and told him so. Each term his report card was covered with As and Ds. There was never a B or C in the bunch. His teacher's comments stated that Josh was *brilliant, creative* and *a pleasure to teach* or *lazy, disrespectful* and a *bad influence*. Josh was proud of both the praise and criticism.

"I'm ambiguous and complex," he had told his bewildered mother last semester when she saw his report card.

The other students at General John Vincent called Josh a loner. Over the years he had cultivated that persona, staying to himself and scoffing at school clubs and athletics. To look cool, he strutted down the halls, sneered in his classes and sat at the back of the room slouching at his desk with his legs stretched out in the aisle. This tough lone-wolf role he played gave Josh a certain amount of capital at the school, which in turn bought his solitude. In a school infested with bullies and hoods, smack-dab in one of the roughest part of the city, he was left alone.

When he entered his French classroom, his teacher Madame O'Hara stood at the front of the classroom. She was in her forties and taught both French and Home Economics. Today she looked as though she had dressed for two different climates: a summery green dress with yellow flowers was accessorized with a pair of black leather boots with woolly white fur around the ankles. She looked at Josh and frowned as if he had incorrectly conjugated the verb *to have*. He handed her the pink slip. Grand-mère est mort, Josh thought as she read his hall pass. *Tres mort.* He tried to remember if there was a superlative for "dead" in French. *Grand-mère la plus mort?*

Madame O'Hara's mouth tightened and her head rose slightly, as if she was telling Josh to keep a stiff upper lip. Josh gave her a weary smile. He wondered if he could make a tear roll down his cheek. But he would probably start laughing if he tried. Since yesterday, when he had heard that Grandmother Moore had died, he hadn't cried. He tried, but couldn't. To Josh, the whole thing didn't seem so much sad as—just natural. Josh walked away from Madame O'Hara and sat down at his desk at the back of the classroom. He opened his yellow French binder and wrote the date on the top of a blank sheet of paper. A few students looked back at him. Perhaps they were annoyed he had interrupted the class again. *Fuck em.*

Josh did not fit in with the other students in the advanced-level University preparatory courses. He had been a better match with the people in general-level classes. After high school the general-level students were destined to go directly to work or head off to Iroquois Community College to take two or three year courses in Advertising, Radio Broadcasting or Computer Programming. Through grade ten, Josh was content to be in the general-level courses, but last year decided that university would be the best and fastest ticket out of Hamilton. To make the move to the advanced level, he had to spend last July and August in summer school upgrading his math, English, and French. Now Josh kept a running timeline in his head. There were only twenty-one months left before he would finally climb on a train or bus bound for a university in Toronto, Montreal or Vancouver, leaving Hamilton behind him for good.

"As I was saying… the Château Frontenac is one of the most beautiful hotels in Canada," Madame O'Hara said. "It's a four-star hotel."

Josh sat up straight at his desk. She was talking about the annual school trip to Quebec City for the grade eleven advanced-level French students. A week earlier they had been given the permission slips for the June trip—it cost one hundred and twenty-five dollars. Now each morning before she started teaching, Madame O'Hara collected students' money and slips signed by a parent or guardian.

Josh was still trying to figure out how he would find the money to get to Quebec City. When he had handed the permission slip to his mother last week, she rolled her eyes and shook her head.

"Do those people at your school think this neighborhood is full of Gloria Vanderbilts?" she had said. "Maybe the rest of us shouldn't eat because you want a big fancy holiday. Maybe you haven't noticed but I'm the only one working in this house. I'd like to get away too, but no one is giving me expensive vacations, you know."

I know I know I know. I know you're a bitch. Josh had gone into his bedroom and slammed the door. From the other side of his door he gave his mother the finger. He would get to Quebec City somehow. He couldn't expect any help from his father, but he wasn't going to miss this opportunity to get the hell out of Hamilton—even for a few days.

Now Josh sat in French class wondering what the chances were that the old woman had left him one hundred and twenty-five dollars in her will. Not fucking likely. There would be no discoveries of rubies stashed in the flour canister or a mattress stuffed with money. Her only bequeathment would be a fist full of bills in her rigor mortised hand. Late the night before, Uncle Carl had come to their house and told Josh's parents that everyone in the family was going to have to chip in just to put her in the ground. Now any extra money his parents had would be going straight to the Bates Brothers Funeral Home. He saw his one chance to get to Quebec City disappearing. *They're never going to let me out of this town.*

A few seats up from Josh, in the next row over, Brent Palmer was biting the nail on his pinky finger and taking notes in a mauve binder. Josh curled up his lip. Brent was too pretty for a boy. He had black curly hair, wet with hair gel, which curled in ringlets over his forehead and around his ears. His eyes were hazel with tiny gold flecks and his thick red lips always looked wet. *Cocksucking lips.* Today he wore a pink sweater with a white collared shirt with the shirttails hanging out of his tan chinos. He wore oxblood penny loafers with argyle socks. Penny loafers in winter! Only a gay guy would do that.

Brent had already handed in his one hundred and twenty-five dollars to Madame O'Hara. That worried Josh. Brent only hung around with girls and since Josh had no guy-friends at General John Vincent either, it was likely that the two "odd men out" would have to share a room at the Château Frontenac in June. Josh wasn't so worried about sleeping in the same room as Brent, but he did not want to share a bathroom with him or catch any disease Brent might have from being queer. Josh would just tell Madame O'Hara that he wasn't sharing a room with Brent. In front of him, Brent bit down on his thick bottom lip as Madame O'Hara read a passage from Zola's *Germinal.*

After school, Josh drove the Malibu home. Since his grandmother had been dying, the ongoing war between him and his father had calmed and an unofficial truce was declared between them. Their house, no longer a battlefield, was now eerily tranquil.

Josh walked in the back door of the house and heard his mother talking on the telephone in the living room. He dropped his head and sighed. That was where she had been when he left that morning. Josh kicked off his winter boots, took off his coat and stepped into the living room.

"The funeral will be this Saturday at two o'clock," his mother said into the phone. Dressed for visitors, she sat on the chair beside the telephone in a pair of black pants, a white blouse and dark green cardigan. A strong scent of her *Estée Lauder Youth Dew* hung in the air. Josh's mother only wore perfume on her days off. It always reminded Josh of holidays. Beside her on the end table, a black address book was open to *H. Jesus Christ, she's not even halfway through the alphabet,* he thought. Josh sat at the end of the sofa and examined a wet patch on the sole of his right sock. *And if a dead grandmother wasn't enough, now I got a fucking hole in my boot.*

His mother finished her call and placed the receiver down. "I took your gray suit to the Chinese cleaners at the mall today." She said gray suit as if Josh had more than one. "They promised it would be ready for you to pick up anytime tomorrow afternoon. The yellow laundry ticket is on the kitchen table—*no tickie, no laundry.*"

"Okay."

"So you can drive me to the funeral home for Grandma's visitation tomorrow evening."

"Alright" Josh said. "Did you make anything for dinner?"

"Auntie Doris brought over a Shepherd's pie. I'll heat it up in a few minutes." Josh wrinkled his nose. "You like Shepherd's pie," his mother said. She turned a page in the address book. "I need to call my cousin Arlene and let her know about the funeral."

"Your cousin Arlene doesn't even know who Grandma was," Josh said. He felt the weight of the word was in his mouth. It seemed cold, numbing what it touched, like a hard white peppermint on the tongue: Grandma was sweet, grandma was sad, grandma was sick, grandma was tired, grandma was old, grandma was unhappy. She was everything except dead.

"Arlene met Grandma at my wedding," his mother said. "She knows who she was."

"Isn't Arlene like four hundred pounds now? She wouldn't be able to get through the bloody door of the funeral home," Josh said. "And don't go and tell her I'd pick her up either—she'd bust the shocks in the Malibu. Then Dad would blame me."

"Will you just get out of my hair, Josh? I'm sure Arlene would at least want to give me her condolences."

Is this a funeral or a sideshow?

Josh turned and walked to the end of the hall. He hesitated at the top of the stairs leading to the basement. His mother's lingering perfume was overpowered by dank earthiness and stale tobacco rising from below. His dog Reefer wouldn't even go down there anymore. It was the smell of limitation.

Only twenty-one months more.

He stepped slowly down the stairs into the basement. It was

freezing. At the end of the room, his father sat in his black Lay-Z-Boy recliner watching an old episode of *I Love Lucy*. He wore a white dress shirt under a light-blue sweater, the pants from his navy blue suit and the plaid slippers Grandma had given him for Christmas. Josh stood silently. He did not know what to say.

Usually Josh did not go into the basement. He always felt too exposed down there, as if the long gloomy room with wood paneling and red shag carpeting was enemy territory that left him vulnerable to a frontal assault or a flank attack. For the last few years, Josh and his father had been like two combustible elements. Any mundane discussion had the potential of growing into an explosive argument. Yet, Josh thought, these cruel clashes between father and son served a purpose; they created some kind of unwholesome glue that adhered Josh and his parents together in a cohesive, if maladjusted, unit; just as long as everyone played their part.

"Mom said the funeral is on Saturday afternoon," Josh said.

His father remained silent staring at the television. He looked confused, like he had when Josh and his mother visited him in the hospital the day after the shock treatments. *Were his shock treatments on Tuesdays or Thursdays?* Josh used to know, but he had been only eight years old at the time. *They were Thursdays.*

"I just can't believe it," his father said. He did not turn away from the television.

He can't believe his eighty-one year old mother died? Josh glared at his father. Old people die. If Josh's mother had died last night, yes, it would be horrible and sad, but it wouldn't be so far out of all comprehension that he would fall apart like his father had. Josh considered this another yellow thread of weakness woven in his father's character.

Josh's father had acted exactly the same way when Josh's Aunt Wilma and, two years later, Aunt Peggy were being eaten up by cancer. Praying alone in the basement for days on end, Josh's father told anyone who would listen that "an astounding miracle was about to happen." The miracle never happened—three times.

"I just can't believe it," his father repeated. Josh wanted to slap his father hard across the face and shake him.

"Mom said the visitation at the funeral home is tomorrow evening and again on Saturday morning. I have to pick up my suit at the cleaners and drive Mom to–"

"Did you put gas in the car?" his father asked.

"No, I just put five dollars in yesterday."

"If you can't look after the car, you're not using it again."

"I said I just put five dollars in yesterday." Josh sighed. He didn't want to do this. But, like flying on an airplane, once you left the ground, there was no getting out until the stewardess opened the cabin door at your destination.

Prepare for takeoff.

"I told you if you wanted to take the car you had to put gas in it. Now the tank's empty."

"It doesn't take five dollars to drive to school and back. If the tank's empty it's because you went out driving up and down the streets of the neighborhood late last night. I heard you leave with *my* gas," Josh said.

"All I ask you to do is put gas in the car when you use it. But you... you expect everyone else to do it for you. God, you're one selfish little bastard."

We've reached our cruising altitude. Be advised that turbulence can occur at any time.

"Hey, don't blame me because... God let you down again." Josh swiped his bangs out of his eyes.

"And I want you to get a haircut tomorrow. I don't want you going to your grandmother's funeral looking like a fruit."

Jesus, he's pulling out all the stops today, Josh thought. "I'm not cutting my hair," he said quietly. "And I don't care how much you scream about it."

"You'll do what I tell you!" Josh's father grabbed the *TV Guide* that sat on the arm of his chair and threw it. It struck Josh below his right eye.

Please return to your seat and fasten your seatbelt, as we've hit some turbulence.

"Then you can carry your own mother's coffin," Josh said. He touched the scratch under his eye. There was a dab blood on his finger. "Oh, I forgot—you can't. It's too far away from the basement."

"Get out of my house!"

"Are you sure about that? If I left who would do all your errands? Who would pick up your wife from work? Who would get your groceries? Who would go see *your* mother when she's dying?"

Josh's father looked at him. His face was red, his eyes bulged and his lips shook like he was on the verge of crying. Josh tasted blood and went in for the kill.

"Next time you're praying, ask God why he stuck me with a father who can't walk out the front door of his house without having a nervous breakdown."

"My God, what's going on down there?" Josh's mother yelled from the landing. "How can I talk on the phone with this racket?"

Please stow your items and prepare for landing.

Josh marched up the stairs past Reefer and his mother and went into his bedroom. Both his mother and dog had the same goofy look of confusion on their faces. He slammed the bedroom door and locked it. *Fuck you all.* He opened the bottom drawer of his dresser and pulled out a saucer hidden, along with rolling papers and a few issues of *Hustler* magazine, far in the back. The saucer, with tiny purple peonies painted around the ridge, was from his mother's wedding china. He wondered if his parents would be angrier knowing that he smoked—or that he used one of their best dishes for an ashtray. He flopped down at his desk, lit a cigarette, and exhaled. Right now he didn't care if his parents caught him smoking.

A few minutes later there was a soft knock at the door. "Dinner's ready," his mother said from the other side. Josh cocked his head and blew smoke rings at the door.

Welcome to our destination. The time is 5:44pm Eastern Standard Time. Please refrain from smoking until you are well into the terminal and then only in designated areas.

⬧

Late that night, Josh sat cross-legged on his bed in the dark. He had just jerked off for the third time and his dick still tingled in his briefs. He smiled and swirled a drink in his left hand. He had poured himself half a glass of Diet Pepsi in the kitchen and then, in his room, topped the glass up with rye from a forty-ouncer of Five-Star rye hidden in his closet. A senior had bought the bottle for Josh in exchange for two packs of cigarettes. Josh raised the glass to his lips and swallowed.

"Mmmmm," he moaned. His guts felt sunburned. Once he was off at university, he wouldn't have to go to such ridiculous lengths just to have a drink; he would have his own bar stocked with rye, gin, and beer right in his room. He saw a bar fridge he liked in the Sears Catalog.

He took a long drag off his cigarette. He had forgotten about the fight with his father earlier that night. He was thinking about lifting his grandmother's body. She would not weigh much. She had dwindled to such a tiny thing at the end. The last time he had seen her was Tuesday, he had stood at the foot of the bed while Aunt Sue sat at her bedside continually wiping the green-black bile she was spitting up off her lips and chin. Every few minutes Aunt Sue would drop another soiled tissue into the garbage can near the bed. When Josh left, the garbage can looked as if it was full of boiled spinach.

Just after midnight, the phone rang in the living room. Christ, what now, Josh thought.

"Yes," his mother said into the phone. "Wait a second." She stomped on the floor once and hung up the phone. Dad must have picked up the extension in the basement, Josh thought.

A few minutes later Josh's father came upstairs.

"I don't want that man in this house," Josh's mother said. Josh tried to figure out who they were talking about. There were lots of people his mother did not want in their house. "The last time he was here he stole from me."

Ah, they're talking about Uncle Dale, Josh thought.

Josh's mother hated Uncle Dale. Five years earlier, some silver dollars that she had been collecting disappeared after Uncle Dale had spent a week sleeping on their couch.

"He took all fourteen!" she had yelled while still holding the lid of an ebony box she kept on her dresser. "Dale's probably out there right now using my silver dollar collection to buy dope!"

Josh rarely saw his Uncle Dale. He was his father's youngest sibling, the twelfth child (thirteenth if you counted poor dead Ruth). Uncle Dale did not look like anyone else in the family, likely because he was the only male product of what Josh called *Family B. Family B* was Josh's grandmother's second batch of children after she "remarried." That was after Josh's own grandfather skipped town with another woman. Not surprisingly, *Family A* and *Family B* meshed like Orangemen and Knights of Columbus.

Josh thought that the robust Viking element in his grandmother's Norwegian ancestry had been concentrated and refined in his Uncle Dale's blood. He was a large man, a few inches taller than the rest of Josh's uncles, with long red hair and wild rusty-colored beard. His eyes were light green, just like all of Josh's uncles and aunts, and he wore glasses with thick black frames. Strange abstract tattoos twisted and turned down both of his muscular arms—the only identifiable image was an emerald eyeball on his left forearm. He had once told Josh that it was Grandma's eye always keeping watch over him. He had joined the army when he was young but was tossed out (Josh's father said that Uncle Dale had never told anyone the reason why). Later, with no wife and children, he shifted between big cites in Canada on his motorcycle working where he could, playing guitar in a succession of bands. For the last few years Uncle Dale had lived in British Columbia, where he worked in a lumber mill and played guitar on the weekends. Josh's mother called him a bum and a ne'er-do-well.

Now, in the living room Josh's father tried to reason with his mother.

"Dale's sick," his father said.

"And how do you know he's not contagious?" Josh's mother replied. "I don't want him near me or Josh—or you."

"We can't stop him from coming to the funeral."

"I don't see why not. I think you and Sue just want the opportunity to jump on him and convert him before he dies. I know this drill inside and out, Ted. You ask him to come to Jesus, he tells you to bugger off, and you get disappointed. Finally he drops dead and your family falls a little more apart. Sound familiar?"

"There are a few skeletons in your family's closet that I could yank out and rattle."

Josh grinned. His father had become more focused and coherent since their earlier fight.

"I don't want to argue with you, Ted. But don't you find it strange that any disease out there always seems to seep into your family tree?" Josh remembered how he had once overheard that his grandmother had contracted syphilis back in the nineteen-twenties and passed it on to Aunt Ruth while she was pregnant. It had killed poor little Ruth before she was a year old. *I wonder if anyone will bring that up in her eulogy.* They should, Josh thought. That old syphilis story and others like it made his grandmother seem like a real living person and not just some dreary lady who sat piously knitting and humming her favorite tunes from the 1944 hit parade. How fucking awful it would be to have people think of you as a saint.

Josh took another sip of his rye and Diet Pepsi and constructed an alternate eulogy for his grandmother in his head. He tossed in stories no one talked about, like the time she ran off with a man and had to be dragged back by Josh's grandfather, and the one about how she had bought her own wedding ring in the bargain basement of Eaton's so her neighbors would think she was actually married to her second husband. Or the one about how she had married a philanderer and then buried the baby he infected in her womb. Or how about the one where she was ultimately abandoned, first by the men she allowed in her life and then by her own children, who complained about it being their turn to have her over for Sunday dinner *again.* For the first time since she died, Josh's eyes filled with tears and he choked back a sob.

"We can't keep Dale away from his mother's funeral," his father said. "But we can make Josh stay home if that's what you want." his father said.

Try and make me, Josh thought. He put his head near the screen of his bedroom window and blew out more smoke into the alley that ran beside the house.

"Josh can't stay home, you asked him to be a pallbearer," his mother said. "And he's seventeen now. If he wants to go to his grandmother's funeral, we can't stop him."

His father grunted.

"I just wish Dale had stayed beneath that rock he was living under in Vancouver. Doing whatever it is he does," Josh's mother said. "He's going to ruin this whole funeral for me."

Josh imagined his mother folding her arms across her chest and pouting. *There's nothing worse than a ruined funeral.*

"Do you know how Dale caught it?" his mother asked.

"I really *really* don't want to know," his father answered.

"I have an idea..." Josh's mother said.

"Shut up" his father said. "Didn't you just hear me say I don't want to know?" He stomped across the living room floor and down the basement stairs.

"I don't care how sick he is, I'm telling him I want my fourteen silver dollars back," his mother said softly to herself.

Josh butted his cigarette on one of the purple peonies on the rim of the saucer and took another sip from his glass.

"Mmmmm."

❖

On Saturday afternoon, Josh sat in a pew at the front of the chapel in the Bates Brothers Funeral Home. To his right, Uncle Carl, Uncle Jack and Uncle Andy whispered amongst themselves. His uncle Carl looked up and winked at him. In front of him, Josh's grandmother was laid out in her coffin. She sported an unsettlingly cheery grin that Josh had never seen during her lifetime. Someone had styled her cheap gray wig and, unbelievably, had given her Mamie Eisenhower bangs. The hairdresser must have worked from some old photograph of Grandma, Josh thought.

Her face was plumper than it had been in the hospital and her cheeks were painted a pink hue that matched her flowered dress. In her thin hands they had opened her black leather Bible with the red tinted-edged pages that Aunt Wilma had given her to Psalm twenty-three and laid it on her chest. It was strange to see all of the rings removed from her fingers. To be divvied up by the vultures later, Josh thought. A large spray of white lilies tied in a cream-colored ribbon were placed on the lower half of the casket. Josh shuddered. The strong scent of the flowers covered something slightly putrid. He tried to turn his attention back to his grandmother's bangs so he would not have to think about it.

Just before two o'clock, a small gasp and whispering swept through the people sitting behind Josh. It was Uncle Dale. He moved slowly down the aisle, steadying himself on a black wooden cane with a silver handle. Taking his place in the pew with the other pallbearers, he sat down slowly next to Josh and placed his cane between his legs. Josh's heart beat fast and his mouth fell open. Uncle Dale had mummified. His long hair had faded from bright red to a dull orange and it hung in wet sweaty strands down his back. Even his green eyes had paled and sunk deep into this skull. He wore a pair of black jeans, a white shirt and a black leather jacket that hung over his flat backside. Josh turned his head. He did not want to inhale the same air being exhaled from Uncle Dale's decaying body.

"How's it hanging, Josh?" he asked. He nudged Josh's side.

"Fine," Josh said. He covered his mouth with his hand.

The pastor rose and spoke but Josh did not listen. He could not stop thinking about Uncle Dale at his side. He wanted to run to his father's Malibu and drive away as fast as that shitty car could move. His mother, sitting somewhere behind him, could get a ride home with Kevin or Troy.

The pastor finally motioned with his hand toward the six men in Josh's pew. They stood. A young handsome funeral director in a slightly worn black suit lowered the coffin lid as taped organ music played *He Walks with Me*. From the back of the chapel someone wailed.

Josh took his place at the back right-hand side of the casket. He touched the side. It felt like a velveteen hatbox. Uncle Dale limped to his place in front of Josh. *He can barely walk, how can he lift a coffin?* Josh used both hands and lifted the coffin off the table. He groaned. It was heavier than he thought it would be. The six men walked the coffin out of the white double doors to the hearse parked outside.

Don't drop it... don't drop it.

The coffin fell to the floor of the hearse with a loud thump and Josh helped shove it in from the end. The hearse door was shut.

⬥

After the burial, Josh sat at a table in the basement of The Good Shepard Baptist Church with his cousins Dana and Beth.

"Oh my God, Uncle Dale looked awful," Beth said.

"It scares me to even look at him." Dana said. "Is it cancer?" She looked at Josh.

"What am I, a doctor?" Josh said.

As he sipped on ginger ale in a plastic cup, Josh examined Dana and Beth's breasts. He wondered if their newly grown tits would end up killing them one day, just like the rest of the women in the Moore family. Josh was glad he hadn't been born a girl.

"Oh shit," Beth said. "Aunt Sue is coming this way."

"Someone hide me from that miserable bitch," Dana said. "At the funeral home she told me I looked *trampy* with my hair dyed red."

"Well, you do," Josh said. "But she shouldn't have said it."

The cousins laughed. They all had the same loud booming laugh. The Moore laugh must be a dominant gene, Josh thought. Like their big-ass horse teeth.

From across the room, Aunt Sue came carrying a paper plate of potato salad and a few slices of cooked ham and turkey rolled up with toothpicks. She wore a black dress with a strand of pearls around her neck. *Fake.* Josh could not remember a time when she did not have that hairstyle, but the gray strands which had been noticeable at Aunt Peggy's funeral were now gone. She had begun to wear more makeup and her peach lipstick bled like spider webs into the wrinkles around her mouth. Down the front of one leg she had a run in her pantyhose. She sat down. For the first time, Josh noticed how very small she was.

"Well at least Grandma is up in heaven with Auntie Wilma," Aunt Sue said to the three younger Moores, "with Auntie Peggy and poor little Ruth too."

"Bullshit."

It was Uncle Dale. He had hobbled over to the table holding a plate with a few slices of cheese and crackers. Josh stood up and pulled out a chair for him at the table.

"Thank you," Uncle Dale said. He put down his plate, took off his leather jacket and threw it on the back of the chair. He had enormous perspiration stains under the armpits of his white cotton shirt.

"It's true," Aunt Sue said. "Mom is up there in heaven right now with Wilma looking down at us." She turned to Josh. "Right?"

Josh shrugged his shoulders. He considered the obsceneness of his dead relatives gathering to look down to watch him jerk off every night.

Aunt Sue swung her head around and stared at Beth and then Dana. "Isn't that right? Right?"

"Sure," Beth said. She looked at Uncle Dale. "I'm going to check out the dessert table. Come with me, Dana." Dana nodded and the two girls quickly walked away whispering to each other, leaving Josh at the table with his aunt and uncle.

Bitches.

"I can see Mom turning to Wilma right now and saying, 'Well Wilma, now we can rest and wait for the others to show up.'" She smiled. Why did a non-smoker have such yellow teeth?

Uncle Dale rolled his eyes. "You may not want to face it, Sue, but when you're dead—*you're dead.* There's nothing else. *Zilch. Squat. Nada. Zip.*"

"That sounds horrible! And very sad," Aunt Sue said

"*Nothing* sounds pretty good to me," Uncle Dale added.

Aunt Sue scooped up a forkful of potato salad and shoved it into her mouth. She turned to Josh. "I made the potato salad," she said. The white mayonnaise made her teeth seem even more yellow. "It was Grandma's recipe. When I was making it this morning, I thought I heard her say to me, 'Sue, you're using too much dill!' You know, Joshua, I don't think Grandma can ever really be gone as long as we have her recipes."

"Oh, brother!" Uncle Dale said. He threw his head back and rolled his eyes.

Aunt Sue put her fork down and looked Uncle Dale in the eye. "You don't want to let Mom down, Dale. How do you think she'll feel when she finds out you won't be joining the rest of us in heaven?"

"She won't *feel* anything because she's dead." Uncle Dale laid his hand upon Aunt Sue's hand. "I'm afraid that there'll be no deathbed conversion with me, Sue. I'm destined to die as I lived, happily in the throes of sin and depravity."

She quickly moved her hand away and stood. "We'll talk later," she said.

"I can't wait," he replied.

Aunt Sue picked up her plate and walked to the food table near the back of the room. "Oh poo!" she said as she walked. She had finally noticed the run in her pantyhose. Parking herself at the food table, she directed people to her bowl of potato salad.

"Can we smoke in here?" Uncle Dale asked.

"I think you have to go outside," Josh said.

"Can you help me?"

Josh's face tightened. "Sure." He held his uncle's black jacket open for him to slip his thin arms into. Josh squinted. On his uncle's back, three dark purple blotches were perceptible under the white cotton shirt. Once his uncle's coat was on, Josh wiped his hands on his pants before putting on his own coat.

When Josh and his Uncle Dale opened the door at the back of the church, they saw Dana and Beth standing against the wall. The girls quickly hid their cigarettes behind their backs.

"I'm tellin'," Josh said, "unless you give me one."

Beth handed Josh a cigarette.

He smiled and zipped up his bomber jacket. "Fuck, it's cold."

"Hey, don't you have asthma?" Beth asked. "I remember when we were kids you were always sucking on that inhaler. You'd be yelling after us, 'Hey guys, slow down! I can't breathe!'" She held her chest and wheezed.

"I remember that, too," Dana said.

"Must have been someone else," Josh said. He smirked. "Speaking of sucking, Beth, I hear you're doing a lot of sucking yourself these days—but not on an inhaler."

Dana slapped Josh on the shoulder and gasped. "You pig!" Her mouth opened wide and she smiled, showing all her teeth.

"I've heard that too," Dana said. "And I live on the other side of Hamilton."

"I even heard it way out in Vancouver," Uncle Dale said. He pulled his cigarette package from the pocket of his leather jacket. As he took out a cigarette, Josh saw two joints in the pack as well.

"You're *all* a bunch of pigs," Beth said.

They all laughed. It warmed Josh up.

When the girls had finished their cigarettes, Beth searched in her white purse and pulled out a roll of mints. She handed one to Dana. The girls popped the mints in their mouths and went back into the building.

"See you in church," Beth said.

"So, was the funeral home too far for your father to travel?" Uncle Dale asked.

"He won't go past the CN railroad tracks."

"That doesn't leave much room."

"Nope."

"I mean for you... not him."

Uncle Dale leaned on his cane. His face grimaced. "What do you plan to do after high school, Josh?"

"I want to go to university... not in Hamilton, some other city. I'm thinking either Toronto or Montreal. Or maybe even Vancouver."

"I went to university."

"I didn't know that!"

"Yep, I went to Brock for one semester. I studied music. But I decided the best way to study music was just to play it."

"Dad said you have a band in Vancouver."

"I did, it was called The Dew-Dads." He smiled. For a second his green eyes shone.

Josh laughed. "Dew-Dads? That's a crazy name."

"I guess it was crazy." He wiped the sweat off his forehead. "So what do you want to do after university?"

"I think I'd like to be a teacher... an English or French teacher."

"Do you speak French?"

"*Un peu*... a little bit. In fact, I'm planning on going to Quebec City on a French class trip in June."

"I fucking love Quebec City. I once drove my motorcycle there... I love Montreal too." He licked his dry pale lips.

"But the trip is going to cost one hundred and twenty-five dollars, so I'm not sure I'll be able to go."

"Ah, you gotta go. And a hundred and twenty-five dollars doesn't seem like too much money."

"It is to my family," Josh said. "But I'd really love to get away for a few days."

"Yeah, I know. Hamilton can suffocate you," Uncle Dale said. He tossed his cigarette butt into a bush. "See you later, Josh" he said. He walked back into the church, leaving Josh outside in the cold alone.

Five months later a friend of Uncle Dale's notified the family that Dale had died in a hospital in Vancouver. Pneumonia.

⬧

In June, Josh received an envelope containing a check for one hundred and twenty-five dollars.

"Why did Dale leave you that?" Josh's mother asked.

"He was probably going loony at the end," Josh's father said.

"I don't know why he left it to me," Josh said. He didn't want to explain it to them. And the reason didn't matter now anyway. In May the teachers went on strike and the French trip was cancelled. Josh wondered if Brent Palmer was as disappointed as he was.

His mother checked the envelope from Vancouver. "Is there a check for fourteen dollars made out to me in there? No last minute remorse for stealing my silver dollar collection?"

Josh smiled. He would never tell his mother that it was he, not his Uncle Dale, who had stolen her silver dollars to buy smokes. But he hadn't taken fourteen dollars, there had only been eight coins in her ebony box. And since his mother lied about the quantity, Josh felt a little more justified in lying about taking them. Maybe one day he'll send her eight dollars out of the blue with a note that says, *now shut the fuck up about it.*

"And what are you going to do with that one hundred and twenty-five dollars?" his mother asked.

"I'm going to start saving for university." Josh said.

"It's going to cost more than that tiny amount Dale left you," his father said. "And don't look at us to pay for it."

"My guidance counselor told me I could get a grant and assistance to help with the tuition… because we're a low income family."

"If you're so worried about our low family income, why don't you get a job and help out?" his father said.

"Maybe I will," Josh said.

"I don't like you going around telling your teachers our business," his mother said. "The world doesn't need to know we're poor."

"He'd get more mileage by putting that money into the gas tank of the car than for university," his father said. "And I'm getting tired of going into the car and always finding it empty."

"I put five dollars in yesterday," Josh said.

"Besides, you'll never even get into university. You're too lazy. And you're barely making it through high school with all those Ds."

"He gets As too," his mother said.

"Yeah, in *art,*" his father sneered, "and *French.*"

Josh sighed. This time he wasn't fighting. "I'm going to my room," he said.

As he walked away, his father looked confused, as if Josh had spoken the wrong words in a play they were performing. Josh grinned and took a deep breath. The unhealthy glue that ensnared his family loosened—slightly.

Sixteen months to go.

Shirts

Before their weekend night shift, Josh and some of his friends from the plant spent the afternoon at a strip club not far from the factory where they worked. The club was housed in what had been a grand old Bank of Nova Scotia building in the heart of downtown Hamilton. Over the last two decades Josh had seen the pink-marbled building go through a number of incarnations: as the swanky French restaurant, *Le Papillion*, a Persian rug store, a thrift shop, and then as *Bingo Palace*. After the police had shut the bingo hall down and prosecuted the owners, the crumbling edifice was left derelict for over ten years. Now the old wooden doors had opened once again.

To entice pedestrians and drivers along King Street, above the front doors of the club hung a glowing sign depicting a half-naked woman. Looking coyly over her right shoulder and smiling like a forties pinup, the woman had one eye shut in a wink and both hands resting on her thin waist. Out of her lower back grew a single green leaf and where her ass ought to be was the outline of an enormous bright neon peach. At the top of the sign, above the woman's curly hair, *The Peach Basket* was written in arching black cursive lettering. Called simply "The Peach" by its patrons, the bar was known for having the classiest strippers in the city because, unlike the rest of the strip joints in Hamilton, The Peach never hired girls with tattoos.

Now, on a humid Saturday afternoon in early summer, Chad, The Peach's doorman stood outside the club looking remarkably cool in a black double-breasted suit and red silk tie. One of his cufflinks flashed in the afternoon sun as he waved Josh and his three friends into the bar without asking any of them for ID. Josh ground his teeth and shoved his unopened wallet back into the left ass pocket of his jeans. This was the first time that he had not been asked to prove he had reached the age of majority. Either, Josh thought, Chad had seen them too many times or Josh, now twenty-two years old, was finally being pushed across the barricade separating youth from adult.

Josh entered through the doors into the darkness of the main room. Music thumped through the empty bar, rattling through Josh's body and vibrating his testicles. The sensation in his loose underpants made the corners of his mouth curl into an involuntary smile. Josh let Steve, Tony and Gary take the lead, their work boots clomping on the floor, toward Pervert's Row, the tables surrounding the square stage in the center of the bar. All the tables in Pervert's Row were empty except for one old man sitting on the far side of the stage.

Josh's friends always sat up front, but he would have preferred sitting near the back by the doors. Close to the stage the four of them would be marked. There would be the constant hustle of girls pushing their way onto their laps and trying to get the boys into the backroom for private dances; trying to bleed them of as much cash as possible. Josh sat down at the end of the table beside Steve and tossed his cigarette package beside one of the two grimy tin ashtrays lying on the tabletop. Josh calculated the distance from the brass pole in the corner of the stage to where he sat and then pulled his chair farther back from the table. He did not want a five-inch heel rammed into his temple during a poorly executed twirl on the stripper pole.

On the stage, a woman with short black hair danced to an old Alice Cooper song. She had a boyish face, a short thick body and small breasts with hard brown nipples. The lights around the stage flickered and washed her in alternating hues of amber, pink and deep purple. She smiled at the four of them and Josh wished that there were more people sitting in Pervert's Row. She moved her hands over her body and cupped her breasts in each palm. Her skin was very pale, unhealthy, as if it had never been touched by sunlight. Josh tried to guess what her stripper name would be. Probably something like *Vampira* or *Creepella*. Bored, he turned away from the stage and began counting the small number of men scattered throughout the bar. No one wants to come downtown anymore, he thought, even for naked women.

Beside their table, an iron staircase corkscrewed to the strippers' dressing rooms on the second story. As her first song began, a girl would saunter down the spiral staircase, rattling it with each careful stilettoed step down to the stage for her set. Tony, who enjoyed seeing the girls' asses as they walked up and down the staircase, sat just to the side of it. Steve, on the other hand, was a breast man all the way, while Gary just seemed to like female skin, anything and everything female. *What about me? Am I an ass man or a breast man?*

The air conditioning must have been turned to "arctic" and the wet marks of sweat turned ice-cold under Josh's armpits and around the neck of his red T-shirt. He crossed his arms. Steve was wearing the same white and blue Toronto maple leaf T-shirt he had worn to work yesterday and smelled strongly of sweat, metal, and *Obsession for Men*. Josh considered the combination a manly scent. But unlike Steve, Josh could not have worn the same T-shirt that he had worked in last night. It was lying in the corner of his bedroom, having been ejaculated into that morning when Josh masturbated before going to sleep. Josh wondered if Steve, now that he was divorced, had done that too.

Since Gary was driving, Josh knew that he could drink as much as he wanted before their twelve-hour shift at Dominion Metal Stamping started at 7:30 pm. He examined his watch and calculated the hours and minutes remaining before he had to be at his machine into an equivalent number of drinks. If the waitress was on her toes tonight, he could down seven or eight before they had to leave. Josh's job wasn't difficult, and he had been doing it for almost five years. He put a sheet of metal in the machine, pushed two buttons, and yanked out whatever was lying there when the press went back up. He could do it in his sleep or, as he often did, when he was half-corked. Once he got to work tonight, he could take it easy for a few hours and sober up. Then later into his shift, after midnight, he could speed up and fill his quota.

When Josh worked the dayshift, the plant was always crawling with "shirts"—managers and supervisors sticking their faces over his shoulder while he worked, so he had to watch himself. During the dayshift there was no drinking or going to the parking lot to smoke pot during their half-hour lunch break. But on nightshift, and especially on the weekend nightshift, a party atmosphere swept through the plant like fresh air blowing away the stale smell of grime that covered both machines and workers. As long as quotas were filled, the machines stamped, and the bins were filled with those goddamned metal parts, the foremen did not care what the boys did behind the shop door in the middle of the night to pass the time. And for Josh, it was getting harder and harder to walk into that plant to start his shift sober. Even looking at that bloody mill was getting difficult. Lately he even avoided driving past the place on his days off.

Josh tried to focus attention on the corpse-like stripper dancing on the stage. *Where's the waitress?*

Steve waved with both arms like a drowning man at a woman holding a tray at her side. She strolled across the bar and leaning against their table, took their order.

"So that's a rye and Coke, two Exports," the waitress said, jotting down their order on a thick white pad on her round tray. "And what are you having handsome?" she asked as she put her hand on Steve's shoulder.

"Molson Golden," Steve said. He studied her breasts and licked his upper lip. It shone glossy in one of the pink stage lights.

"And a Golden for the golden boy," she said. She ran her fingers through the thick blonde hair that ran down past Steve's shoulders. "You look like that Swedish tennis player," she said. She walked away toward the bar slapping her tray against her thigh in time to the music.

"Looks like you made a friend there, Goldilocks," Josh said, gruffer than he intended. He was irritated by her stupid, outdated tennis reference.

Tony took a cigarette out of his Player's Light cigarette package and offered one to the other three. Josh held up the lit cigarette already between his fingers and stared at Tony. "I only smoke one at a time."

"Hey man, I wasn't looking at you," Tony said. He lit his cigarette, leaned back in his chair and rolled his eyes upward waiting for the next girl to walk down the stairs.

"I guess we can't let the same thing happen as last time, can we, Gary?" Steve said, jabbing Gary in the side with his finger. "The wife might never let you back in the house."

"Fuck off," Gary said and looked away.

Last month, the four of them had decided to stay at The Peach and skip their Friday night shift. It seemed like a good idea at the time, since all of them were loaded, but they could not do that again without some major hassle from their boss—and for Tony and Gary, some major hassle from their wives. Gary's wife, Robin, was so pissed off when he staggered home that night (when his ass should have been at work) she would not let him in the house. Gary ended up calling Steve on a payphone asking to crash on his couch.

Now the dark haired woman on stage was on her last song. Josh sighed. The strip was always the same. Each woman would be on stage and dance for three songs. She kept all her clothes on for the first song, stripped down to her waist for the second and then stripped totally naked for the third. The first two songs were usually upbeat and the third, the "beaver song", was always a slow ballad. On stage, the dark haired woman was lying on a dingy yellow blanket with her legs in the air wiggling to *Only Women Bleed*. A glint on the stage caught Josh's eye. He squinted and saw a gold ring piercing the girl's labia, reflecting in an amber stage light like gold in a prospector's pan. Shivering, Josh twisted the single diamond stud in his left earlobe and turned away from the stage.

Mimicking Steve, Josh slouched in his chair and stretched out his legs under the table. Guys always like to take up as much room as possible when they sit or stand, he thought. Arms out and legs open wide. Unlike women, who try to make themselves look as tiny as possible with their legs together and hands folded, men always want to look twice their actual size. *Must be a Darwin thing.* Josh extended his right arm out and rested it over the back of an empty chair beside him.

"Let's hear it for Taboo," the DJ shouted half-heartedly from his booth.

The older man on the other side of the stage clapped enthusiastically. Tony and Gary clapped politely as Taboo walked off the stage with her blanket bundled up like a baby under her arm. Josh remained silent. He took a long drag on his cigarette then blew the smoke toward the stage.

Beside their table, the iron stairs rattled. Tony smiled, sat back in his chair and watched a pair of meaty tanned legs walk carefully down the spiral steps. Josh watched Steve's eyes grow larger as they settled on the woman stepping carefully on the stage. She was tall with long curly bleached blond hair, huge breasts and wore white bikini bottoms and a white men's dress shirt tied across her midriff that shone violet under the purple light. Her full red lips pouted as she glanced toward their table. And as she waited for her first song to start, she put her right hand to her mouth and blew a kiss toward them. Although Tony, still looking up the spiral staircase to watch Taboo's white thin legs climb tiredly up to the second floor, missed it.

"Okay, boys, next on the center stage we have Country Comfort," the DJ said as a guitar began to twang through the speakers of the bar.

"She's new," Josh said, impressed with the country music gimmick. That's better than that creepy Taboo shit, he thought as the waitress finally came with their drinks.

"Let the backup supervisor pay," Steve said. Gary and Tony snickered.

Josh grimaced and dug in the front pocket of his jeans and felt four crisp twenty-dollar bills he had just taken out of the ATM and pulled one out. He threw the bill on the waitress's tray.

"Keep the change," Josh said. "And you might as well bring the next round now."

The waitress nodded and Josh considered giving her an outdated compliment like "did anyone ever tell you that you look just like Hope Lange?"

Josh gulped down half of his rye and Coke. He enjoyed how the alcohol seemed to flush away any dust still lingering from last night's shift from his throat and a sensation of relief swept over him as the liquor burned deep in his stomach.

Steve raised his bottle of Golden to his lips and swallowed. He wiped his light-brown mustache with the back of his hand and laid his bottle down on the table. Although Josh had the same long hairstyle as his buddies, he was the only one of the four men at the table who did not have a mustache. Last year he had tried to grow one like Steve, but could only manage a sparse patch of pathetic whiskers over his top lip. The guys at the mill had teased him mercilessly until he finally shaved it off. Josh tried to blame his inability to grow any decent beard or mustache on the large dose of Native blood he had inherited from his mother. "Yeah, right," Steve had said.

On stage, Country Comfort had started her second song and was about to peel off her bikini top.

"Oh yeah," Steve shouted as the white shirt was unbuttoned and finally dropped to the stage floor. "And they're real."

Josh looked over toward the pink neon VIP sign shining over a silver metal door at the back of the bar. Would Tony or Steve go back there tonight? Gary, worried that his wife would find out, never went into the VIP room.

"Man, look at those tits," Steve said, his mouth open as if he were hoping she would slide her nipple out and feed him beside the stage. She picked her breasts up, brought one nipple to her mouth and stuck out her tongue. He's hooked, Josh thought.

An hour and a half later, Josh was finishing his sixth rye and Coke when Country Comfort appeared beside him. She had changed into a pair of white spandex shorts that showed off half her ass cheeks and a lacey bra that struggled to hold in her huge breasts. She placed a towel on Steve's knee and sat down. Here we go, Josh thought, the hustle begins. The act was always the same, the girls waited until the men had a few drinks in them and then came over and asked if they wanted a private lap dance for ten dollars a song. Many of the girls would do more, whispering in your ear, "thirty for a hand job, and fifty for a blowjob." Sometimes, if Josh had the money, he would go back there for a dance and a hand job, but he would never let any of these Peach girls suck him off, like Steve and Tony did. Josh was too afraid of catching herpes—or worse. *And why do these girls always go for Steve first?*

Steve whispered into the girl's ear and the whiskers of his moustache brushed against her. She giggled and rubbed her earlobe with the fingers of her right hand. "You're tickling me!" Her left hand slipped between Steve's thighs.

Across the table, Tony and Gary were discussing the new plant manager. "He's a fag," Tony said. "Do you see how he prances around the plant floor in his pink shirt and clipboard?"

"And when he goes to the lunchroom, he'll wipe the seat with a napkin before he sits down," Gary said.

"So he won't get any of our dirt on his pretty pink shirts," Tony answered. "That really pisses me off."

"And I heard that the prick is planning on raising the nightly quota of parts we have to make again," Gary said.

"Like fuck," Steve said not turning away from Country Comfort. "I'll quit."

"Me too," Josh said.

Of course Josh would never quit. And they all knew it. Josh had been promoted to backup supervisor last year and would likely be made a shift foreman soon. He had already been told as much. A few months ago the new plant manager had stopped by Josh's machine and asked him whether he could handle the problems that would come with the foreman's job.

"The boys might not be so nice once you became salary," the plant manager had said rolling up his pink shirtsleeves.

Josh smiled. "I can handle it," he had said.

"We think you can handle it too," the plant manager had said. "You're a damned good worker and one of the few people here with a high school diploma. But..."

Josh chewed the inside of his mouth and looked down at one of the red buttons on the side of his olive-green press machine.

"The only problem would be a few things in your personnel file."

"Yeah... I knew you were gonna say that," Josh said.

"You've been written up for drinking," the plant manager said. He tapped his pencil on his clipboard. "You've also been sent home a few times for being drunk on the job."

Josh did not know what to say. It was all true. The plant manager stared at him, waiting for an explanation.

"I... um... I don't do that anymore..." Josh said. "And I haven't been written up in months." He could not let this opportunity slip away; becoming a shirt was the only way Josh could see of ever getting away from the machine. He felt his face grown warm. *Now my face is as pink as his fucking shirt.*

The plant manager smiled. "So obviously that nonsense would have to stop," he had said cheerfully.

"Yes, sir," Josh said.

"And we'll be watching you, Josh," the plant manager said as he walked away. "So save the booze for when you get home—like the rest of us."

In his throat, Josh had stifled a cheer. Soon he would be free from the machine. When the plant manager had left, Josh kicked the side of his machine with the tip of his steel-toed work boot. It clanked and echoed through the plant. Across the shop floor on his own machine, Steve had squinted at Josh and cocked one eyebrow.

At first Josh hoped that he would be able to become a foreman *and* keep his friends in the plant. This was the first time in his life that he had made male friends and, although he always felt a bit like a hanger-on with the three of them, he did not want to lose them. Josh had always felt odd and slightly delicate with other men before starting work at the mill, but being around Steve, Gary, and Tony made him feel masculine. By watching them, Josh had learned how to act, how to dress, and how to speak. He even put his long hair in a ponytail at the start of the shift to keep cool like they did. Now, after almost five years of emulating their speech and mannerisms, he had begun to forget that he was imitating them at all. He had become just like them. And for a long time, they were all good friends. Two years ago, Josh, Tony, and Steve were all groomsmen at Gary's wedding.

But since his promotion to backup supervisor, Josh could feel that they were pushing him away. Now they only ever called to ask him to go to The Peach before their night shift. Probably because they liked to make fun of him or because Steve liked to have a fellow lush to get pissed with, or maybe because Josh was generous when he drank and picked up the tab for most of the rounds. Soon they wouldn't even ask him to come to this filthy place, Josh thought as he finished another rye and Coke. They didn't want to be around a shirt any more than he did. And now Josh was becoming a shirt. Fuck em. "Where's the waitress?" Josh snapped.

"Country Comfort, that's a cool name," Steve now said putting his hand around the girl's naked waist and nuzzling against her neck.

"It was Southern Comfort, but I got a cease and desist order," she said in a maritime accent so strong it sounded almost Irish. She'd have no problem getting the meat out of a lobster shell, Josh thought.

"I like it," Steve said. "Country is dirtier than Southern; it's got a *cunt* in it."

Country Comfort tossed her head back, cackled like no one had ever told her that before and leaned her lips closer to Steve. Her long blonde hair hung down into Steve's face. He does look like Björn Borg, Josh thought. Josh butted his cigarettes into the ashtray, making the table wobble.

"Another round, Steve?" Josh asked, intruding into their conversation. Country Comfort frowned at Josh and crossed her arms over her large chest. Was she seeing her fifty dollars in the VIP room disappear into thin air? Josh smirked and tapped his empty glass against the table to the beat of a Bon Jovi song that was booming from the speakers.

"Sure," Steve answered.

"I'll have a double this time," Josh said to the waitress after waving her over. Why do we have to keep waving her over in an empty bar? he wondered. From behind him, Taboo walked up and leaned against Josh's shoulder.

"Nice piercing you have down there," Josh said. "At first I thought you were just really wet."

"Do you like it?" she asked putting her arm around him.

"Oh yeah," Josh said. She put a towel on Josh's lap and sat down. As she whispered in his ear, he put his hand around her waist.

"I'll be back in a few minutes guys," Steve said getting up. The outline of his erect penis was noticeable in his pants as he stood. Then Country Comfort took his hand and led Steve into the VIP room.

As she walked to the VIP room with Steve, Country Comfort looked back at Taboo, shrugged her shoulders and smiled.

Taboo nodded at her and snickered. Now the hustlers are laughing at their dumb marks, Josh thought. He wanted to throw Taboo off his knee.

"What's so funny?" Josh asked her.

"Did you see her trying to hide her tits?" Taboo whispered into Josh's ear.

"Who? Country Comfort?" Josh asked.

"Yeah, her real name is Caroline," Taboo said. "She began leaking—lactating—while she was talkin' to your friend." She snorted a laugh. Josh bit his bottom lip. It was one of the saddest things he had ever heard.

"The same thing happened to me last year—but it happened right on stage."

Josh stared at the VIP sign. Everything seemed wrong.

Taboo leaned over again and whispered in his ear. Her bottom lip flicked his earlobe.

"Okay, a hand job for thirty," Josh said too loudly. He stood and stumbled toward the VIP room and Taboo had to break into an unsteady trot on her stilettos to keep up with him. Tony and Gary looked at each other and burst out laughing. On stage a young girl stripped to Aerosmith.

Josh's eyes struggled to adjust to the darkness. The room smelled like stale cigarette smoke mixed with sweat and semen. Taboo waved to a huge man who stood on guard just inside the entrance to the private room. The man nodded and frowned at Josh, as if to say, "I'm watching you, boy." Taboo took Josh's hand and walked him over to the long benches along a mirrored wall. Josh pulled down his green work pants and underwear and sat down on the red crushed velvet seat. He felt a cold wet spot on his right ass cheek and quickly became erect. Taboo grabbed his penis and began to jerk her hand up and down quickly, hurting the skin of Josh's shaft.

"Easy, easy," he said, putting his left hand over hers to demonstrate the easy gentle movement he wanted over his penis. Taboo sighed with what Josh interpreted as impatient exasperation.

"Cum or three songs... whichever comes first," she said. "I can't be in here all night."

Suddenly Josh didn't want her to work any harder than she had to either. *She probably hates working on my dick as much as I hate working on that fucking metal press.*

On the other side of the VIP room, a few feet away on another dirty bench, Country Comfort knelt between Steve's legs. Steve's T-shirt was pulled up over his chest and his head hung back over the back of the seat.

"Mmmmm," Steve said suddenly looking up. He stared across the VIP room at Josh and grinned.

"I have an idea what you'd like," Taboo whispered. She slid the index finger of one hand against Josh's anus while continuing to jerk him off with the other.

"Oh yeah... just like that," Steve moaned. Still he was looking into Josh's eyes and smiling as Country Comfort's head continued to bob between his legs.

Josh felt the cold wet spot on his ass warm and melt like butter against his body and before the end of the second song, he ejaculated onto the black floor.

An hour later, the group was in Gary's car on their way to the plant for the night shift. In the backseat, Josh laid his head against the window. The coolness felt good on his head.

"You gonna be okay to work?" Steve slurred.

"Yeah, what if they need a backup supervisor tonight?" Gary

asked from the front seat.

"I shouldn't have had those doubles," Josh said.

"That was your first mistake," Tony said laughing.

Gary drove his rusty Honda into the Dominion Metal Stamping parking lot and parked near the back by the chain link fence.

"What's say we meet back here at lunch for a quick smoke," Tony said. "I have some new stuff that will knock you on your ass." Josh's head spun. He would not be out here at lunch.

They punched in and walked to the men's locker-room. Josh sat down on a bench in front of his locker and tried to focus his eyes while rolling a pair of heavy wool work socks over his white cotton socks. He was allergic to wool and would get a rash if his work socks touched the skin on his leg. He laced up his steel-toed work boots, tied back his long brown hair into a ponytail with a rubber band, and slid on his yellow plastic safety glasses. Standing on his toes and swaying, Josh reached deep into the top shelf of his locker. In the back, hidden in a brown paper bag, he had a few hundred amphetamines.

"Can I get one?"

Josh jumped. It was Steve looking over his shoulder. Steve, also with his hair in a ponytail, looked drunk. His blue eyes were cloudy and appeared to focus somewhere over Josh's shoulder. "I hope I don't look as drunk as you do," Steve said swaying from side to side. He had sprayed on more *Obsession for Men*.

"Fuck, man. You scared me," Josh said.

"Think I was a shirt?" Steve leaned into Josh's face and laughed through his teeth. He smelled like beer.

Josh grinned and pulled back his fist like he was going to punch Steve. Then he gently tapped Steve's upper arm with his fist. Josh looked around the locker-room and then reached into the top shelf of his locker. He pulled out five white pills, handing them to Steve. "For the rest of the weekend," Josh said.

"Thanks, man" Steve said. "I'll pay you later." He put the pills in the front pocket of his jeans and stumbled out of the locker-room into the adjacent washroom.

Josh locked his locker and walked onto the plant floor. His eyes rolled back in his head. The day had been hot and the plant was like a furnace. Josh hoped the night would be cool. In an hour and a half, he would have his first smoke-break. By then the sun should be down. He stopped at the water fountain near the double doors and swallowed the pill he carried in his hand. If he didn't puke it up, he would feel better in about thirty minutes. He walked slowly between the yellow lines along the rows and rows of machines that stamped out different shapes and sizes of metal car parts. Not any interesting parts though— mostly gaskets and rings. The largest pieces stamped at the Hamilton plant were oil pans.

Josh stopped at a machine near the middle of the factory. This was his machine. It was not a hard job. For the press to work, all Josh had to do was push down two greasy red buttons on each side of the machine and the ram, the huge metal press, would come down and stamp out the car part from a piece of sheet metal. Then Josh would grab the newly made car parts and toss them in a big metal bin. Since both buttons had to be pressed at the same time, the operator could not (unless he had three hands) accidentally have one hand in the machine when the stamp came down. *Any monkey could do this job.*

Josh looked over the ugly green mechanism that towered over him. He was going to have to have it oiled sometime that night. The asshole from the day shift was long gone and had left a mess behind him. Josh made a mental note that he would leave the floor early as well. Then he put a yellow earplug into each ear and stared into the mouth of the press. The machine had been making the same ashtrays all summer and Josh was sick of looking at them. He would love to stamp anything other than ashtrays—even for just a few days.

He picked up a piece of sheet metal from the pallet beside him and put it in the machine. He stopped and swallowed down a mouthful of rye-tasting vomit. *I'll feel fine by midnight.* He pushed the red buttons and the ram came down with a pound so loud that Josh closed his eyes and clenched his teeth. It was going to be a long night. He pulled out the six ashtrays stamped from the die and threw them into the metal bin to his right. They set everything up for right-handed people, he thought, annoyed again. The scrap was tossed to the left side into a larger rusty bin.

Josh placed another piece of metal into the machine and pressed both buttons.

BAM

There was enough sheet metal to last most of the night before he'd have to get a forklift driver to bring over another pallet. He looked at the clock. It was almost midnight. When the ram of the stamp machine rose, his eyes began to drift to the left and he saw twelve ashtrays instead of six. He was falling asleep. He dug in his pocket and took out a second amphetamine and popped it in his mouth. Two pills were more than he should take but he needed to wake up. Soon his scalp began to tingle and he felt his eyes bulging in their sockets. Finally, the speed in his bloodstream was working.

BAM

Josh wondered how many parts he had stamped out in the four and a half years he had been there. It was supposed to be a summer job before university and then... what had happened? He had liked the money. He had been tired of books and teachers. He had been lazy. But right now he did not want to think about what he had lost. He began to imagine the number of bins of ashtrays he would fill after forty more years in the plant, stretching out over the city and down the highway toward Toronto, but disliking this picture, he stopped himself from thinking about it by humming an Alice Cooper song.

BAM

Josh looked at the bin of finished ashtrays. He was behind. He would have to work harder and faster right until morning. The drugs had geared him up and he began to work fast. No one worked faster on that machine than he did.

Just before 2:00 am, Steve appeared. Not slowing down, Josh continued throwing in the sheet metal and stamping parts.

BAM

"Feeling better?" Steve asked.

Josh took out one earplug. "Much better... did you guys go smoke a joint at lunch?"

BAM

"Oh yeah, Tony wasn't kidding. He really did have some amazing shit," Steve said. "I'm so stoned." Steve must have been working hard on his machine too. His hair was wet and his Maple Leafs T-shirt was sweat soaked. Through the wet fabric the hair on his chest was visible. Josh wished that he looked like Steve did in a T-shirt. If it wasn't for being a quarter Indian, he would have hair on his chest too.

"Are we going to The Peach again tomorrow?" Steve asked. "I wanna see that Country Comfort again." He grabbed his crotch, squeezed and stuck out his tongue.

"I'm game," Josh said. His chest tightened and his breathing quickened slightly, thinking of Steve and the VIP room.

As Steve babbled on about Country Comfort, Josh reached into his machine to dislodge a piece of scrap metal that had become stuck in the die. Still unsteady, Steve staggered and leaned against the red button on the right side of Josh's machine. How could Steve have known that to work faster, Josh held his left finger down constantly on the other red button?

The press jolted and fell.

If Josh had known that he would never see his hand intact again, he would have looked at it one last time. He would have admired the five fingers, the calluses, and even the greasy dirt under his fingernails. But Josh was not looking at his hand. He was looking at Steve, in his Toronto Maple Leaf shirt, staring back at him with a goofy grin and smelling like pot and aftershave.

Suddenly Steve's face began to change. His light blue eyes grew wide and bulged out from his skull as if he had taken all five of the amphetamines Josh had given him. Then Steve's smile distorted into something else. Josh tried to read this weird in-between place in Steve's face and decipher where it lead. Was it terror?

Then the stamp connected. A strange hollow sound echoed through Josh's body into his ears. The machine had sprung to life. As the press crushed through Josh's hand, he could hear each bone snap, one after the other, like a telegraph machine tapping out a short bloody message. A sensation of pressure built in his finger and grew to a burning white pain that fed on what air Josh still had in his lungs. He tried to breathe in but his throat had seized as the agony in his arm eclipsed the pleasure Josh had felt from Steve's presence. He tried to yank his arm from the grip of the machine. *Help me.* Beside him, Steve took a step back.

The head of the machine rose and Josh fell to his knees. Still, he did not take his eyes off Steve.

◈

Josh sat alone drinking at The Peach, where he spent most of his days. His hand, still wrapped in bandages and a cast, hung in a navy blue sling over his chest. He had been off work for almost two months. There was no way that the doctors could have saved the entire finger on his right hand, since most of it had been crushed into mush, but they were able to save it just below the knuckle.

"You've broken a few bones and lost most of your pinky finger, but it could have been much worse," one of the doctors had told Josh. "And you were really lucky that it wasn't your dominant hand."

The only time Steve called Josh was to tell him that the company had installed safety guards on the machines to ensure that no one else could accidently lean on the button again. Now the index finger had to slip through the safety guards to push the buttons. "That's fucking swell, Steve" Josh had said. Later that month, Gary called to tell Josh that Steve had been named the new backup supervisor. "Can you believe Steve becoming a shirt?" Gary had said. Dominion Metal Stamping had given Josh a small settlement, and since they had found a bag of amphetamines in his locker, they thought it best that Josh accept the settlement and leave quietly—even the union had cut Josh loose and told him to just take the money he was offered and go.

But now Josh was running out of cash.

In Perverts Row, Josh waved off a fat stripper asking to sit at his table. I'm no mark, he thought as he stretched his legs out under the table. Josh had recently heard from a few of the dancers that The Peach was in trouble. It would probably close soon, they had told him. To top it off, the vice squad had been nosing around the VIP room. It would be the last nail in the coffin for The Peach, Josh thought. He would not be sad to see the Peach close, but Josh did wonder what would open next in the old Bank of Nova Scotia building. *Maybe it will be something really great again, like Le Papillion.* On stage, a woman with a tattoo of a tiger crawling down her back danced away on stage to an empty bar.

Josh looked around. "Where is that fucking waitress?"

King of Fools

"Look to your left and then to your right," Miss Rogers said. A faded and rumpled middle-aged woman with fat ankles and overgrown eyebrows, her mousy appearance looked coordinated to match the institutional beige-colored classroom she presided over. Miss Rogers paused, giving her words dramatic effect. She wiped her straight stringy bangs away from her dark sunken eyes, making the three green plastic bracelets on her right wrist clacked together with a cheap hollow sound when she lifted her arm.

To Josh's left, a chubby redheaded girl in a white blouse and black wool skirt turned her head and smiled. Josh, dressed in his old green workpants and a faded black Def Leopard T-shirt, gave her a tired half-grin. On Josh's right, a young man sporting a bowl haircut stared wide-eyed straight ahead at the instructor, quickly nodded eight or ten times, and then scratched down some notes on a new pad of paper. At the end or their row of desks, a Native man in a light blue denim jacket, looking bored, rested his chin on his palm. Josh sighed. Almost everyone in the class was younger than him.

"Only one out of the three of you will finish this course," Miss Rogers continued with a grin. She raised a bushy eyebrow and stared at Josh and the others sitting in the back row as if to say, "Will you be that one?"

Smug bitch! How many times had she given this little speech of hers to the first year students? Josh wondered. He leaned back in his chair, reached behind his head and, gently grabbing his ponytail, let it slide slowly through his fingers like a cat's tail. Then remembering his wounded hand, made a fist and crossed his arms over his chest.

"Get into computers," the woman at the Workman's Compensation Board had said after Josh had completed the physical rehabilitation on his hand that spring. As if *computers* were a warm bath or a new pair of Levi's jean he could slip into, he thought. And though he wasn't really sure he wanted to pursue a career in computers, Josh took the woman's advice and applied as a mature student to a computer programming course at Iroquois Community College. In early May, he received a letter from the college on official-looking watermarked paper that began with an overzealous *Congratulations!!*

But Josh had doubts. Throughout the summer, he had sat alone on the balcony of his east end apartment, drinking beer and staring off toward the steel mills down around the bay wondering if he was smart enough for college. Maybe he had been smart enough once, but during those five years he had worked in the factory his brain had shrunk. He had felt it shrivel in his skull. Things that he knew—that he could easily reach out and take hold of at any time—were harder to grasp. It took a few seconds for him to remember what season comes after summer, how to convert miles to kilometers, and even how old he was. Remembering took effort now. The constant banging of the machines had, it seems, chopped up his mind into mush, just as it had his finger.

In an attempt to reboot his mind, Josh decided he would read a couple of books before school started in September. One of these books, which Josh had found under "Nonfiction Bestsellers" at a bookstore in the mall, was about the Iran/Contra scandal in the United States. But Josh had to put it aside when it became just too difficult. He didn't understand the politics involved and he couldn't keep track of all the shady characters or the intricacies of the convoluted plot. He did, however, finish reading the second book he bought—a paperback copy of *Lord of the Flies*. Still, after finishing the book, Josh felt that he had missed some deeper meaning. Books like that always have some hidden meaning that has to be explained. So he went back to the mall and bought *Lord of the Flies Cliff Notes* and was surprised to discover that the novel wasn't about a bunch of school boys acting like little shits, but was really about education and human nature. "The main question the novel raises is, of course," the *Cliff Notes* stated, "did the boys revert back to some basic State of Nature, or were they simply acting out exactly what the English school system had taught them *up to that point*?" Josh had no idea why "up to that point" was put in italics, and he had no one to ask.

Now, after his first microcomputer class with the dumpy Miss Rogers (where they didn't even turn on a microcomputer), Josh sat eating fish and chips and sipping chocolate milk from a carton at one of the brown tables in the smallest of the college's three cafeterias. The small cafeteria was the only one of the three where smoking was permitted and a thick haze of cigarette smoke hung in the room, irritating Josh's eyes. Someone should do something about the ventilation, Josh thought as he dipped his fish in a greenish-white goop said to be tartar sauce.

"You're in my class," someone said.

Josh looked up. A man with hazel eyes stood across the table carrying a wrapped submarine sandwich and a bottle of apple juice on an orange plastic cafeteria tray. Josh swallowed a mouthful of deep-fried halibut.

"Yep," Josh said. He smiled without showing his teeth and wiped the grease from the corners of his mouth with a white paper serviette. Josh had seen this guy sitting in the middle of Miss Roger's class beside some girl with big tits. The man had a handsome oval face, long strong nose, thin lips, and the last remnants of baby fat on his cheeks. His long hair, parted at the side and curled slightly on his shoulders, was a shiny chestnut brown. He wore desert boots, a new pair of blue jeans and a gray T-shirt that, because it was a little too tight across his chest, showed the outline of the cross on a chain he had around his neck.

The guy laid his tray on the table across from Josh and sat down on one of the gray cafeteria chairs with an air of familiarity.

"My name's Rob."

Josh nodded and gave his name. He was relieved when Rob didn't extend his hand. Although Josh had taught himself to shake hands with the stub of his baby finger dug underneath into his palm, he wanted to keep his right hand firmly on his white plastic knife. Why the fuck couldn't it have happened to my left hand, Josh thought, not for the first time.

"So you're into computers, eh?" Rob said. He looked annoyed as he searched for the end of the cellophane cocoon wrapped around his sandwich. Finally, Rob brought the sandwich up to his mouth and ripped at the wrapping with his teeth.

"No, I wouldn't say I'm *into* computers," Josh said. "I'm being retrained 'cause...um... I got injured at work."

"You mean your finger there?"

"Yeah," Josh said. He quickly spread out the fingers of his right hand to acknowledge it, but Rob, who was sprinkling a tiny package of salt on top of his sandwich, did not look up. Josh closed his fist. "It was crushed by a machine," he said.

"Ouch!" Rob said. He bit down on the end of his submarine sandwich.

"It could have been a lot worse, though," Josh said. "I could've lost my whole hand." He cut another piece of his greasy battered fish and scooped it into his mouth with the plastic fork.

"You can hardly notice it," Rob said.

"I tell people I got carried away with the nail clippers," Josh said. He had told that joke many times before and everyone, except his mother, had laughed.

Rob chuckled, put down his sandwich and leaned over the table toward Josh. Josh's muscles tightened around his neck and down his arm. Rob slapped Josh lightly twice on his right shoulder.

"That's funny," Rob said.

He's a *toucher*, Josh thought. The lingering scent of Rob's cologne hung in the air even after Rob's hand retreated back to his side of the table. The scent wafted, mingled briefly with the cigarette smoke and fish, before finally dissipating into the haze.

"I'm not one of these *computer geeks*," Josh continued. "I'm just taking his course for the money. All I want is a nice clean office job that pays me the big bucks when I'm done." He grinned and slapped what was left of the greasy battered fish that still lay on his plate with the back of his fork. *Smack Smack.*

"I didn't think you looked much like a computer guy," Rob said.

"Hell, I'm the guy who used to beat up computer geeks back in high school," Josh said.

"And now you are one."

"Yeah, and so are you," Josh said. He bent his elbow, flicked his wrist effeminately at Rob and changed the register of his voice to a bizarre falsetto, "Hey boys, wanna see my floppy disk!"

Two seats down, two men looked over at Josh with disdain.

"I can't stand their little businessman haircuts and calculator watches," Rob said.

"I know!" Josh said. "Every fucking guy in our class has one of those calculator watches. Every hour, on the hour, the entire class goes *beep!*"

Rob leaned forward and Josh thought for a moment that he was about to slap him on the shoulder again, but Rob only reached for his apple juice.

"That's so fuckin' true," Rob said. He craned his neck over and peering over Josh's head, scanned the room with his hazel eyes. "Well, I guess I'm being retrained too. I was in Engineering at the University of Toronto, but dropped out after two years."

"Why," Josh asked. "Didn't you like it?"

"I was more what you might call *pushed* out. The math killed me." Rob sunk his teeth into his sandwich again. His teeth were perfect, except that the front two crossed over each other slightly.

"I'm shitty at math too," said Josh. "Maybe I should get me a calculator watch."

"And I partied too much too," Rob said. "I mean if there's a choice to be made between partying and sitting through some lecture, well... the flesh is weak, isn't it?"

"I know mine is," Josh said.

"So now I'm here... at *Community* College," Rob said with his mouth full. "Yippee." He raised his half-eaten submarine sandwich and waved it around like a scepter. Stray pieces of shredded lettuce fell to the table like used ticker tape. He had large hands with fingernails chewed down to half the normal size. Josh had stopped biting his own fingernails back in high school when he got braces put on his teeth.

"I party way too much too," Josh said. "If it weren't for my union, I probably would have been fired from my job way before my accident."

"You were in a union?"

"I was a member in good standing of the Steelworkers Local 260." Josh rolled his eyes. "What a fucking joke that was."

"So you're a union man!"

Josh chuckled. "No, I was never a *union man*. In fact, if I could have opted out, I would have. It always bothered me that I had no choice about it—I had to join the union to work there. All it ever did was make sure that lazy bastards couldn't be fired. What bothered me even more is that they sent a hunk of my union dues to the socialists in the New Democrat Party—now that really really *pissed* me off."

"So you're not an NDP supporter, I take it."

"No way! You're looking at one of the few Conservatives in Hamilton," Josh said. He waited for the usual reaction of disbelief or disgust and was surprised when Rob held out his apple juice in a toast.

"That makes two of us," Rob said.

Josh picked up his carton of chocolate milk and tapped the side of Rob's juice bottle with it. *Maybe college isn't gonna be so bad.*

"So you liked working in a factory?" Rob asked.

"It was alright. It was mostly boring—but the money was good."

"That always helps, eh?"

"And why did you decide to get into computers?" Josh asked, lighting a cigarette.

"I forget," Rob said chuckling. "It seemed like a good idea at the time. And after all, this is the Computer Age, isn't it? Well, that's what they keep saying, anyways."

Josh wondered when exactly the Computer Age had started. Whenever it was, he'd missed it; he had been too busy feeding that punch press for the last five years to really notice. *Now I have to catch up.*

"After I left university I took a job at a gym. And I've been doing that for three years now."

Josh slowly sucked in his stomach under the table and pushed his tray to the side with a swoosh. "What's that like? Working at a gym?"

"It's a pretty cool job, actually," Rob said. "I work the front desk and do some training. I'm the guy who yells at housewives to move their asses."

He looks like someone who spends a lot of time at the gym, Josh thought as he followed the thick vein that ran over Rob's bicep with his eyes until it disappeared under the sleeve of his T-shirt.

"Then this year, Allison and I decided to go back to school," Rob said.

"Who's Allison?" Josh asked.

"She was the girl sitting beside me in microcomputer class this morning. She's pretty, has long dark curly hair..."

Josh nodded his head. And big tits, he thought.

"Where's she now?" Josh asked.

"She's a keener. She went to the bookstore to buy a copy of our microcomputer textbook. Christ, I told her she could wait 'til the line died down. It's not like she's new to this—she just spent four years in university."

"Did she drop out too?"

"No, not Allison! She has a degree in Art History from McMaster."

"Art History?"

"Yeah, how completely fucking useless is that? I mean, how often does someone ask you to explain the difference between baroque and rococo?"

"Hardly ever," Josh said.

"And then she discovered, after a year without being able to find a job, that it might be a good idea if she actually got some training in a *real* profession."

Four teenage girls with salads on their orange trays, looking like some lumpy eight-legged herbivore with a multi-pitched hyena laugh, walked between the tables behind Rob. Josh heard one of them say *fox*.

"So now Allison and I are the two old folks in this class of youngsters."

"How old are you guys?" Josh asked.

"I'm twenty-five and Allison's twenty-four," Rob said. He finished his sandwich.

"I'm twenty-three," Josh said. He watched as Rob's Adams apple bounced every time he swallowed a mouthful of apple juice.

"Just a tad older than your average collegians," Rob said.

"But did you see that really old broad in our class?" Josh asked.

"The one who was carrying every textbook for every class on the first fucking day? Yeah, I saw her."

"She must be pushing forty, but she was trying to dress like she's sixteen." Josh said.

"Man, I noticed that!" Rob said. "It's pathetic, really. She probably didn't even finish high school. I think the only criterion for getting into a technical college is having the nine hundred and fifty dollars tuition." Josh wondered if *criterion* was the same thing as *criteria*.

"So you and Allison are a couple?"

Rob nodded and swallowed. "Yep, we met at the gym. I was her trainer."

"Cool," Josh said. He had recently rented a porno movie with that plot. It was called *Working up a Sweat* or something like that.

"We're going to get married after we finish this course," Rob said. He pulled a slightly crushed cigarette package out of the back pocket of his jeans and lit a smoke. "Are you married, Josh?"

"No way," Josh said. "I came close once... but escaped by the skin of my teeth." Josh chewed the side of his mouth and wondered why he had just lied. Now he would have to remember that story whenever he talked to Rob. Already college was way more complicated than he wanted it to be. Still he continued to concoct the phony tale of his failed relationship in his head as he finished his carton of chocolate milk. Her name was Eileen—no—her name was Annette. She was from North Bay, they met when they both worked at the factory, Annette's parents hated him on sight, he fooled around with her older sister and got caught, Annette broke up with him—end of story. He could remember that. The older sister could be called Eileen.

"Do you live near campus?" Rob asked.

"No, I have an apartment down in the east end by the lake—The Bay View Apartments. I've been living there for five years—since I started at the mill right after I graduated from high school. How about you? Do you live nearby?"

"I rent a room in a house with five others," Rob said. "They're all students. Last night we had a big start-of-term party. I'm still so fucking hung over."

"Does Allison live there too with you?"

"Nah, she still lives with her parents in Ancaster."

Ancaster. Josh was impressed with the word. Ancaster was the rich part of town. It had the best schools, nicest houses and cleanest streets. It was as far away from where Josh grew up as you could get and still be in the same city. He didn't even see Ancaster for the first time until he was sixteen and was able to drive there himself. Growing up, Josh had imagined it as a magnificent place where the air did not smell like smoke, trucks did not rattle down the streets and the parks were kept safe and clean.

"Allison's parents have a big house there," Rob continued. "Her father's a real estate lawyer and her mother's a divorce lawyer."

"With all those lawyers in her family, I'm guessing that if you two ever get divorced then Allison will probably get the dog."

"Ha ha, probably," Rob said.

From behind Rob, a woman entered the cafeteria holding a large Styrofoam coffee cup, a red textbook, and hanging from her elbow, a black leather purse which bounced against her thigh. Josh watched how the other men in the cafeteria watched her in her tight jeans and shiny deep-purple blouse. Ignoring all wolfish glances, she walked over to Josh's table, slightly favoring one leg as she walked, as if she had a tiny pebble in her shoe. Her dark hair had been teased up held into place over her ears with gel, making her hair appear wet at the sides of her head. She wore pale pink lipstick and on her chin she had a small mole. She touched Rob gently on the shoulder and sat down in the empty chair beside him. Her fingernails matched her blouse. As she laid down her textbook on the table, her eyes fell on Josh. She smiled.

"This here's Allison," Rob said.

"Ah, it's Ponytail Guy!" Allison said.

"It's who?" Josh asked, intrigued.

"That's what Rob and I called you when you walked into class this morning," she said. "You walked to the back of the classroom and sat near Injun Joe and Monkey Face, right?" Josh waited for her to take her shoe off and shake out a small stone, but she only pulled herself up close to the table.

"Monkey Face?" Josh asked.

"Didn't you notice that he looked like Mickey Dolenz from The Monkees?" she said.

"He did look like Mickey Dolenz, didn't he?" Josh said. Allison laughed. Her laugh seemed indecent.

"Though I've always thought Mickey Dolenz looks like an actual monkey too," she said.

"I'm Josh. You can call me Ponytail Guy if you want but I should warn you that I don't always wear one."

"With those cheekbones, you should," she said.

Josh silently thanked his mother and her Ojibwa blood again for his cheekbones. It was, along with his ability to tan, the only thing he thanked his native ancestors for. Otherwise I might have been called Injun Joe, he thought.

"I love your name," she said. "My little brother's name is Joshua too. Well, he's not really little anymore, he's almost twenty."

She sipped on her coffee. As her eyes were bent downwards, Josh looked over the curves of her body. *She could be a stripper.*

"Anyway, what are you guys talking about?" she asked. She put her coffee down in front of her. "Art? Literature? Philosophy?" She pulled out a package of cigarettes and a yellow plastic lighter from her purse. "And what's this I hear about an election coming up?" She put a cigarette between her pink lips.

"We were discussing our ages in comparison to the rest of the class," Rob said. He leaned over and took a cigarette from her pack without asking.

"We're the *mature* students," she said. "But if you look at it in geological terms, we are all the same age." Allison lit her own cigarette, and then lit Rob's.

"In geological terms, we're the same age as Charlemagne," Rob said putting his arm around Allison's shoulder.

They'd look good in bed together after fucking, Josh thought, trying to imagine the scene. Rob pulls out of her and falls back onto his pillow with a grunt. She reaches for a cigarette and the sheet falls away from her big tits to her waist, showing her big brown areolas, swollen and ruddy from being sucked and chewed on all night. The tent in the middle of the sheet below Rob's hairy belly starts to collapse and fall to one side as his dick, covered in semen and pussy juice, turns soft. Allison nestles her head into Rob's chest. His dick starts to stir again under the sheet.

"I really like your ponytail," she said. "I've tried to get Rob to wear one. He'd look good with one." She reached over and held Rob's hair back. "See?"

"Looks good to me," Josh said.

"When I was getting my coffee, I saw some of the people from our class in the non-smoking cafeteria. It's about four times the size of this one," Allison said.

"That's prejudiced," Josh said, "against people who smoke."

"I think we may be the only smokers in the class," Rob said.

"Maybe the younger generation is finally listening to all those anti-smoking campaigns," Josh said.

"Oh my God, those ads were so annoying!" Allison sat up straight in her chair. "Remember the one that went... *smoking makes your teeth yellow! Smoking makes your breath smell-o!*"

Rob smiled and shook his head. "I don't remember that one," he said.

"I remember it," Josh said. *"You've heard, you've learned... smoking you'll get burned."*

"That's it!" Allison said. "Those ads were so retarded. In fact, I think I may have started smoking just out of spite."

"I shouldn't smoke," Josh said. "I have asthma."

"Shame on you!" Allison said. She leaned over the table and slapped his left wrist. *She's a toucher too.*

"So what made you get into computers, Josh?" she asked.

"He was hurt working in a factory," Rob said. "So he came back to college to be a computer geek."

"How were you hurt?" Allison asked.

"I lost a finger," Josh said. He held up his right hand. "Now I can only count to nine and a half." He picked up his chocolate milk, and then remembering it was empty, put it back down on the table.

"That's nothing," Allison said. "I broke my back."

"Are you serious?" Josh said. His eyes widened. Rob's mouth fell open and Josh knew it was true.

"I fell down the stairs a few years ago and fractured my back," she said. "This was before I met Rob. I spent almost six months in a body cast and now I have a limp."

"A *slight* limp," Rob broke in, "so slight that she has no trouble power walking on the treadmill at the gym."

"As long as I'm careful," she continued. "And I have back pain from time to time. But they give me Tylenol with codeine so I really don't care so much." She grinned.

Josh tried to come up with a theory of why she fell down the stairs. *Was she drunk or is she just a klutz?*

"I need two handsome men like you to carry me around in a chaise lounge all day. What do you say, Josh? Would you and Rob carry me around for the rest of my life? I could lean on one elbow and look... regal?"

"She just wants to pretend she's Manet's *Olympia*," Rob said. "She likes to do that in bed." Allison gasped good-naturedly and nudged him with her elbow. He put his arm around her shoulder and kissed her cheek.

"So you two met at the gym," Josh said. "That sounds nice and healthy. I met most of my girlfriends in much less healthy places... like smoky bars and strip joints." Josh spoke to both of them, starting with Allison and then moving his eyes to Rob.

"Well, we didn't meet at just any gym, it was Rob's gym."

"Your gym?" Josh asked.

"Rob's family owns Northern Fitness," said Allison.

"Your family owns Northern Fitness gyms?" Again, Josh was impressed. "All of the Northern Fitness gyms?"

"Yep," Allison said. Rob put his hands over his face and moaned. "Oh don't be shy, Robbie," Allison said and she pried his hands from his face with her right hand. She held Rob's hands and looked over at Josh. "His grandfather started Jordan Sports in Niagara Falls, selling basketballs and hockey equipment back in the fifties and now they have... what's the count now? Is it eight or nine gyms from Niagara Falls to Toronto?"

"Something like that," Rob answered.

"There's a Northern Fitness right by my apartment on Barton Street," Josh said.

"Rob can get you a huge discount on a gym membership if you want one," Allison said.

Rob nodded. "No problem at all," he said. "If you want you can come with me to work out a few times before you decide to buy a membership."

Are they saying I need one? Josh wondered. He had gained weight in his year off work.

"I'd like that. I've never been a member of a gym before" Josh said. He quickly reconsidered as the thought of Rob yelling at him to get his big ass moving like one of his fat housewives.

"Okay then, we'll go to the Barton location next week and workout for a few hours. It's the only location with a pool, so bring your swim trunks."

Josh wiped his mouth once more and tossed the greasy serviette on top of his empty plate.

"Yes indeed! I got my claws into Robert Jordan, heir apparent to the Northern Fitness Empire," Allison said. She began singing the radio jingle. *Get fit, get strong, get happy at Noooorthern fitness! Dee-da-da-dee..."* She turned back to Rob. "Or is it the heir presumptive? I always mix those two up."

For the rest of the day, Josh sat beside Rob and Allison in the middle of the classroom while Allison taught him the nicknames that she and Rob had christened everyone else in their class. And that evening, after school, Josh went alone to the college library and opened the enormous dictionary that lay on the wooden card catalog. Digging in his front pocket of his green workpants, he pulled out a list he had written in pencil on a crumpled paper napkin that afternoon: *geological, criterion, Rococo, Baroke, Manay and Sharlemain.*

◈

Within a month, the three of them had become good friends. At first, their friendship seemed somewhat peculiar as they had little, except their ages, in common. Unlike Josh, Rob and Allison had been to university, traveled to Europe and talked about books and artists Josh had never heard of. For a while, Josh felt a little stupid around them, as if their friendship was undeserved, but by spending so much time together, Josh seemed to be learning from them through some kind of osmosis. *Osmosis.* That was another word Josh had learned from them. And from the day they had met in the smoker's cafeteria, Allison called the three of them "the little gang." Josh liked it when she called them that, although neither he nor Rob ever called themselves "the little gang". It would have sounded dumb if a guy said it out loud.

Now Josh drove his old Chevy Cheyenne pickup down a tree-lined road to Rob's house, not far from the college. The lush green front lawns of the houses along the street were peppered with blue Conservative Party signs for the upcoming election. Josh never saw blue signs down in his part of the city, where red Liberal Party signs and the orange signs of the leftist New Democratic Party dominated the lawns and apartment balconies. It was as if Rob and Josh lived in two different cities. These blue Conservative signs looked stronger than the others, he thought. *This here is where I belong.*

Josh parked his truck on the street and, after grabbing a case of beer from the passenger seat, carried it up the front steps of Rob's house. He reached the front door and kicked on the base with his foot. The door swung open.

"Hey there!" Rob said. He held a bottle of Molson Canadian beer by the neck with his thumb and index finger. "*Entrez vous.*"

Rob wore only a pair of gray track pants, a blue University of Toronto T-shirt, and deck shoes without socks. He had taken out his contact lenses and was wearing a pair of thick black-rimmed glasses Josh had never seen Rob in eyeglasses before and found Rob's athletic features juxtaposed against the nerdiness of the glasses endearing. Rob reached out his left arm and embraced Josh roughly around the neck somewhere between a hug and a headlock.

"I always hug the beer man," Rob said. "I had to steal this bottle from one of my roommates. Luckily he doesn't count his beers—like I do." Rob laughed too loudly for the neighborhood.

Rob waved Josh into the house and, ignoring two guys watching television in the living room, led him down the hallway into the kitchen at the back of the house. Josh was surprised to see the kitchen so clean. He had expected dirty dishes piled up in the sink and empty beer cases stacked to the ceiling, but the room—except for two pizza boxes on the kitchen counter—was tidy. Still, the faint smell of cheese mingled with something sour lingered in the air. Josh put the beer on the rickety wooden kitchen table.

"Should I put the beer in the fridge?" Josh asked.

"Nope," Rob said. "Just bring the case outside. These roommates of mine would suck 'em all up before we even finished our first."

Rob grabbed his blue nylon jacket and they walked out the back door to the patio. As Josh put the case of beer in a shaded spot, Rob opened two lawn chairs and put them side by side on the pink patio stones that formed a square outside the back door. The grass needed to be cut.

"There won't be many more nice October days like this," Rob said as he sat down.

Josh twisted the top off his bottle, drank a few mouthfuls, and then put it down beside his chair where a small weed grew between the patio stones. "This is a nice part of town," he said. "I wish I had a yard like this. All I got is a balcony with a view of the steel mills."

"The house is okay," Rob said. "But my roommates are goofs. They'll be out here once they sniff the beer."

"Are they in computers too?"

"No. All of them are F-Wingers." Josh knew what that meant. Every course at Iroquois Community College was in a different wing of the college: the computer students were in A-Wing, business students were in B-Wing, communications students were in C-Wing, and engineering students were in E-Wing. At the far end of the school, F-Wing was for the music and art students. "Fairy Wing," the computer students called it.

Rob handed Josh another beer out of the case beside him.

"I can't drink too much, I'm driving." Josh said.

"What? No way! It's like the last nice day of the year, probably. I'll tell you what, why don't you spend the night here. We can drink, watch the hockey game, and then you can crash on the floor in my bedroom."

It wouldn't be the first time they had slept together. Two weeks earlier Rob and Allison had come over to Josh's apartment to watch *Fatal Attraction* after class and ended up spending the night when Rob and Josh had gotten drunk on tequila shots. Josh made up a bed on his couch for Allison while Rob just passed out on Josh's loveseat. The loveseat's tan crushed velvet fabric still smelled like Rob's cologne. Now Josh wondered how much sleep he would get on the floor of Rob's bedroom.

"And your roommates won't mind?" Josh asked.

"Why would they?" Rob said. "People crash here all the time."

"Yeah?"

"It's like a fucking flop house."

The two men continued to drink and talk through the afternoon until they had almost finished the entire case of beer Josh had brought. As the sun slid behind the trees at the back of the yard the air grew cold and Josh began to do up the buttons on his faded denim jacket.

"Hey, do you have another one of those things for your hair," Rob asked. He pointed an unsteady finger at Josh's head."

"What thing?" He moved his hand to the top of his head.

"That elastic thing you tie your ponytail up with."

"Oh yeah, I've got a bunch of 'em at home. They make you buy them in packages of like a hundred. You want this one?"

"Yeah."

Josh pulled out the red elastic hair band from the back of his head. His fine brown hair fell over his shoulders.

"Show me how to tie it," Rob said.

Josh stood and walked behind Rob's lawn chair. The effect of the alcohol hit him all at once and his head felt like it was floating on his shoulders like an apple bobbing in water. He scooped up Rob's thick hair in his left hand and tied the elastic band around it twice.

"That's not too tight, is it?" Josh asked.

"No, it's fine," Rob said. "How's it look?"

Josh smiled. "Allison was right—you do look good with a ponytail."

When the sun set, Rob picked up the remaining bottles of beer left in the case and lead Josh to his room. The room smelled of his cologne, moldy gym clothes, and fermenting sperm, like some strange overripe fruit. Rob's room was the largest in the house; "because I pay more rent than anyone else," he had said. There was a double bed in the middle of the room with a small television on a table against one wall. On a desk by the window were textbooks, cassette tapes and a ghetto blaster but no computer. Clothes and paperbacks were scattered over an old matted down blue shag carpet. Josh searched the titles for *Lord of the Flies* but didn't see it. Beside the bed, a bottle of Ralph Lauren's *Polo* cologne was on a small nightstand.

Rob turned on the television, kicked off his deck shoes and sat on the floor with his back propped up against the side of the bed. He crossed his legs and scratched the heel of one foot with the toes on the other. Josh took off his running shoes and jacket and sat down on the floor beside Rob to watch the hockey game.

"Two Canadian boys drinking Molson Canadian beer and watching hockey," Rob said. "You can't get more fucking Canadian than that, eh?"

"Except by adding some hot Canadian fox," Josh said.

"Or a sweet Canadian beaver," Rob said laughing.

After the first period, Rob ordered a pizza. When it finally arrived deep in the second period, they ate it off of paper towels with the last of the beer.

"No problem, my boy," Rob said after finishing the last bottle. He crawled over to his closet and dug into the back. "Pizza and merlot is a perfect match," he said, pulling out two bottles of red wine.

"Christ, we're gonna be smashed," Josh said.

Rob staggered into the kitchen and came back with two large Tupperware juice glasses and a corkscrew. He filled up both glasses to the rim and, spilling some onto the blue shag carpet, handed it to Josh.

Josh tried to sip from the yellow plastic drinking glass without dribbling anymore onto the carpet.

"So what do ya think of the wine, Josh?"

Josh was always startled when someone said his name out loud. Rarely did people actually say other people's name. A strange feeling shot through Josh as he heard his name roll around in Rob's mouth and then slip out through his lips.

"It's good," Josh said, taking another sip.

"I stole them from a wedding Allison and I went to last month."

Rob refilled the glasses and put the bottle down beside him.

Josh had only had wine a few times. He had gotten sick from some lousy Niagara white wine when he was in high school and had also had some sparkling white wine at a cousin's wedding but had not touched it in years. This was the first time he had ever tried red wine though. Unlike beer, the red wine sucked the moisture off Josh's tongue as though he had a teabag in his mouth. He gulped it down and shoved a piece of spicy pizza into his mouth to kill the taste.

"Allison and I fought this morning... before she went to her grandmother's in Niagara Falls," Rob said. "Nothing really big, but I hate fighting."

"Everybody fights, Rob." Rob's name felt round and white in his mouth.

"I know everybody fights, but... sometimes she acts like she hates me."

"No she doesn't," Josh said.

"She said I was lazy. There she is at the top of the class... and you're doing well too... but I'm gonna flunk out, I know it. It's like university all over again."

"We won't let you flunk out," Josh said.

"She called me stupid too." Rob leaned over close to Josh's ear. "You wanna know how she broke her back?" he whispered.

Josh was stunned. Neither Rob nor Allison had mentioned Allison's back since the first day they had met in the smoker's cafeteria. It seemed to have become (like Josh's mashed finger) something unmentionable

"Yeah," Josh said. "I do wanna know."

"She was seeing this guy... a mean fucker. And one night they were fighting and he threw her down the stairs. And then he got in his car and just drove away, leaving her there at the bottom of the stairs. She had to crawl to the phone for help."

Josh began to feel ill. He tried to remember the route to the bathroom. "Holy Fuck!" he said, holding the glass of wine close to his chest.

"Allison always liked the bad boys," Rob said. "Her parents were really worried that she would marry some creep—since creeps were all she ever dated until her accident. They were really happy when she met me. They like me. I love her... but I think she's getting tired of me, Josh."

"I don't believe that, Rob."

"I think our little gang is about to dissss-sintegrate," Rob said. His left eye was half closed. He leaned over and put his head on Josh's shoulder.

"No it isn't," Josh said.

"What are you two doing in there?" one of the roommates yelled from the hall.

Rob lifted his head. "None of your business," he shouted at the door.

"Are you gonna share any of that pizza or what?"

"Fuck off!" Rob yelled. "If there's any left, I'll put it on the kitchen table." He turned to Josh and lowered his voice, "but there won't be." The roommate stomped away from Rob's door and down the hall toward the kitchen.

Josh continued to look at the hockey game on the television but without paying attention. From the corner of his eye he watched Rob stare at him. Josh turned to Rob, who was now only a few inches from his face.

"What are you looking at?" Josh said. He tried to grin.

"Can I ask you something?" Rob asked.

"Sure," Josh said softly. He swallowed and his breathing grew shallow in his chest.

"Can I see your finger? You always hide it by making a fist."

Josh opened his right hand and held it out toward Rob. He took Josh's hand and held Josh's pinky between his two fingers, examining the soft pinkish end.

"Did it hurt?"

Josh was surprised. No one—not even doctors had ever asked him that question before. "Yeah, it did… but it's funny, I really can't remember the pain anymore. I mean, I remember that it hurt; I just forget what the pain actually felt like. Does that make sense?"

"I think so," Rob said. He gently touched the tip of Josh's finger. "There's something so macho—even cool about it," Rob said. He let go of Josh's hand. "Promise me you won't hide your hand from me anymore."

"You're drunk," Josh said.

"I am," Rob said and giggled like a little girl. He leaned over and rested his forehead on Josh's head. "And I know I get sloppy and sentimental when I'm drunk. But I'm tellin' you the truth. I'm your friend, Josh, and I don't want you to feel like you have to hide your hand—or anything else—around me. Promise me that you won't."

"I promise, I promise," Josh said. He forced a phony-sounding laugh from his throat.

After the hockey game ended, Josh lay in a sleeping bag on the floor beside Rob's bed. As Rob snored away loudly above Josh in his bed, Josh imagined Rob's big hands roaming over Allison's body, holding her big breasts in his hands, gently twisting her nipple as another hand slips between her legs. Josh reached out for one of Rob's gym socks lying on the floor beside him and quietly ejaculated into it.

◈

A few weeks later, Josh, Allison, and Rob sat in Josh's small living room at The Bay View Apartments in the east end of the city.

"Okay, boys, what are we going to be for the Halloween pub?" Allison asked. She sat on one end of the tan couch with her legs crossed under her. On the other end of the couch, Josh sat smoking a cigarette with his feet on the coffee table.

Having just eaten two helpings of the spaghetti Josh had made for dinner, Rob spread out on Josh's matching tan loveseat opposite the couch flipping through the television channels.

"What about the three of us go as *The Brothers Karamazov?*" Rob said, without turning from the television. "But I want to be Ivan, the moody atheist." He turned, looked at Josh, and then, as if seeing Josh's confusion, looked down at his own feet dangling over the end of the loveseat.

"Ah, he's such a book snob," Allison said. "A few survey courses on Western Literature and he thinks he's an expert." She turned to Rob. "Tell us the truth, Robbie. Did you even finish *The Brothers Karamazov?*"

"Of course, I did."

"Then tell us who killed the father?"

Rob smiled. "You're such a bitch."

"And you're *so* busted!" she said.

Josh studied their banter and looked for the signs of anger in Allison that Rob had described the night in his bedroom. Rob had said she hated him, but if she did, she never showed it in front of Josh.

"I love this book," Allison said as she picked up *Lord of the Flies* from the end table beside Josh's chair.

"It's a great book," Josh said. "I was just re-reading it before school started." Josh tried to remember the right words. "But the question is... were the boys reverting back to some primitive state or... um... were they just acting out what they'd learned *up to that point*?"

"That's a good question," Allison said. "Do you read a lot, Josh?"

"I used to. I was accepted into McGill University in Montreal after finishing high school and was planning on studying English... but got sidetracked." He stood. "Does anyone else need another beer?"

Rob raised his arm in the air. "I do, I do!"

From the kitchen, Josh snatched two beers from his refrigerator. "You know, if I could have been anything, I would have wanted to be one of those university English professors. The kind of professor that's charmingly alcoholic... teaching James Joyce with those leather patches on their elbows."

"I could *totally* see you doing that," Rob said as he took the beer bottle from Josh.

"Yeah, sure, the alcoholic bit, right?" Josh said.

"No, seriously, I could see you doing the professor thing."

Could he really see me teaching? Josh wondered. He tried to remember if he had ever said anything really smart in front of Rob. There was the time Josh had made an argument for Free Trade. That was really smart. But he had stolen the whole thing from a Barbara Amiel editorial in *The Toronto Sun*.

"You know, Rob," Allison said. "I think it's time we found this boy a girl." She stood and opened the balcony doors. "It's too smoky in here," she said. A cool breeze blew in the apartment. "And not one of those stripper girls he likes to go out with, but a nice well-read well-traveled young *lady*. Though, I don't know if I want any more female energy competing with mine in our little gang."

"Yes, let us find a true lady-love for me." Josh said, in an English accent. "I must find my very own Queen Guinevere to ravish."

"Hey, that's not a bad idea," Rob said. "Why don't we go as Arthur, Guinevere, and Lancelot?"

Rob grabbed the purple crocheted afghan from the back of the loveseat. He stood in front of the television and draped the afghan over his shoulders. "I'm King Arthur of England!"

"You look like the King of Fools," Allison said. She picked up a beer cap off the coffee table and threw it at him. Rob threw the afghan over her head.

"And I'm not wearing one of those long pointed hats all night like someone in the chorus of *Falstaff*," she said under the afghan. "But I'll do it if—and only if—Rob goes as Guinevere and I go as King Arthur. It is Halloween, after all."

"Not on your life," Rob said pulling the afghan off her head. "You just want to humiliate me in front of the class."

"You don't need any of my help to humiliate yourself," she said.

Now *that* sounded a bit mean, Josh thought.

On Halloween night, the little gang changed into their costumes at Josh's apartment and then took a taxi to the college. Since the three of them would be taking another cab back to Josh's after the dance, they could all drink as much as they wanted. "No designated drivers tonight," Josh said, though it was always Allison and never he or Rob who ended up being the designated driver whenever they went out.

"I think we look great," Allison said as they drove toward the college pub. Her short white cotton dress rode up her thighs as the taxi bounced them slightly in their seats. She had made her costume too short.

"My feet are *freezing*," Rob said. "Maybe we didn't think this out as well as we could have, wearing sandals in October is fucking crazy."

"Oh stop whining," Allison said. "We'll warm up when we get to the bar."

It was Allison who finally came up with the idea for their Halloween costumes. She said she had worked on the costumes for a few musicals when she was at Ancaster High School. Of course Ancaster High put on musicals, Josh thought. The only entertainment in his high school was drug sniffing dogs in the halls and the occasional sexual assault. "And this won't be very difficult," she had said. "We only need to buy four colors of material for the costumes... orange and black for Rob's, brown for Josh's, and of course white for mine. It'll be a lot easier than what I had to do for *Pippin* and *The Boy Friend*."

Over the last week the three of them had spent most of their free time at Josh's apartment with Rob and Josh standing on kitchen chairs while Allison kneeled on the floor and pinned the bottoms of their costumes. After days of sewing and ironing, earlier that afternoon Allison had finally finished all three costumes: Rob was Fred Flintstone, Josh was Barney Rubble, and Allison was Wilma. As a finishing touch, Allison sprayed each of their heads with a can of temporary hair dye she had bought at a costume shop—first the black on Rob's hair, then the powdery blonde on Josh's hair, and finally the bright florescent red on her own. "This should wash right out," she said.

Now, in the backseat of the taxi, Rob reached across Allison and tried to yank up Josh's costume. "You know the girls will be pulling up your bearskin to see how hung Barney is," Rob said.

"Hey, hands off the merchandise," said Josh. He swatted away Rob's hand and held the bottom of his costume down over his knees.

When they arrived at the college pub, they found two tables at the front of the large room near the dance floor and ordered two pitchers of draught beer. As the room filled, other people from their computer programming class sat down at their table.

"Coming?" Allison asked as she and Rob walked toward the dance floor.

"Later," Josh said.

While Rob and Allison were dancing, Lynn, the older woman in their class sat down at the table. She was wearing a red plastic cape and devil's horns. Josh had seen that costume, along with Dracula and a French maid, at Shoppers Drug Mart, on sale, for $7.99.

"Great costumes," Lynn said." She took a sip of her bottle of beer and put it down in front of her on the table.

"It was Allison's idea," Josh said. "I thought the three of us should have come as the Brothers Karamazov."

"The what?" she asked.

"Never mind," he said.

Josh picked up the pitcher of beer and refilled his brown plastic cup. He watched the dance floor. Allison danced well enough. Even with a bad back, she moved easily on the floor. Rob, however, was a terrible dancer He moved one leg out and then the other, continuously sipping his glass of draught. And he never strayed from his spot on the floor, leaning left and then right out of time with the music. Josh grinned.

"So are you dating a couple, Josh?" Rachel, a fat girl with bad skin and an upturned nose asked. She was not dressed in a costume, but was wearing the same black wool skirt she had worn when she sat beside Josh on the first day of school.

"What's that?" Josh asked.

"Tell the truth," she said, leaning close to him. "If Rob wasn't in the picture... you'd be all over Allison, wouldn't you?"

Josh leaned back and smiled. Should he tell her that their nickname for her was Porky?

"Barney does not do Wilma," he said.

"Well, I don't think Wilma would mind," Rachel said. She ran her hand through her curly red hair.

The dance music suddenly stopped and a slow ballad began. On the dance floor, Rob reached out and, putting his arms around Allison's neck, pulled her close to him.

"Beaver song," Josh said quietly to himself.

"What?" Rachel said, leaning in close to Josh again.

"Hey Rachel, you wanna dance?" Josh asked.

"Sure!" she said standing up.

At the end of the night, Josh and Rob staggered toward one of the taxis parked in a queue in front of the bar. Allison had run zigzagging drunkenly ahead to grab one before they were all taken. Josh's ears were ringing from five hours of pounding dance music.

"Over here, guys!" she yelled as she opened the back door of a Yellow Cab.

Together, Josh and Rob leaned on each other to keep their balance as they walked toward Allison.

"The three of us should get a two-bedroom apartment for next term," Rob said.

"Yeah, we should," Josh said. "But somewhere up around here... I don't wanna live down in the east end anymore."

"It's not so bad," Rob said. "It's just a little grungy down there."

"Come on!" Allison yelled. She climbed in the backseat of the cab.

As Rob and Josh stumbled toward the car, a group of guys pushed quickly past them, bumping into Rob.

"Fags," one of them, dressed as a cowboy, said as he passed.

Josh flew toward the cowboy. Reaching him near the line of taxis, Josh punched him hard twice in the face, knocking off his black cowboy hat.

"Who you calling a fag, fag?" Josh said. He punched the cowboy again in the side of the head knocking him down while Rob, apparently oblivious to what was happening, stood weaving by the taxi. The cowboy held his bloody face as Josh turned, worried that his friends would jump him, but each put their hands up in surrender. The cowboy lifted his head and Josh finally had a good look at him. He was just a kid. He looked too young to even get into the bar.

"Come on and get in the car!" Allison yelled.

Shame and adrenalin sobered Josh up as he walked shaking toward the cab. He noticed a splash of blood on his hand as he and Rob climbed into the car beside Allison.

The taxi driver looked at them suspiciously in the rearview mirror. He must have seen what happened, Josh thought.

"What the hell was that all about?" Allison asked. "Did he say something?"

"It was nothing," Josh said holding his sore hand. "Just a little scuffle." He tried to smile and hoped that Rob and Allison did not think he was some kind of east end hoodlum. *Why do so many of my stories end the same way?* It was as if he was stuck in an endless computer loop. It had to stop.

"Hey, let's order a pizza when we get to your place?" Rob said. He closed his eyes. "I'm fucking *starving*."

"Okay," Josh said. "And we've got some beer left too."

Allison, put her head on Josh's shoulder. "None for me," she said. "I'm afraid I'll throw up. I can't drink like you two lushes."

He looked so young, Josh thought, and forgetting about the greasy spray in his hair, he pulled at his ponytail and got a handful of blonde dye. *Shit.* He wiped his hand on the seat of the cab.

When they arrived at Josh's apartment, Josh immediately jumped in the shower and washed out the blonde spray from his hair. Washes right out, my ass, he thought as he lathered up his hair for the third time. Then he threw on a pair of red plaid pajama bottoms and a T-shirt. While he was in the shower, Allison had staggered, still in her Wilma costume to Josh's bedroom and passed out on his bed. Josh sighed. He hoped that the red hair dye wouldn't stain his pillowcases.

While Josh ordered a pizza, Rob showered. He came staggering out of the bathroom wearing only his white and blue boxer shorts. He hadn't been going to the gym these last couple of months and a slight beer belly was beginning to show.

"Too bad I don't have merlot for the pizza," Josh said when the pizza arrived.

"Beer will do just fine, Joshua," Rob said.

Josh smiled. "Well it had better, Robert, because there is nothing else to drink."

After they had eaten, Rob laid on the loveseat, his bare feet hanging over the armrest, singing old Mamas and Papas songs. Josh tried to harmonize on *California Dreaming*, taking Mama Cass's part, but he was too drunk to hold a tune. Soon their voices faded and they fell asleep.

It was still dark when Josh woke up. Rob was curled up on the loveseat snoring as an infomercial for a hand-held mixer ran on the television. Josh's hand was throbbing. He wondered if the kid he punched was alright. Maybe he used a fake ID, Josh thought. He just looked so *fucking* young. But then again, as Josh was getting older, kids were looking younger and younger. Still, he didn't look more than sixteen or seventeen.

"I'm not going to think about this anymore," he said.

Josh sat up, lit a cigarette, and drank the half a bottle of beer he had left on the table. It would be morning soon. When he was done, he stood and walked over to the end table beside where Rob laid. He picked up what was left of Rob's beer up and finished it as he watched him sleep. Then, taking the purple afghan off the back of the loveseat, Josh placed it over Rob's long frame.

King of Fools.

He walked into the kitchen to get another beer and as he stood at the open refrigerator holding the cold bottle on his swollen knuckles, Allison came up behind him and laid her chin on his shoulder. Josh jumped.

"Any more beer?" she asked quietly.

"Sure," Josh said, leaning down to the bottom shelf.

Allison put her arms around Josh and, sliding a hand down the front of his pajama bottoms, began massaging his penis and testicles.

"You shave your balls," she whispered in his ear. "I love that." She dug deeper in his pajamas and held Josh's loose heavy scrotum in her hand. "Rob shaves his too."

I know he does, Josh thought. He had seen Rob naked in the locker room when they went swimming together at Northern Fitness. Josh's penis grew hard in her grip.

Josh turned and kissed her. She tasted of stale beer and smelled of Rob's cologne. Josh lifted up her short white dress and slipped his hands under her underpants, cupping her buttocks in both hands. Her ass was soft and smooth. A hand slipped between her thighs.

In the living room, Rob continued to snore.

◈

Now, almost two years later on Graduation Day, it turned out that Allison would be the only one in their little gang to get her computer programming diploma. Robert had left school after the first term when he found out about Josh and Allison. Josh chose to take a job as a data entry clerk for an insurance company and did not return to Iroquois College after the first year.

So that afternoon, when Allison walked across the stage at the Iroquois College Auditorium, Josh sat alone in his Bay View apartment, finishing his second bottle of merlot and reading *Bleak House* in his loveseat. He had decided not to go to Allison's graduation ceremony. And since every graduate was given only two tickets to the ceremony, he told her to take her parents. "I don't mind," he had told her. "And to be honest, I don't want to see those people again." That was true. After Rob had dropped out of school the whole class, having learned every detail of their story it seemed, had chosen sides. And no one, not even porky Rachel, was on Josh's side.

As the sun set, Josh grabbed one of the wedding invitations that Allison had stacked on the coffee table and, using it for a bookmark, closed his thick paperback novel and tossed it on the table. Even on her graduation day, Allison could not stop planning their wedding. *In a few months I'll be a married man.* Darkness enveloped the apartment and laying his head down on the arm of the loveseat, Josh pressed his face against the tan crushed velvet fabric. He inhaled deeply. Then, pressing his face harder into the fabric, he inhaled again… and again. He sighed. Not a hint of *Polo*. The only thing he could smell now was Allison's perfume.

Mount Sinai

The late summer sun beat down on Josh's back and shoulders as he stood waist deep in the shallow end of his backyard swimming pool.

"Christ, that sun is hot," he said to himself.

He reached down and, cupping his hands, picked up a handful of water and tossed it over his back, cooling his sunburned shoulders. He felt like an ant frying under a magnifying glass. The sun was hotter than it used to be, must be the hole in the ozone. Still, he had to stand in the pool for another ten minutes. Allison may be timing him from the kitchen.

All that summer Josh had the same routine; after work each day, before he cleaned his backyard pool, he would stand waist deep in the shallow end for half an hour while Allison cleaned up the dinner dishes. What would he do next month when he closed the pool for the winter? If nothing had happened by then, he would have to sit in a cold bath. Josh shivered in spite of the sun. Most days he would kill time reading the newspaper as he stood in the pool. Still, the neighbors would look over his backyard fence with suspicion. *I must look like a fool.* He always made sure that his hands were out of the water.

Josh didn't actually know if he had a low sperm count. The problem may lie with Allison. Sometimes it takes a while for women who had been on the pill for a long time. And Allison had been on the pill for the first four years of their marriage; even before that. Who knows, Josh thought, maybe there was a problem with both of them.

Shirts and Skins

After trying to get pregnant for over a year, Allison's family doctor suggested Josh take cold baths. That might do the trick. Cooling down his testicles would increase his sperm count. And, the doctor said, if that didn't work then he would send them to a specialist and have Josh and Allison tested. But there were long wait times to see a fertility specialist. "It seems like everyone's having problems having babies these days," the doctor had said.

Maybe the baby was just being smart, Josh thought.

Josh swam across the length of his pool to the deep end and floated on his back in an area shaded by one of the maple trees that grew in a wooded park on the other side of his backyard fence. He frowned. There was a hint of a chlorine smell in his pool. He would take a sample and check the water after he and Allison finished fucking. Josh prided himself on having the perfect pH balance in his pool. He liked it at 7.5, the exact pH balance of the human eyeball. No one could say that their eyes burned after swimming in his pool.

With his back against the output return jet, he spread out his arms along the plastic pool ledge and rested his head back on the edge of the pool. The sky is so blue this time of year, he thought and then gathering his strength, he looked around his backyard. When he and Allison moved into their large house in Ancaster, Josh had the backyard professionally landscaped with a variety of perennial flowers. This ensured that something was always in bloom, starting with daffodils and tulips near the small pool house in early spring, irises and peonies along the walkway in June, daylilies of crimson, copper, gold and yellow in the flowerbeds July and August, and finally the mauve obedient plants and purple dahlias blooming now around his fence. There was always something to tend.

Beside the fence on the south side of the yard, a lilac bush was growing larger, changing from bush to tree. He had to cut it back. But you were only supposed to cut lilac bushes back in the spring— or was it the fall? Josh couldn't remember. He would have to check. He would have to remember to ask that young guy who worked at White Rose Garden Center, the one with the soul patch who always wore work boots and cargo shorts. He was even wearing shorts with a bomber jacket last December when Josh bought his Christmas tree. Duncan was his name. He had sold Josh a clematis plant earlier this year and seemed to know what he was talking about.

"Alright, that's enough," Josh said.

He pulled himself up on the aluminum steps. He could feel the water in the pool yank at his red swim trunks as he pulled himself out, revealing a few inches of the crack of his ass. He walked across the deck, pulling up his trunks as he walked, leaving wet footprints on the deck. He took a towel off the back of a patio chair and dried off his arms, torso and legs and then steeling himself, hung the towel around his neck.

"Al?"

"Don't get water on my floor," Allison said from the kitchen as he came into the living room through the patio doors.

"I won't," Josh said. He shut the patio doors behind him, stripped off his wet bathing suit and walked naked into the kitchen dangling his swimsuit on his index finger.

Allison smiled. She had changed from her business suit into a pair of shorts and a mint-green T-shirt.

"The neighbors will see you," she said as she washed a pasta pot in the sink. She tilted her head toward the bay window in the dining room that looked over the backyard pool.

"I don't care. It would be the most exciting thing to happen in this neighborhood in years."

Josh walked up beside her, rubbing the head of his penis against her leg. "I think I'm chock-full of sperm now," he said. "I can feel the little fuckers swimming around in my sack." He began to grow stiff.

He undid the top button of her shorts and sliding his hand under her left breast, felt the weight of it in his hand.

"Your hands are cold," she said, pushing his hand away.

"Let's do it here," Josh growled. "Let me fuck you in the bay window."

"Get out of here!"

"Remember when we'd turn off the outdoor lights and go skinny dipping at night when we first moved in?"

"Barely," she said, smiling. She placed the pot into the bottom rack of the dishwasher and looked up at the clock on the kitchen wall.

"And wouldn't it make a great conception story to tell the kid? How Mom and Dad made him right here on the kitchen floor? Maybe he'll grow up and be a great chef."

Allison closed the dishwasher. "And when we're done, I'll just toss my legs up over the stove? No thank you! Now go upstairs and call me when you're ready."

Upstairs in their bed alone, Josh stroked his penis. It was more difficult since the doctor started prescribing him Prozac. He closed his eyes and thought about the old strip clubs he went to when he was single. Each one had a backroom where the girls would do whatever you wanted, right there in the open, for a few extra bucks. He imagined one of his neighbors, Craig, watching him fuck Allison through the patio door. At some point in his fantasy, Allison disappeared completely and it was only Craig, watching Josh. He slowed down. *Spill not your seed upon the floor.* Once he had cum too quickly, shooting in Allison's mouth while she was attempting to get him hard. Pissed off, she had spit out his semen onto her fingers and gently pushed it into her vagina. "Sorry," he had said.

"What's with the goofy smile?" Allison asked as she came through the double doors of the bedroom.

"I didn't know I was smiling," Josh said.

She pulled off her shorts and white cotton panties but left on her shirt. She had shaved her pubic hair that morning.

"I'll be glad when I'm done ovulating for the month," she said, pulling the comforter to the bottom of the bed. "I'm getting tired of making up the bed two or three times a day."

Josh stroked his penis until he was ready to ejaculate while watching Allison in the mirror. As she flipped through the channels on the television with one hand, she absent-mindedly rubbed a water-based lubricant from a plastic bottle onto her light pink labia.

"Okay," Josh said. "I'm ready."

Allison put the remote control on the nightstand, laid back on one of the many emerald and gold pillows on the bed and spread open her bent legs like she was having a pelvic exam.

Josh lay on top of his wife, thrusted a few times, and ejaculated into her vagina. He held the base of his penis and milked out the last of his semen into the folds of her labia. He pulled out. His dick was already quickly reverting to its normal state. He studied her face but if she was disappointed by the quantity of sperm she didn't show it. It didn't feel like much. Josh thought it would be better just to fuck once a day with one big load; doing it two or three times reduces the amount. On the upside, as he had learned as a pubescent boy, each subsequent orgasm in a given day feels better than the one before it. Ah well, he thought, a few more days and she wouldn't bother him for sex for a month.

Josh kissed Allison on the cheek and rolled over and out of the bed, his feet landing on the floor with a thud. Lying on her back with her legs in the air, she reached out for the remote beside her on the bed and began flipping through channels.

"Not too hot a shower!" she yelled as Josh stepped into the ensuite shower stall.

He felt sorry for her. Sitting still was difficult for Allison. For the first few weeks, Josh had held her as she had laid with her legs in the air, using gravity to point the little buggers in the right direction. But after a few months, the act of procreation had become, if not more effective, at least more efficient. Now while she lay for half an hour in bed and watched television, he would clean the pool.

After showering, Josh dried off and, deciding against a pair of boxers, slipped a dry pair of khaki shorts right over his bare skin.

"I gotta test the pool water," he said. "It smells too much of chlorine."

Outside again, Josh kneeled at the side of the pool and dipped a clear plastic tube into the water to get a sample to test. He squeezed a few drops of bright phenol red liquid from a small plastic bottle into the test water. Perhaps their sperm and egg sensed something between them which kept them apart, Josh thought. Last year he had spent six months sleeping in the spare room down the hall. His winter sweaters were still there in the guest room closet. But since they had started this attempt to get pregnant, things were better. The distance between them was still there, but instead of a void, there was now something else—a project.

The water test kit read 7.7 pH.

"We can do better than that," Josh said.

⬥

In early September they got pregnant.

From the beginning of her pregnancy, Allison had trouble sleeping. So to make things easier for her, and to remove himself from her nocturnal tossing and turning, Josh offered to move back to the spare bedroom. They both slept better after that. Sometimes Allison would climb into his bed early in the morning and Josh would hold her close to him. Or they would make love. During those first months, Allison suddenly grew aggressive during intercourse. Her hands grabbed greedily at Josh in the mornings, her mouth pushing deep into his as she rode his cock. At one point she even demanded to be fucked from behind in the dining room window. Josh did everything she told him willingly, even allowing his wife to put her dildo up his ass one night after he'd polished off two bottles of wine.

But after the first trimester Allison's sexual appetite disappeared as quickly as it had come. If she came into Josh's room in the morning, she would just lay silently in Josh's arms. Josh loved those mornings. With his hands on his wife's stomach, he imagined his child's heart beating in unison with the faint pulse he felt on his lips while gently kissing Allison's neck. But by Christmas, she had stopped coming into his room altogether.

"You're going to have a boy," Josh's mother, Gloria, said one night in February. "That's because you're carrying the baby up front, just like I did."

Josh shrugged his shoulders and sipped his tea. They had just finished a dinner of overcooked pot roast with mashed potatoes and now he, Allison and his parents sat together in the living room of his parent's east end Hamilton house, waiting for the frozen cake his mother had bought for dessert to defrost.

"And I should know," Gloria continued. "I've had three boys." After all those years of working in mills and factories, she still looks good for her age, Josh thought. And even at sixty she was still working. She couldn't stop; they had no money. Josh's father hadn't worked in twenty years.

"If you know what you're having, why not tell everyone?" Josh's father, Ted, said. He had taken the large chair by the window and set his cup on the window ledge, as if reaching over to the coffee table would be far too much effort.

"We want it to be a surprise," Josh said.

"But I was a lot bigger than you are," Gloria said. "You hardly look pregnant at all." She brushed some crumbs off the front of her red sweater. Sneaking cookies while she made the tea, Josh thought.

"Did you tell your parents what you're having?" Josh's father asked, looking at Allison.

Josh clenched his teeth and wondered how much longer it would be before he and Allison could remove themselves from his parent's home. *There's still a whole goddamn Pepperidge Farm cake to eat.*

"We haven't told anybody," Allison said.

Josh looked down at the tea in his cup. It had been his idea not to tell anyone the baby's sex. Allison's parents didn't seem to have a problem with not knowing—and it was their first grandchild. This would be his parent's fourth, but after three girls they were itching for a grandson.

"It would just be easier for everyone if they knew what color the baby things they buy should be," Ted said. Josh was going to ask what it was his father was so desperate to buy for the baby but decided not to. He wondered when the last time his father had been in a store—or bought anything at all for that matter, except cigarettes and Pepsi.

"You can buy baby stuff in any color you want," Josh said. "We'll use it."

"That's stupid," Ted said. He leaned over to the coffee table with a grunt and picked up his cigarette pack. "You can't put pink on a boy or blue on a girl."

"I can do whatever I want," Josh said.

"You usually do," Ted said.

"And I don't think a newborn baby will care much about the color of the clothes," Allison said. She put her empty cup down on the coffee table and laid her hands on her growing stomach. Her smile was beginning to fade.

"I can tell, it's a boy," Gloria said. "But I'm only buying things that are white and yellow... and a few light green things. That's what we did in the old days before ultrasounds when nobody knew what we were having."

"Have you chosen a name?" Ted asked. He took a cigarette out of his pack, placed it in his mouth and then tossed the pack on the windowsill beside his cup.

"Yes, we have," Josh said.

"But you want it to be a surprise," Ted said, frowning. He lit his cigarette, picked up the remote control and turned on the television.

"It's more fun not knowing," Josh said.

"The last time I was at your house I sneaked upstairs to see if you had painted the baby's room," Gloria said. She lifted her shoulders mischievously and grinned. "But you hadn't painted it yet."

I'd have no problem spending a day and fifty bucks painting that room the wrong color just to irritate them, Josh thought. The more he thought about it, the more he liked the idea. Allison wouldn't think the elaborate practical joke was funny, though. But she wouldn't stop him. Then again, it would be a lot of work and then they'd just end up with a ton of baby clothes in the wrong color. So who would get the last laugh?

"Oh, I have something for you," Gloria said. She stood and walked down the hallway to the kitchen. Josh wondered if she was eating more cookies on the sly. She came back with something wrapped in yellowed newspaper and handed it to Josh. Intrigued, he pulled off the faded newsprint.

It was a porcelain baby bowl.

"Do you remember it?" his mother asked. She smiled and bit her lower lip.

He did.

"It's the bowl Joshua used when he was a baby," she said. "Actually all three of my boys used it for their Pablum."

The bowl was creamy white with a baby blue rim. In the center of the bowl, a mother robin wearing a kerchief tied around her head was standing above a nest with three baby robins, all with their little beaks open, waiting for their dinner. One of the robins had yet to completely hatch and only his head was sticking out of the top of a blue egg. Below the rim, on the side of the bowl, "*tweety-tweet! Hungry birdies need to eat!*" was written in yellow.

"That's sweet," Allison said. She picked up the old yellow newspaper Josh had thrown aside on the couch. "What's this? *The Socialist Worker?*"

Josh picked up the paper and checked the date. *January 12 1972.* "Didn't you know my dad was a socialist?"

"I was not a socialist," Ted growled.

"And you never had me picketing either," Josh said. "I suppose now you are going to tell me I wasn't at the National Day of Protest with you?"

"When I was a child I spake as a child," Ted said, not turning away from the television.

"Not if you used words like 'spake' you didn't," Josh said.

"I remember the National Day of Protest," Gloria said. "It was in October. I forget the year. And you did bring Josh with us. I told you to leave him in school but you just had to have him there."

"Someday I'll tell you that story," Josh said to Allison.

"Socialists ruined this country," Ted said. "Atheists, mostly..."

"You know you can be Christian *and* a socialist, don't you? Tommy Douglas was a socialist and a Baptist preacher. And he was the one who brought socialized medicine to Canada," Josh said.

"I was never a socialist!" Ted said. He smashed his cigarette into the ashtray. "Is there any more tea?"

"Revisionist history!" Josh said. He turned to his mother. "Like his time in the army. When I was little it was the worst thing that ever happened to him; it ruined his life he said. Now it's like the best thing ever."

"I didn't say it was the best thing ever."

Allison gave Josh the undetectable but undeniable touch of a wife on his hand that indicated she was ready to leave. They would have to skip the cake.

"I just know you're going to have a boy," Gloria said.

⬥

On a Saturday in early March, Josh was on the Stairmaster at the Ancaster Fitness Club reading a *People* magazine that someone had left behind. He had hoped to work off a hangover but after twenty minutes climbing to nowhere, he was feeling worse. Josh had only joined the gym a month earlier and his muscles were aching. He hadn't really worked out since Rob had taken him to Northern Fitness those few times way back in college. Josh grimaced. He wasn't fond of the Ancaster Fitness Club. It was too expensive and, to make matters worse, he had to drive twenty minutes out of his way to get to there even though a brand new gym had just opened up right down the street from his house. But of course it was a goddamn Northern Fitness. And even after all these years he didn't want to run into Rob again. Irony can be a real cunt, Josh thought.

Josh flipped a page of his magazine. *Sharon Stone's Chiffon-and-Champagne Wedding to Newspaper Editor Phil Bronstein Leaves Guests in Awe.* Must be nice, Josh thought. All we had at our wedding was a chicken dinner and *Blue Nun.*

Josh checked the clock on the control panel on the Stairmaster. *Eighteen more minutes.* Once he was done here, he would shower, hit the sauna and then pick up a turkey sub and a couple of bottles of wine on his way home. I refuse to use the term 'hair of the dog,' he thought. There was no need to rush today. Allison was spending the afternoon in Toronto shopping for baby clothes with her mother.

Freezing rain had started about an hour earlier and the gym had been emptying out steadily since. With him on the second floor mezzanine where the cardio equipment was located, one lone woman ran on a treadmill and below Josh, on the ground floor, two men were lifting free weights in front of the wall-length mirror.

One of the men was on his back, legs astride, on one of the benches doing dumbbell flys. The weights clinked each time they met over his chest. Josh knew that the man's name was Charles and he was some kind of a doctor. Josh had spoken to him briefly when they shared the hot tub in the men's locker room the week before. Charles was an older man, forty-five or fifty with a middle age plumpness his time at the gym had yet to rectify. He had thinning blonde hair and a bald spot that looked much larger in the shower when his hair was wet. He was married to an Australian woman who taught junior high school and had a couple of grown daughters. Josh had also noted (from witnessing Charles' exit from the hot tub) that the doctor had the biggest set of nuts Josh had ever seen on a man. They looked odd compared to his average-sized dick. A ball to dick ratio of at least 3:1, Josh had thought. He turned the page of his *People* magazine but his eyes wandered again down to the floor below. *Maybe even 4:1.*

A few benches down from Charles, another younger man was doing dumbbell curls. Josh had seen this other man around the gym but didn't know his name. However, having seen him in the parking lot, Josh did know that the man drove an old 1970s-era blue Ford Fairmont with a child's car seat in the back. He was a tad younger than Josh, in his mid-to-late twenties, with dark curly hair and dark eyes. He looked Italian and had a short stocky build with a red tattoo on his left calf of something Josh couldn't make out from the mezzanine. Maybe a maple leaf, Josh thought.

But even from the second floor, Josh could see that both men, like him, were wearing wedding bands. Why, Josh wondered, are wedding bands always visible at fifty paces?

Charles finished his set, dropped his weights and sat on the end of the bench to rest. The younger man walked past Charles a few times looking over the rack of free weights and then, resting both hands on the top of the rack at waist-level, bent slightly over the weights as if deciding which to pick up. He reminded Josh of one of the perennials in his garden as a honey bee hovered by. Charles looked over at the stocky younger man and then back at the floor when the younger man, deciding not to take any weights at all, sauntered back to his own bench. The younger man, seemingly catching Charles' glance in the mirror, grinned and looked away. Did they know each other? It didn't appear so. They hadn't spoken to one another. But it seemed, Josh thought, that the younger man's movements were almost—rehearsed.

Josh studied how Charles glanced at the younger man in the mirror. They were nothing like the looks you would give someone you did not know. Each time Charles looked at the younger man, his glance carried a strange gravitas that, Josh thought, should be accompanied by a word but wasn't. As if Charles was about to say, "Hey, your wallet dropped out of your back pocket." Or "Didn't we go to Queen's University together?" Every so often the same question was silently asked again. Suddenly Charles turned his neck to look up at the second floor, making Josh look down at his *People* magazine.

In what could be described as some kind of an odd mating dance, Charles ogled the younger man while in return the younger man sipped on his silver water bottle and stared back at Charles with, what seemed to Josh, little interest. Had he received the response he wanted from old Charles and could now relax and let nature take its course? Though the whole scene seemed, at first, a little comic to Josh, it had become more natural— and intriguing as he continued watching.

The younger man walked away toward the window but looked back a few times while Charles continued to stare, with his head cocked, in his direction. The younger man returned and, smiling, sat down on the bench beside Charles. Josh slowed down on the Stairmaster and strained to hear down to the first floor.

"Lousy day out, eh?" the younger man said. He put his towel around his neck.

"That's March for ya," Charles said.

"Sure is a mixed fucking bag, eh?"

"But I always say that if I can get through February," Charles said, smiling, "then I can handle anything March throws at me."

The younger man laughed. He sat down on the bench beside Charles and wiped his face with his towel.

"Hi," a woman said to Josh as she stepped on the Stairmaster beside him. Fumbling with the controls, she entered forty-five minutes into the machine.

"Hey," Josh replied. He had seen this woman before but had never spoken to her. She was attractive, around thirty-five who, Josh had noticed, always had on a different stylish outfit when she worked out. Today she had on black track pants and a gold T-shirt. She didn't have a wedding band.

"What are you reading?" she asked.

"Oh," Josh answered, sheepishly. "It's a *People* someone left behind. I'm not really reading it." When he looked back down to the first floor the men were gone.

Even though the control panel showed he had almost ten minutes left, Josh stopped the Stairmaster, grabbed his towel and hopped off the machine.

"Did you want to read this?" Josh held out the magazine to the woman.

"If you're done with it, sure!" she said, smiling.

"Absolutely," he said. He handed her the magazine. "Sharon Stone got married".

The locker room was empty except for a man cleaning the toilet stalls in the area off the showers. Josh stripped out of his shorts and T-shirt, wrapped a towel around his waist, and walked to the showers. Surprised to see no one was in there, he jumped into one of the empty stalls and quickly showered. After toweling off, he hung the towel around his neck and walked naked past the empty hot tub to the far end of the locker room and opened the sauna door.

A cloud of steam wafted out as Josh stepped inside. From the other end of the sauna Josh heard movement, but, since the sauna was large and the steam so dense, he was unable to see across it to the other side. As not to burn his ass, Josh put his towel on the tiled bench near the door before he sat down. This was the best part of joining a gym. As the steam began to disappear, Josh saw two figures, one larger than the other, sitting together across the sauna. They were moving. Suddenly a burst of scalding steam from above fogged up the sauna. Then slowly, over a few minutes, the fog began to dissipate again. Now the figures appeared closer. Over the next ten or fifteen minutes, Josh watched as the silhouettes of the figures would appear ghostly before his eyes for a few seconds before again disappearing behind another partition of haze as the sauna's steam generator kicked in. Each time the figures looked to be moving closer to each other. And then, as the fog was disappearing slightly for the fifth or sixth time, the figure looked, for just a moment, like the outline of one large animal. But then, as if sensing it was being observed, it quickly broke apart like an ameba in mitosis. There was a cough somewhere in the mist before the steam rushed in again, blinding Josh to only a few inches from his face.

Below the hissing of the steam, Josh heard shallow breathing. His own heart was beating hard. His penis grew. And then for just a second—less than a second he would tell himself later—he wished he wasn't married or about to become a father.

Unable to stand the heat any longer, Josh wrapped his towel tight around his waist in a feeble attempt to hide his hard on and left the sauna for the showers. About five minutes later, as Josh was standing under a cool stream of water, Charles came into the shower room. His body was pink and glistening with sweat. And then, a few minutes later, the younger man entered as well.

I was right, Josh thought, it was a maple leaf tattoo.

◈

Josh had just arrived home from the gym when Clara his mother-in-law called. Allison's water had broken while they were searching for baby clothes in a downtown Toronto baby boutique. She had been taken by ambulance to Mount Sinai Hospital, not far from the Baby Gap in Yorkville where, as his mother-in-law put it, Allison "broke down."

"The doctors are trying to delay delivery as long as they can," Clara said. "They're hoping with drugs they can hold off for forty-eight hours... but it won't be any longer than that. Any time will help, they say, because she's only twenty-five weeks along."

She'll be twenty-five weeks on Wednesday.

Josh wasn't exactly sure where he was going as he raced toward Toronto in his silver Pontiac Grand Am. Mount Sinai Hospital was somewhere on University Avenue, Clara had said. He planned to just head straight downtown and then ask someone for directions to the hospital. His head was spinning; at one point he thought he may have to pull over since he had become so lightheaded. Perhaps he should have asked someone to drive him. He had not even phoned his parents—or anyone else in his family—to let them know what was happening with Allison and the baby before he left Ancaster. If he had, his mother would have asked him to pick her up and take her along, and then he would have lost at least half an hour driving to the east end of Hamilton to get her. The drive was slow enough because of the wet snow that was starting to fall. But luckily the freezing rain had stopped.

When Josh arrived in Toronto an hour later, Clara and her husband Frank were both in the hospital room with Allison. Josh pushed his way past Frank and took Allison's hand. She began to cry. She looked pale and somewhat smaller than she had that morning. She only had the tiniest remnants of her light pink lipstick left on her lips and her dark hair, with the new auburn highlights Josh loved, was fanned out on her white pillow.

"I'm so scared," she said. Josh leaned over and hugged her. He wanted to climb into the bed with her, hold her in his arms and cradle her stomach.

His in-laws quickly rattled off as much information as they could. The doctors would not be able to stop the baby being born. It was only a matter of time now. They were hoping they could hold off for forty-eight hours but it was unlikely. It would probably happen later that evening or maybe the next morning. Allison was given a shot of steroids to help the baby's lungs develop quickly.

"The doctors are in and out all the time," Clara said. "If you have any more questions."

Questions? Yeah, I have some questions, Josh thought. Like how the fuck did Frank get here before me? Josh decided that Clara had called her husband before calling him. He would talk to them about it later.

"They have about six or eight doctors helping her," Frank added in his lawyer voice, as if he'd personally assigned them to her.

"It'll be fine," Clara said. She was holding Allison's other hand "Premature babies are born all the time now. They're used to it here. It's almost lucky that this happened while we were in Toronto and not in Hamilton. The best doctors are in Toronto."

"That's what I say," Frank said. "If Hamilton doctors were any good why would they stay in Hamilton?"

"Did you call your parents, Josh?" Clara asked.

"I didn't have time."

"We'll go down and call them now... if you want," Clara said. "I have their phone number in my PalmPilot."

"Yes," Josh said. "Thanks."

Clara motioned to Frank with one finger to get up and he quickly obeyed. "And we'll get a coffee as well." She bent over Allison and kissed her. "We'll be back soon, Sweetie." Josh had never heard his mother-in-law call Allison 'Sweetie' before; it didn't really suit a tough divorce lawyer like Clara and, he thought, sounded pretty stupid too.

After they left, Josh sat on Allison's bedside and held her hand as she cried. From deep in the pit of his stomach, a cry of grief and anger grew. But not wanting to cry in front of his wife, he choked down the wail of pain, allowing only the tiniest whimper escape from his lips.

"I just keep waiting for the baby to move," she said. "When it does I feel okay for a second, but then I want the baby to move again."

Josh noticed that after all those months of trying to keep the baby's sex a secret by saying "the baby" instead of a gender-specific pronoun, it was difficult for Allison to stop now.

"It's going to be fine. Your mom is right; they do this all the time now. Early babies are nothing these days."

Finally, sometime after midnight, a male nurse came into the room and gave Allison something in her IV to make her sleep. "She'll need her rest," the nurse whispered. "Even if she only gets a few hours... it'll help."

Once Allison was sleeping, Josh left his wife with her parents and took the elevator down to the ground floor to get a coffee from one of the vending machines near the security desk. Outside, University Avenue was quiet. Josh walked to the front doors, peeked out, and stopped. He was never comfortable in Toronto. It intimidated him. He looked around to see if there was someone outside that he could bum a cigarette from. Josh hadn't smoked for years, but wanted one now. Seeing no one, he walked slowing around the ground floor sipping his coffee. It tasted like hot water and dirt.

Walking past the closed cafeteria, Josh saw a sign on the wall pointing visitor's toward the hospital synagogue. Josh followed it to a large oak door.

The chaplains at Mount Sinai Hospital are trained to offer multi-faith spiritual care and support. We are represented by a Rabbi, an Ecumenical Chaplain, a Roman Catholic Chaplain and a Chaplain specializing in ICU and the Women's and Infants' Health Program. If you want us to call someone from your own faith group, we will try to contact such a person. However, belonging to a religion is not necessary for chaplaincy support.

Josh wondered if St. Joseph's Hospital back in Hamilton would provide a Rabbi. Probably not, he concluded and opened the door of the synagogue.

It was empty.

He sat down at the back of the room, covered his face and sobbed into his hands. For the first time Josh allowed the pain and anger to escape, and his wails echoed off the walls of the synagogue and reverberated in his ears. He tried to remember a prayer from Sunday school—and he almost did pray—but he couldn't. He knew no one was listening.

Early the next morning his son was born.

"It's fifty-fifty," a doctor said to Josh and his in-laws in the hospital. "Twenty-five weeks is really at the cusp. But it's much better odds than it would have been even a week or two ago... but then again the odds would have been a lot better two weeks from now."

Fifty-fifty, Josh thought, that's like tossing a coin.

Heads you live; tails you die.

An hour later, Josh, with Allison in a wheelchair, was taken down the hall to the neonatal intensive care unit to see their son. The baby was red, like a newborn hamster, and tinier than Josh ever imagined a baby could be. He was lying, wrapped in a white blanket, in an infant incubator sleeping quietly. His head, covered with a white cap to limit heat loss, looked too large on his tiny body and taped to his face was a respirator tube that went down his throat to help him breathe. Tubes and wires ran from his chest to machines that monitored his heart rate, blood pressure and temperature. Under his fragile skin, Josh could see the blood vessels that ran over his son's body.

"That's because there hasn't been enough time for him to develop any fat underneath," the stout Jamaican nurse said. She gave them a reassuring smile that seemed to Josh sincere. "But he'll grow some fast enough. Like the rest of us"

Josh watched Allison stroke the baby's leg through one of the plastic sleeves in the incubator's porthole as she hummed a lullaby. The baby's leg did not move with the caresses except for the occasional quiver in the toes. Josh counted his son's ten tiny toes over and over through the glass. He did not want to touch them through plastic.

Josh looked around the white sterile room, there were other babies in the NICU, but his son was the smallest. He wished they would bring in a baby that was even tinier. His son's chest moved up and down slightly with each *shwoosh* of the respirator. Such little lungs must need so little air, he thought. How do they know how much to give him? Across the room a young couple was taking turns feeding a larger baby with a bottle. Maybe their baby was this size too once. Josh tried to find hope in the couple and their healthy-looking baby, but he could only hate them.

Later that morning the chubby Jamaican nurse took a photo of Allison beside the incubator. It would be the only photo they would ever have of their son. A short time later, after the baby died, they let Josh and Allison take turns holding him in their arms. Holding his son for the first and last time, Josh held each little toe between his fingers and counted them one-by-one to ten.

That afternoon Gloria arrived at Mount Sinai Hospital by bus from Hamilton. Even though she had taken the day off work she still looked tired; older. She ran to Josh and held him tightly as he sobbed in her arms.

"Oh, Joshua, no!" she said.

"His name was Daniel," he said.

※

Josh kneeled at the side of his pool checking the pH balance. It was a little low, at 7.4. Inside his garage, between his apothecary of various dry chemicals and blue gels for his pool, he still had a pair of tiny water wings he had bought at Christmas.

"You can try again," the doctor had said. That was after the tests they do when you lose a baby; tests that require scalpels and microscopes. Josh knew if he thought about the tests too long he would lose his mind.

Daniel had died of sepsis.

Sepsis was a word that sounded just as revolting as it was. The bacteria started in his lungs and went through his body, shutting down his tiny organs one by one. Allison had stayed by their son the entire time, still caressing him when they turned off the respirator. And with his arm wrapped around his wife's waist, Josh stroked her back tenderly as their son slipped away.

Shirts and Skins

They never actually said that they would wait before trying to have another baby—not in words anyway. But a month or two after Allison had come home from the hospital, Josh moved back down the hall to the guest bedroom. They didn't speak much. The marriage had changed little, except they didn't fight anymore. There was just silence.

Josh poured a cupful of "shock", a white granular chlorine powder used to kill any organic matter that made its way into his pool, into a dish and walked back to the pool. He wondered how often they had used the pool this summer. Two or three times, maybe? He tossed the white powder out of the dish into the pool and sat down on the deck with his feet in the water. He dipped the dish in the pool to rinse it. The chemicals were already eating away at the mother robin and her chicks at the bottom of the bowl, turning them green.

"Well that's enough of that," Josh said as the sun fell behind the trees in the park at the end of the backyard. And leaving the bowl at the side of the pool, he headed upstairs for a hot shower.

A Mere Matter of Marching

Josh reached up and switched on the round light above his airplane seat. Beside him, a fat bald man with the sagging face of a snoozing bulldog suddenly jerked and opened his eyes as though startled by a loud noise. The man wiped a spot of drool off his chin with his palm, huffed a series of incoherent words, and then rested his flabby head back against the window. Josh looked at his watch and stretched his left leg out into the aisle. He had nodded off for only twenty minutes but his neck was as stiff as if he had been sleeping slumped over for hours. Must be getting old, he thought. He rubbed the kink in the back of his neck and stared at the dark sky through a small piece of window not blocked by the bald man's head. Thousands of feet below, a million tiny electric lights shone in bright conglomerations like galaxies across a black landscape.

He was flying down to Washington D.C. two days before the actual start of the conference because it was cheaper than flying out Monday morning. By staying over a Saturday night, his boss had explained, Josh would save the company almost a thousand dollars on the cost of the airplane ticket. Josh didn't object. He and his wife had separated a few months earlier and though he had moved into his own apartment, they still spoke every day on the telephone, just as Todd, their marriage counselor, had suggested. Todd also advised that Josh and Allison meet every Saturday night for what Todd called dates. So for the past two months, Josh has been dating his wife—a movie, a dinner, and maybe a quick fuck in his old bed before Josh drove back to his apartment. Todd thought the sundered spouses were making good progress.

But now Josh looked forward to a week of freedom and relished the idea of having hundreds of miles and an international border between him and Allison. A male flight attendant, who had taken off his blue suit jacket during the flight, came down the aisle pushing a trolley and collecting garbage. He was tall and slim with wide brown eyes and short black hair, which had begun to recede slightly, cropped close to his head. A smile stretched easily over his teeth displaying two deep dimples in his cheeks. Josh marveled at how genuine his smile still looked after a two hour flight. His graceful movements, like a ballerina doing pirouettes in a phone booth, seemed too broad for the confines of the narrow aisle. With precision, he would narrowly miss hitting the overhead bins with his hands each time he reached out for a passenger's empty soda can or peanut wrapper. When the man approached, Josh handed him a clear plastic cup containing a few melting pieces of ice, the remains of two gin and tonics, and smiled shyly back, but the flight attendant's head had already turned toward someone else on the other side of the aisle. As he passed, his starched white cotton shirt brushed against Josh's cheek.

Outside Washington National Airport, Josh stood on the train platform with his black suitcase at his side studying the city's subway map. He moved his hand through the greasy gel in his short brown hair and scratched the bald spot that was beginning to grow on the back of his head. He had been planning this for months. The confusing colored lines that made up Washington's subway system looked like a multi-armed Hindu god. He studied the stops on the orange line until he found one on the other side of the Potomac River.

That's it.

He opened a zipper on the front of his suitcase and took out a glossy color brochure: *The Electronic Data Business Exchange (EDBX) Spring Conference, Arlington Hilton.* The Hilton was right above the Balston Metro Station on the orange line. He had to take two trains from the airport to his hotel in Virginia and, although he was thirty years old, Josh had never been on a subway.

After ten minutes and two yellow line trains, a blue line train Josh was waiting for finally rumbled to a stop at the platform. He pulled his suitcase with a clack onto the silver subway car and sat by the doors. He rode the blue line past the Pentagon and through Arlington cemetery to Rosslyn Metro Station where he changed over to the orange line. A few minutes later he was standing in The Arlington Hilton. That was simple enough, he thought.

The lobby was large and elegantly furnished with tan leather chairs and dark brown tables. Around the perimeter of the lobby were a number of stores including a coffee shop, a hair stylist, and at the far end, a gift shop brimming with burgundy and gold Washington Redskins shirts, sweaters, and ball caps. Beside the gift shop, a restaurant was opening for the evening. The smell of burning hickory drifted out of its doors.

After Josh had checked in, a black man in a maroon blazer slid Josh's room access card and a small gold key across the gray marble counter.

"Enjoy your stay," the man said.

"Thanks," Josh said. He put his access card and key in the front breast pocket of his yellow shirt. "Oh, is there a liquor store nearby? I'd like to get a bottle of wine."

"Yes there is," the man said. "Go out the front door, turn right, and walk down one block. There's a liquor store beside The Waffle House on the corner." He leaned across the counter toward Josh and lowered his voice. "But you know... if you order a bottle of wine from room service, it just shows up as *Restaurant* on the bill."

Josh blushed. He's got me pegged, he thought. No boss would question a travel expense for *Restaurant.*

Josh rode the elevator up to the eleventh floor. He entered room 1125, and quickly threw his suitcase onto the bed. He had to piss. As he stood in the bathroom and emptied his bladder, he noticed some little plastic bottles of assorted complementary shampoos and soaps in a wicker basket on top of the toilet tank. Lavender, almond, patchouli. While his stream splashed in the bowl, Josh grabbed the bottle of almond body wash, unscrewed the tiny white cap, and put it under his nose. He sniffed and jerked his head away. It smelled like the marzipan icing on his wedding cake. He put the cap back on the bottle and tossed it back into the wicker basket. *I'll use the lavender.*

He finished pissing, shook, and zipped up his fly. On his way out of the bathroom, Josh saw his profile in the mirror. Even though his new yellow shirt had perspiration marks under the armpits and was wrinkled from the flight, he still looked good. Since he and Allison had separated, he had been going to the gym regularly and lost some weight. And last week, he had made a special excursion to the shopping mall near his new apartment. It was the first time in a long time that Josh had chosen his own clothes, and he had come home that afternoon with a heavy pair of black leather Doc Marten shoes, two pairs of blue jeans, and this bright yellow shirt with a fancy designer emblem on the chest. "My independence shirt," Josh had said to himself when he put it on for the first time that morning before heading to the airport.

Josh's hotel room had a worn royal blue carpet and cream-colored striped wallpaper. Near the window there was a cherry wood desk and chair and in front of the bed, a matching cherry wood armoire held a large television set. A gold cardboard note placed on one of the pillows of the king-size bed boasted that the sheets had a two hundred and fifty thread count.

"I'll count them later," Josh said to the armoire.

He walked toward the window and opened the curtains. It was too dark to see the surrounding landscape, except for the glowing sign of the Waffle House down the street. Then, as if he remembered something, he clapped his hands together and turned around.

"The mini-bar!" He leaped to the front of the bed and the floor vibrated slightly. "Sorry, room 1025!" he shouted to the floor. He shoved the tiny gold key they had given him at the front desk into the lock of the small refrigerator sitting on a shelf under the television in the armoire. He opened the refrigerator door wide and smirked. "Decadence!"

Dancing in place, Josh took out two tiny vodka bottles and a can of tonic. After a few seconds of hesitation, he also grabbed a box of chocolate covered almonds and walked to the desk. I hope this shows up as *Restaurant* too, he thought, as he crunched the almonds between his back teeth. Standing at the desk, he mixed himself a drink using one and a half bottles of the vodka and half a can of tonic. He took one sip and poured what was left from the second little bottle of vodka into his glass. He took another sip and then laid down on the emerald and ruby bedspread. Although he would have preferred the drink with ice, he was not going to search the Hilton hallways for an ice machine right now.

As he finished his vodka tonic, Josh debated whether to call Allison. Todd would want you to call now, he thought. He chewed on his thumb nail. Ach! His fingers smelled like marzipan.

"Later," he said, rolling out of bed.

He put his empty glass down beside the phone on the night table and walked out of his hotel room to the elevator. Back down to the hotel lobby, he marched toward the scent of grilling meat and hickory. The vodka from the mini-bar was already soothing Josh's head but the stark lights of the hotel lobby yanked him back into an unpleasant pseudo-sobriety. Above the entrance to the restaurant, a large red, white and blue electric sign flashed *Yankee Steak House and Bar*. Josh grinned and swung open the wooden saloon-style doors.

Inside, sports photos and memorabilia covered the walls. At one end of the dark room, a big-screen television was showing a boxing match and beside the television, a framed number seven Washington Redskins football jersey hung on the wall. Josh tried to focus. Joe Theismann's signature was scrawled in black magic marker across the front of the shirt. That must be worth a couple of bucks, he thought. *If it's real.*

Josh walked to a long oak bar in the back near the kitchen and sat down on a barstool with his back to the television. There were only a few people scattered around the dark room. It was unlikely that anyone else from his convention had come two days early. Seeing Josh, the bartender put down the Chuck Palahniuk paperback novel he was reading and walked over.

A swarthy man in his early twenties, he had short black curly hair parted to the side and combed back over his head with styling gel, which made his hair look as if he had just jumped out of the shower. His dark almond-shaped eyes looked clear and intelligent and around his mouth, he sported a sparse goatee. He wore a black pair of Levis and a red shirt with a black vest and matching black bowtie. His shoes were shiny black leather with a thick rubber sole. In his right earlobe he had a small gold stud. His nametag read *Ricky.*

"What can I get you," Ricky asked. He had a crooked smile and a tiny gap between his two front teeth. His voice was much deeper than Josh had expected. I wonder if he has Indian blood too, Josh thought.

"I'll have the porterhouse steak and a vodka martini," Josh said.

"Sure thing," Ricky said. "How would you like your steak cooked?"

"Rare," Josh said. He grabbed his left earlobe and felt a small ancient hole. *I wonder whatever happened to my diamond stud earring?* It didn't matter. The hole in his earlobe had closed up years ago.

As Ricky shook Josh's vodka martini in a shiny metal martini shaker, Josh noticed that Ricky wore a thick silver ring on his thumb. When did they start making thumb rings?

"Your steak will be ready in a few minutes," Ricky said as he put Josh's martini in front of him. He had a slight Southern accent. Josh wondered just how far south one had to travel in the States before they started to hear a Southern accent. Kentucky? Ohio? His Aunt Wilma had picked up her feeble Southern accent by living in Georgia for twenty years. Maybe Ricky was from Georgia too.

Josh sipped his drink. The martini was so cold that it numbed the back of his throat.

"Mmmmmmmmmm." He closed his eyes and the last bit of tension disappeared from his body as the vodka and vermouth flowed from his stomach out through his veins. First his gut warmed and his head grew wonderfully hazy. Then his arms and fingers tingled with a familiar pleasure. The fear he had carried along with him from home was being slowly eclipsed by something else. His penis grew erect in his jeans.

Josh stared off at a framed *Sports Illustrated* cover on the wall beside the bar. The photo was of a football player in a Washington Redskin uniform catching a football in midair. Beside the football player the word *WOW* was written in big white letters. What would the headline be for me and my life? Josh wondered. Something like *WASTE* or *ZZZZZ*. He chewed on an olive and, taking the pit from his mouth, placed it on a napkin by his martini glass. What has he been doing for almost a decade? He worked, he ate, he slept and sometimes he even fucked the wife. He tried to remember when that had been enough.

While Josh waited for his steak, the vodka continued to push at dams he had built in his head. The past wafted back to him as if he had caught the scent of long forgotten cologne. Another few sips and the barricades broke, sending debris from the last eight years into Josh's frontal lobe. *If only...*

Ricky placed a plate on the bar in front of Josh. The aroma of a rare porterhouse steak, baked potato, and chopped grilled zucchini wiped all other thoughts from Josh's mind like a wet cloth over a dusty chalkboard. Now he could only focus on his dinner.

As he ate, Ricky stood close swaying to the classic rock music coming from speakers above the bar. "Is the steak okay?" he asked.

"Perfect," Josh said.

"Another martini?"

Josh looked at his empty glass. He had promised Todd to try and cut down on his drinking.

Fuck Todd.

"Yes," said Josh, and then as if suddenly remembering his manners, added "please."

As Josh continued eating his steak, Ricky fixed another martini. This time he dropped two olives into the glass before placing it in front of Josh. The olives looked twice their size through the cold clear liquor.

"You must be British," a voice beside him said.

Josh turned his head toward a man sitting two stools to his right. The man interlocked his fingers and placed his hands carefully on the bar. He grinned. The man was a couple of years older than Josh and had the beginnings of crow's feet growing around his eyes and faint laugh lines around his mouth. He had short wavy light brown hair, amber eyes, eyes, a round nose, and full fat lips. Leaner than Josh, he was only about one hundred and forty pounds, and wore a dark gray suit, white shirt, and a deep purple silk tie. A five-o'clock shadow was appearing on his face.

"Huh?" Josh said.

"Americans never cut their food that way," the man said. "They cut five little pieces off a steak, put their knife down, switch their fork to their right hand, and then eat all five pieces." The man mimed the procedure with invisible utensils. The lights over the bar reflected in his manicured nails.

Josh smiled as he continued to chew his food. You should see me eat soup, he thought.

"But British people cut off one piece of steak at a time," the man continued. "They also somehow get a little bit of everything on their forks... a little meat, a little potato, a little vegetable—it's a skill I'm quite envious of." Josh listened for any hint of an accent but there was none.

"I'm not British," Josh said. "I'm Canadian."

"Oh really?" the man said. "My grandmother was from Montreal. In fact, I've always considered myself to be part Canadian. I think that's why I'm one of the few people I know in San Diego who watches hockey."

"What can I get you?" Ricky asked the man.

"A glass of tawny port, please," the man said.

"Sure thing," Ricky said. He turned and searched the bottles lined up on a shelf over the bar. Josh watched the man's eyes bend upwards and gaze at Ricky as he reached for the bottle and took it down from the top shelf. Before pouring the port into a glass, Ricky ran a damp cloth over the bottle to remove the dust.

"My grandmother was from Minnesota," Josh said, "but I've never considered myself part American."

"Where in Minnesota?" the man asked. He turned and looked at

Josh. His eyes looked golden close-up.

"An Indian reserve called Nett Lake," Josh said.

"You're Indian?"

"You mean you can't tell?" Josh flashed his smartass half-smile and watched the man try to decipher it. Then he snickered and took a sip of his martini.

"No," the man finally said, chuckling. "You don't really look very Indian."

"Yeah, I've been told that before."

Ricky placed a glass of port in front of the man, folded his arms, and leaned back against the bar. Josh wondered why port was served in such tiny glasses.

"So, who taught you those British table manners, your mother?" the man asked. He picked up his small glass, stood, and shifted himself over to the empty barstool next to Josh.

"Actually," Josh said, "it was my wife, Allison."

Like the devil, Josh felt her presence the moment he uttered her name. In the corner of the restaurant, near the kitchen doors, she materialized out of the hickory smoke and stood shaking her head slowly from side to side, looking disapprovingly at his martini with two olives and new yellow shirt. *Be gone! You have no power here!*

"My wife insisted that I learn the right way to use a knife and fork before I met her parents," Josh said. "So she sat me down at my kitchen table one night and taught me how to cut my food using a slice of pizza."

"Would she slap your hand with a fork if you made a mistake?" the man asked. He picked up a white cardboard coaster off the bar and tapped it lightly on Josh's wrist. He laughed through his teeth.

"Now Allison likes to tell people I ate with my hands before I met her." Josh took another sip of his martini. "So check out this execution of the full-fork move you dig so much," Josh said. He cut off a piece of meat onto his fork and then using his knife, added a piece of potato and then a final bit of zucchini. Josh held up his fork but before eating it, tried to show off by twirling it around his thumb. He lost control and almost dropped the fork on his lap but caught it in midair with both hands. A piece of zucchini flew off the prongs of his fork onto the front of his yellow shirt.

"*Ta da*," Josh said. He shoved the fork into his mouth while across the bar Ricky held a cocktail napkin under the faucet.

"And I'm doing that with only nine and a half fingers," Josh said.

"I'm impressed," the man beside him said.

"Me too," said Ricky. He pointed down to the spot on Josh's shirt. "Can I try and clean that off your shirt before it stains, Canada?"

"Yes... please," Josh said. He pushed out his chest toward Ricky. He liked being called *Canada*.

Ricky ginned, reached over the bar and dabbed the front of Josh's new shirt with the damp napkin. His thumb ring tapped against Josh's plastic shirt buttons.

"Yep, I'm one classy fucker now," Josh said. A water spot grew on his shirt and felt cold on his chest. His brown nipple appeared under the spot where Ricky was dabbing as the wet area became semitransparent. "But since my wife and I split up, I'm *seriously* considering becoming uncouth again."

Josh realized that he was acting too familiar. *Get a few drinks in me and I always treat strangers like the best of friends.* Once when he was in Atlanta on business, he had traded jackets with a stockbroker from Chicago he met in the hotel bar. After half a dozen scotch and sodas, the stockbroker had walked away with Josh's favorite denim jacket while Josh went home with a too-big navy blue blazer with gold buttons.

Down at the end of the bar, a man and woman sat down. The man opened a menu and placed it on the bar between them.

"That oughta do it," Ricky said, smiling. He stopped dabbing the front of Josh's shirt and walked toward the man and woman at the end of the bar.

Beside Josh, the man with amber eyes took off his jacket, folded it, and put it on the stool beside him. Josh wondered how he kept his white shirt so unwrinkled. *And no perspiration marks under the arms either.*

"Ah, that's better," the man said. He turned to Josh and held out his hand.

"My name is Mark," he said. "Mark Cooper."

Josh shook Mark's hand. He was surprised at the strength of his grip.

"I'm Joshua Moore... Josh, actually."

"Are you here on vacation, Josh?" Mark asked. He sipped on his port. Josh wondered how he and Mark would look wearing each other shirts.

"Nope," Josh said. "I'm here for a conference, but it doesn't start until Monday."

"The EDBX conference?" Mark asked.

"That's the one," said Josh.

"My company is one of the sponsors for the conference this year." Mark dropped his head into his hands. "And it's driving me *crazy*."

"Why is it driving you crazy?" Josh asked.

"Well I'm—get this title, Josh—The Manager in Charge of Lunches, Tickets, and Receipts."

"As titles go... that's a nice long one." Josh's face warmed.

"I'm the liaison between EDBX and the hotel. And it's been a colossal pain in the ass."

"So if the food's bad I can blame you?"

"You can put the blame on Mark," he said. "Everyone else is."

Josh finished the last of his dinner and looked at his martini glass. There were only two or (if he took tiny ones) three sips of his martini left. He really shouldn't have another. What would Todd say?

Fuck Todd.

"All done?" Ricky asked.

"Yep," Josh said. He leaned back, away from his plate. The wet mark on his shirt was beginning to dry.

Ricky picked up Josh's plate and napkin. "Another martini, Canada?" he asked.

"One more," Josh said. Immediately, he wished he hadn't said that. What if he decided he wanted two—or more? Then he would have to go to his room and order from room service.

"Luckily it shows up as *Restaurant* on the bill," Josh said under his breath.

"What's that?" Mark asked.

"Nothing," Josh said.

"Yeah, this conference has been one big headache," Mark continued. "But at least I don't have to stick around until it ends on Friday. I'm flying back to San Diego Tuesday night."

"What do you do when you're not seeing to food and tickets and… whatever the hell else at EDBX conferences?" Josh asked. His tongue felt heavy.

"I'm part of the management team at a company called Southern Technetics in San Diego. Have you ever heard of it, Josh?"

"No. I don't think so."

"We are a computer consulting company. So right now, as you would expect, we're doing a lot of Y2K stuff."

"Ah," Josh said.

Ricky put Josh's third martini down on the bar in front of him. Josh wondered how many of those tiny glasses of port would fit in a martini glass.

"And what do you do, Josh?"

Josh stuck his fingers in the glass and pulled out an olive. The alcohol burned a hangnail on his index finger. "I'm a systems analyst at a metal fabrication plant in Hamilton, Ontario," Josh said. He popped the olive in his mouth.

"Where's Hamilton?" Mark asked.

"I tell people it's thirty miles—and about twenty years away from Toronto," Josh said as he chewed his olive. "Our clothes may be decades out of date, but we're ambitious."

"And what do you fabricate in Hamilton?" Mark asked.

"We make car doors," Josh said. "Well, we don't actually *make* car doors. We only chop the steel into the shape of a car door. Then we ship it to the Michigan where it's made into a door." He spit his olive pit into his palm and placed it on a napkin.

"That sounds interesting." Mark looked intently at Josh.

Josh shrugged his shoulders and frowned. His job wasn't interesting and he stopped trying to make it sound so a long time ago.

"And I thought getting into computers would get me away from steel," Josh said. "I guess it did for a whole, after college I worked for an insurance company for a while but—ah well—whatever. In Hamilton, steel is the only game in town... my parents even met in a steel mill."

"They did? That's funny," Mark said.

Josh wondered why that was so funny. "Yeah," he said. "I guess I've got chromium in my blood."

A man wearing a maroon blazer and a hotel nametag came up to Mark, whispered something in his ear, and then left. Mark sighed, picked up his suit jacket from the stool beside him and stood up.

"I have to go discuss the semiannual EDBX dinner with the hotel," Mark said. He handed Josh a business card from the breast pocket of his suit jacket and then finished the rest of his port in one gulp. He reached out his hand and placed it on Josh's shoulder. "I'll see you at the conference on Monday."

Later that night, when he got back in his hotel room, the message light on the telephone was flashing. Josh knew it was Allison. He wondered if either of them still believed they were going to get back together. Best to put this marriage out of its misery, he thought—just like back when his golden retriever, Reefer, got old and sick. Josh conjured up the image of the last time he saw his dog. It was over ten years ago, now. Reefer's head was sticking out the car window as his older brother drove him to the vet to be put down.

And that dumb dog was smiling.

❖

"Is Ricky working tonight?" Josh asked.

"No," said the blonde woman behind the bar at The Yankee Steak House the next evening. She wore the same black vest and bowtie as Ricky had.

Josh's face fell. He ordered a vodka martini from the woman and then turning around on his barstool, looked over the crowd of people in the room. Soon the place would be crawling with people here for the conference. It was never too difficult to sniff out other computer geeks. They had a certain look. Josh looked down at his own clothes. He knew that he had acquired that geek look himself—short hair parted to the side, nice white dress shirts, and beige Dockers. So fucking drab, he thought.

He squirmed on his barstool. He had walked too much that day and now his back was aching. He decided that he would finish his drink and then head back up to his room. There was a call to make. There had been two messages for him while he was walking around Washington DC. I'll order room service—a bottle of wine and a meal—and afterwards make the call, Josh thought. He just needed a little Dutch courage first. He was about to leave when Mark sat down beside him and ordered a glass of port.

"Hi Josh," he said.

"Hey, what's up Mark?" Josh said too loudly. "How are the lunches, tickets, and whatever's coming?"

"A nightmare." Mark put one hand up and shook his head like he did not want to discuss it. He was wearing a navy blue suit, a light blue shirt with a white collar and a gold and gray striped tie. Dark stray chest hairs poked out of his shirt collar while his tie, tied too long today, hung between his legs over the bar stool. He smells like patchouli, Josh thought.

"I did a little tour of your capital today," Josh said.

"Oh yeah? What did you think of it?"

"It's very nice—and very clean—except the reflecting pool at the National Mall. For some reason it was kinda grubby. I was surprised."

"They'll clean it before summer," Mark said. "So where did you go on your tour? I went to college nearby so I have some civic pride in Washington."

"Well, the usual tourist stuff, I guess. I walked around the Mall, saw the White House, and a few of the memorials."

"Uh huh."

The bartender returned with a glass of port and put it in front of Mark.

"She needs her roots done," Mark said when she left. "What else did you do during your tour?"

"I walked around the Smithsonian."

"Did you see Archie Bunker's chair and Fonzie's leather jacket?" asked Mark.

"And Dorothy's ruby slippers," Josh said.

Josh wondered if Canada had an equivalent to this kind of pop junk. What sort of Canadiana would they put into our national museum in Ottawa? Perhaps Finnegan the puppet from *Mister Dressup*? Or Al Waxman's jacket from *The King of Kensington*?

"Those television exhibits always have the biggest crowds around them," Mark said. "What else did you see?"

"I saw a flag from the War of 1812. The one that inspired Francis Scott Key to write The Star Spangled Banner."

"Ah… the enigmatic War of 1812," Mark said.

"Well it's not really an enigma," Josh said.

"No, I just mean that Americans don't really learn much about the War of 1812," Mark said. "So it's more like a mystery than an enigma." Mark put his thick lips to his tiny glass and sipped. "Why dwell on wars without a clear winner?"

Josh wondered why the sight of a grown man drinking out of a tiny glass looked stupider now than it had the night before.

"I think all we did in history class during junior high school was talk about the War of 1812," Josh said. "How we Canadians repelled your American invasion and forced your armies back across the Niagara River." Josh lifted his arm and swept the air with his hand.

"Do you live near Niagara Falls?" Mark asked.

"Yep," Josh said. "And one of the major battles of the war, the Battle of Stoney Creek, was fought just a couple of miles from where I live."

"I always wanted to see Niagara Falls," Mark said. "Have you been on that boat that takes you right up close to the falls?"

"Yeah, I have. It's called the Maid of the Mist."

"Sounds like a poem by Longfellow, doesn't it?" Mark said. He repeated the name slowly, "The Maid of the Mist."

"Did you know we set the White House on fire during the War of 1812?" Josh asked.

"Did you?"

"That's why it's white... it had to be repainted."

"That wasn't very neighborly of you." Mark said. "I thought Canadians were supposed to be nice!"

"Hey, it was *you* that invaded *us*." Josh pointed first at Mark then to himself for emphasis. "Did you know Thomas Jefferson said that taking Canada would be *a mere matter of marching*?" I'm getting drunk, Josh thought. There was a fine line between Dutch courage and stupidity. "Did you say that you went to college around here?" Josh asked.

"Yes," Mark said. "I went to law school at Georgetown."

"You're a lawyer?"

"I sure am."

"Then why are you managing lunches and semiannual dinners for computer geeks like me?"

"I stopped practicing law a few years ago. I decided I'd rather get in on the business side of things so I went back to school and got my MBA. Now I'm finally doing what I enjoy as a VP at this computer consulting firm. This conference dinner is the exception of course—I don't enjoy this."

"Did Georgetown prepare you for planning dinners?"

"Not at all, but it had other things going for it." A slight smile grew on Mark's lips which had turned even redder and fuller from the glass of port he was drinking.

"Isn't Georgetown a Catholic university, like Notre Dame?" Josh asked.

"Yes indeed it is—and since I'm half-Catholic and half-Jewish, it was a somewhat confusing three years."

"Just like Proust!" Josh said.

"Just like Proust?"

"Marcel Proust was half-Jewish too."

"That's right, he was," Mark said. "But I've never read any Proust... have you?"

"I had to read *Swann's Way* for a course in World Literature I took at university," Josh said. "But I wonder... can someone actually be half-Catholic or half-Jewish? After all, they're religions not races." Josh stopped himself before telling Mark that he had not met a Jewish person until he was well into his twenties.

"Where did you go to university, Josh?"

"I went to a small college in Hamilton."

"Majoring in computer science?"

"Yeah," Josh said. He was not going to tell Mark that it was a technical college, or that he had never graduated. "But over the last two years I've been taking courses part-time at university."

"That's cool," Mark said.

"Yeah, my marriage counselor thought that my lack of achievement in life goals was causing my marriage to fall apart. So now I'm working on a literature degree. But since I can only take one or two courses a year, it'll take a long time before I finally finish. At the pace I'm going, I should graduate sometime around my ninetieth birthday, I think."

"But you like it?"

Josh nodded. "I do."

"And have these university courses helped your marriage any?"

"Not a bit."

Josh thought about the phone call he had to make. It was getting late and if he intended to call Allison, he had better do it soon. It was just so hard to get up from a barstool once he sat down.

"My undergrad is in American Literature," Mark said. "I guess books are another thing we have in common besides computers. Do you and your wife have any kids, Josh?"

"No. We lost one and then—I don't know..." Josh motioned for the bartender and ordered another martini. Christ, she does need her roots done, he thought.

"Were you at the last EDBX conference in Napa Valley, Mark?"

"No, I was supposed to come but I couldn't get away. I heard it was pretty good though. I know a lot of work was done."

"It was great," Josh said. "They had a wine tasting with all these

Napa wines after the semiannual EDBX dinner and everyone got completely smashed. And just like this time, my company shipped me down two days early to save money. I told them if I had to bum around for two extra days, I wanted to stay in San Francisco during the weekend."

"I lived in San Francisco about ten years ago. Did you like it?"

"It was fucking wild. I was there over Halloween and the town was totally crazy. I ended up walking around the gay area with all the other tourists. It was a total freak show."

"You were in the Castro for Halloween?" Mark looked at Josh and squinted. "That's pretty adventurous."

"It was an adventure," Josh said.

The waitress came with Josh's martini. It had only one olive. *Aren't we stingy?* He sipped. It wasn't as good as the ones Ricky had made the night before. Josh looked at his watch. Was he going to make that phone call or not? This is my last martini, he thought.

"You know, I lived in the Castro when I lived in San Fran in the late Eighties," Mark said. He stared straight ahead at the bottles of alcohol on the shelf. "Actually, I lived there with my partner—my ex-partner."

"Ahhhhh," Josh said, "so you're..."

Mark nodded. "Just like Proust."

Josh stared down at his Doc Martens. His face warmed. "You know, Mark, I kinda figured that out the first time I met you. I think it was your glossy fingernails—and the way you kept staring at Ricky."

"Ricky?" Mark looked at his fingernails under the bar lights.

"The bartender from last night... young guy, black hair, goatee..."

"Ah yes... Ricky, the bartender." Mark said.

Josh finished his drink. "But it's cool," Josh said, trying to sound disinterested. "I don't have a problem with gay guys."

"Well, I'm glad you don't have a problem with us, Josh... would you like another drink?"

"Sure... thanks."

"Have you ever had port?"

"Never," Josh said.

"Then it's time you did." Mark ordered two glasses of port. "Is this the first time you ever had a gay man buy you a drink?" He grinned.

Josh laughed. "I guess it is."

When the bartender brought them their glasses, Mark raised his glass.

"Cheers," he said.

"Cheers," Josh said. He sipped the port. It was sweet and tannic with, Josh thought, a strange hint of immorality in it. "I like it," he said.

"Now," Mark said. "I don't want to offend you, Josh, but when I saw you here last night I thought you were gay too."

Josh tried to laugh. "I'm not offended," he said. "I've been told before that I have... an ambiguous sexuality."

Mark grinned. "There's nothing ambiguous about you, Josh."

It was just before midnight when Josh left the bar. Mark walked with him through the deserted lobby to the elevators. Inside the elevator, alone for the first time, Mark reached up and caressed Josh's cheek. Josh jerked his head away. A bolt of electricity shot through Josh's body and the voltage boiled the last drops of port in his mouth and sizzled on his tongue. Josh stopped breathing. The elevator doors opened and Mark stepped out onto the third floor. He turned and stood staring at Josh until the elevator doors closed. Later, Josh would wonder at what floor he had started to breathe again.

⬥

That next night, Josh walked into the Yankee Steak House and Bar smelling of lavender body-wash and wearing his blue jeans, brown loafers, and his yellow shirt. He had already drank half a bottle of red wine that he had ordered from room service before coming down for dinner. Josh had only seen Mark once that day; he had been making notes on a pad of paper during a lecture on electronic purchase orders when he saw Mark come into the room. He had looked around, waved at Josh, and sat down in the row directly in front of Josh. A few minutes later, Mark had stood and disappeared out the back door. He didn't wave goodbye.

When Mark came into the bar, Josh was finishing his second vodka martini. He walked toward Josh, sat beside him, and sighed deeply. He wore the same suit as the night before but with a shiny lime-green tie. On his chest, an enormous blue ribbon, displaying his host status, hung down from his nametag. Josh chuckled.

"Looks like you just took first prize at the county fair," Josh said.

"It's ridiculous, isn't it?" Mark said. He looked down at the ribbon and shook his head.

"How were you feeling this morning?" Mark asked.

"I was a little shaky," Josh said, "but I'm better now.... I don't usually drink that much."

"We did drink a lot," Mark said. He carefully unpinned the blue ribbon from his chest and placed it in his inside breast pocket.

"And I think I may have given you the wrong impression last night," Josh said quietly. He looked around at the smattering of people around the bar.

Mark brushed the front of his green tie, folded his hands on the bar, and shook his head from side to side. Close up, Josh could see tiny yellow and gold paisley prints in the tie. "No, I don't think you did," Mark said.

Josh quickly finished his martini in two big gulps and put his glass on the bar. "Anyway," Josh said, standing up. "I should get to my room."

"How about one glass of port before you head up to bed, Josh?"

Josh thought for a moment and then sat back down on his stool. "Okay, one drink. Then I have to get to my room and call my wife."

Mark ordered two glasses of port from the same woman who had tended bar the night before. She took down the bottle from the top shelf and poured two tiny glasses. Josh looked at the shiny clean bottle and wondered how long it would take before it was thick with dust again.

An hour later they had each finished three glasses of port. His tongue loosened, Josh had told Mark about his wife, their house in Ancaster and the separation. He had even told him about his crazy family back in Canada. In return, Mark had told him about his brother and sister, his father, and his mother who had recently passed away.

Soon we'll be wearing each other's shirts.

Josh looked around the bar for eavesdroppers and then leaned in close to Mark's ear. "Hey Mark... aren't you afraid of... catching AIDS?"

"No, not really," Mark said.

"I'd be terrified," Josh said. "I'm terrified for you."

"I used to be terrified," Mark said. "I even stayed in the closet until I was twenty-five because I was so afraid.... but... eventually a person has to live their life. You know what I mean, Josh?" He softly placed his hand on Josh's knee.

Josh grinned, shook his head, and brushed Mark's hand away. Mark shrugged his shoulders and grinned.

"So do you have a—what do you call it—a boyfriend?" Josh asked.

Mark chuckled. "No, I'm single..."

Josh put down his port glass and laughed. "I was sure you were about to say *single and ready to mingle.*" Josh held his head. "Oh shit, I'm drunk. And I really *really* have to go now."

"Let me walk you to your room," Mark said.

"No. I'm fine."

"Look, either I'm going to walk you to your room or you're walking me to mine."

Josh sat silently for a second as Mark continued to stare at him. Some conventioneers were drunk and talking too loud behind them.

"Okay," Josh said. "I'll walk you to your room."

They took the elevator up to the third floor and walked down the hallway. The whole fucking floor smells like patchouli, Josh thought. Mark unlocked the door of his room and entered. Josh followed. In the dark, Josh allowed himself to be taken by the hand and gently maneuvered onto the bed. Mark fumbled with Josh's pants and quickly had them down around his ankles. Josh's penis was already hard when Mark fell to his knees and took Josh in his mouth. Josh gasped. He ran his fingers though Mark's hair. *His hair is so soft.*

Mark stood and turned on the lamp by the bed. A warm glow illuminated the room. Mark took off his suit jacket, folded it in half, and placed it over a chair in the corner of the room. Slowly, he began to unbutton his white shirt. His torso was lean and covered with light brown hair that glimmered gold like his eyes in the lamplight. Josh laid motionless on the bed as Mark carelessly tossed his shirt across the room in a bundle on the floor. Then he unzipped his suit trousers and stepped out of them. He walked slowly to the bed and lowered himself on top of Josh. His mouth moved toward Josh's lips.

"No," Josh whispered. "I can't."

"Yes," Mark said. "Yes, you can."

Josh looked into Mark's eyes and saw his own image. It was the first time he saw himself content in someone else's eyes. Somewhere, a border that had terrified Josh for most of his life was being crossed. He couldn't retreat now. Josh reached out and put his arms around Mark's waist and then, purposely, he moved his hands down under the elastic of Mark's white and burgundy striped boxers. He squeezed Mark's furry buttocks between his fingers. Mark kissed him. He tasted like port and steak.

Mark unbuttoned Josh's yellow shirt and pulled it off. He lowered his head and kissed Josh's chest, licking both his nipples. They grew hard under Mark's tongue. Josh groaned. Mark moved downwards and unlaced Josh's new shoes. The heavy black shoes fell to the floor. *Thud.*

"I can't believe I'm doing this," Josh said.

Thud.

Mark stripped off Josh's socks and then reaching up, pulled off Josh's pants and underwear in one motion and let them fall to the floor. As Josh lay naked on the bed with his arms folded behind his head, he watched Mark pull down his own boxers and dropped them on top of Josh's clothes at the front of the bed. Mark's large penis had grown semi-erect in a thick patch of light-brown pubic hair. Gingerly, he crawled on the bed and laid his body again on top of Josh. Like a winepress, the weight of Mark's body pressed down on Josh and any remaining apprehension he had was wrung out of him into the emerald and ruby bedspread and onto the floor.

"Like the War of 1812 all over again," Mark said.

He stroked Josh's hair and kissed his ear. His breath warmed Josh's neck. As the blood raced under his skin, Josh's face and body glistened and turned pink. He tried to speak Mark's name but it only rolled deep in his throat like a pre-linguistic growl.

"It's a mere matter of marching," Mark whispered.

Josh pulled him close and slipped his tongue into Mark's mouth. The whiskers of another man scratched against his face, tingling his cheeks and mouth. Mark rolled over and Josh laid his face on his hairy stomach, gently squeezing Mark's nipples. As Mark laid his head back on the pillow, Josh moved his big clumsy hands between Mark's legs. They opened to his touch. Josh had never touched another man's penis and testicles before and was surprised at the weight of them and how smooth the skin felt in his hand. Mark moaned. Josh massaged Mark's penis with his hand, enjoying the twitches of pleasure that moved throughout Mark's body each time Josh stroked him. Josh looked up at Mark and a grinned. Then, lowering himself on the bed, he slid the head of Mark's penis into his mouth. It was as natural as breathing.

That night Mark allowed Josh to examine his entire body. Inch by inch, Josh moved over Mark. He wanted to know how Mark's body felt, smelled, and tasted. Josh moved his hands up Mark's body, feeling the wiry hairs on his lean legs and the soft brown pubic hair that smelled of fabric softener and Ivory soap. He examined the small purple veins in Mark's nose, the mole under his ear, and the tiny bald spot at the back of his head that, just like Josh, he tried to cover up by styling his hair over it. He ran his finger around the areola of Mark's small nipples, partially hidden under a thick coat of chest hair. He kissed one nipple and then the other. Moving down his torso, Josh noticed a saltier taste as he ran his tongue around Mark's navel. Lower, it was saltier still. Then at some point Josh put his head on Mark's hairy chest and listened to the thumping of Mark's heart until he fell asleep. Still, even as he slept, Josh did not let go of Mark's penis, holding it in his fist all night.

The next morning, Mark laid in bed as Josh picked up his clothes scattered around the floor and dressed. Josh knew that upstairs the red light on the phone would be flashing. How would he explain this? Just tell her I got drunk and passed out, he thought. Nothing unusual about that, that's for sure.

"So you're okay?" Mark asked.

"Oh sure, I'm fine," Josh said, a little too quickly.

"I was afraid that when you woke up... you'd freak out or something."

"No," Josh said, buttoning up his yellow shirt. "I'm not freaking out." He leaned over the bed and kissed Mark on the mouth. Mark's morning beard scratched his mouth. Josh's penis stirred. For the first time in his life, the stimulus didn't frighten him.

Mark grabbed him by the shoulders and pulled him into the bed. "I have a meeting at nine-thirty" he said. "But I wish I could just stay here with you until my plane leaves."

"What time are you leaving?" Josh asked.

"My flight's at two o'clock," he said.

Josh snuggled up close and put his head on Mark's shoulder. "Want to hear something funny, Mark?"

"Sure."

"I planned on having sex with a man this week," Josh said. "As soon as I got off the airplane on Saturday, I was checking out the subway map to see how I would get from the hotel to Dupont Circle... that gay section of Washington."

"Well, well, well," Mark said.

"I made up my mind after I came home from San Francisco. I knew that if I didn't do something soon, I'd regret it for the rest of my life. I always thought I had too much to lose... but now... now I think that by starting this late, I've already lost way too much—time-wise, I mean. So last month I bought one of those gay travel guides and picked out some places to go while I was here. I knew it was now or never."

Mark pulled Josh closer. "I'm not really surprised, Josh. You took to the whole thing like a duck to water. It's as if you had been rehearsing it in your head for twenty years."

"Maybe I was just looking for the right person to seduce me." Josh smiled.

"So you had your eye on me since Saturday at the bar?"

"Um… actually no," Josh said. "At first I had my eye on Ricky the bartender. That first night at the bar, he wrote his phone number on my credit card receipt. I was going to call him up—but then you showed up."

"Almost on cue," Mark said.

As Josh was sitting on the bed putting on his shoes, he noticed about two-dozen neckties of every color and pattern hanging in the closet by the door. Josh stood and walked over to the closet.

"Why did you bring so many ties with you for a four day conference?" Josh asked.

"Oh," Mark laughed quietly. "I know it's dumb, but I have this *thing* about ties. I grab one everywhere I go. Last year I was in Lisbon and they sell them everywhere there. So I bought all these knockoff Boss and Armani ties from tie vendors on the streets and came home with about twenty new ties."

Naked, Mark got out of bed and walked up behind Josh. The two men looked at the ties hanging in the closet. "I even bought two at the airport on my way here," Mark said. "I can't help myself."

Josh was silent.

Mark put his arms around Josh's waist and kissed the back of his neck. "Pick one out to take home—as a gift," he whispered.

Josh reached out and gently pulled the long silk and satin pieces of blue, green, red, and paisley cloth towards him. He let them drop. In an airy sweep, twenty ties waved a shimmering goodbye as they floated back into the hotel closet. Josh held back a sob. They were all so beautiful his heart was breaking.

✦

Shirts and Skins

That night, after Mark had left for the airport, Josh took the orange line to Dupont Circle just like he had planned. He was heading to one of the dance clubs on P Street. It wasn't hard to find, he felt the club before he saw it. A bass beat thumped through the sidewalks and adjacent buildings. Walking up to the doors Josh could almost see the wall pulsating with the beat of dance music. He marched in, checked his jacket, and bought a bottle of beer. He looked at his watch. It was early.

After drinking two beers, Josh plucked up the courage to head to the dance floor. *I haven't danced since my wedding night.* First he stood and swayed to the music on the periphery. A strange smell of sweat and solvent drifted in the smoky air, making Josh slightly dizzy. Finally he waded into the bodies on the floor and tried to dance like the younger guys. But why did all the songs sound the same? It was as if the DJ just played one long song.

Heat from the bodies on the jammed dance floor began to rise and many of the men took off their shirts and tucked them into their pants. Josh unbuttoned the top three buttons of his yellow shirt. His chest was wet with sweat. The pounding of the music vibrated deep inside him and he felt his heart beat in time with the swarm of men. They had become one large animal, writhing in the heat and hazy smoke.

"Hey, Canada!"

It was Ricky the bartender. He looks shorter than he did the other night, Josh thought. Maybe the bar was on a platform.

"Hey, Ricky!" Josh yelled over the music. "No bowtie tonight?"

"Fuck no!" Ricky said. He took a swig from his bottle of beer and smiled. His eyes were so dark, they looked black. *This must be what they mean by smoldering.* Tonight he wore a pair of khaki cargo pants covered with pockets and a kelly green Abercrombie and Fitch T-shirt with gold trim around the neck and arms.

Together they danced in the middle of the dance floor and slowly, over a number of songs that still all sounded the same to Josh, Ricky moved closer. They embraced. Ricky stood on his toes and kissed Josh on the lips. Josh noted how he tasted different than Mark. Now he wanted to see Ricky naked too. Josh slid his hands down Ricky's back and, taking hold of his ass, pulled him close. Josh felt Ricky's erection on his leg.

"Do you want to head back to the hotel?" Ricky asked.

"Let's go," Josh said.

As Josh stood with his arms around Ricky's waist in front of the coat check waiting for his jacket, he imagined the telephone flashing away in his room. *Let it flash.* The beating of the music had shaken something loose inside him. For the first time in his life he felt as if he belonged.

Josh took his jacket and walked hand-in-hand with Ricky to the front door of the club. These were his few first baby steps into a new fabulous world. His life was finally waking up. *This is just the beginning. Everything is open to me.* Sure, he thought, it would have been better if he had come out when he was younger, but thirty was still young! From now on, if there was a headline on his life it wouldn't be *WASTE* or *ZZZZZ*, it would be *SEX!* or *DANCE!* or *COCK!* He wanted to howl from the top of the Washington Monument. Then, as they were walking out the front door of the club, Josh was startled by someone shouting behind them.

"Oh my God, Ricky!" the voice screeched. "Where are you going with that *old* guy?"

Suddenly, as Josh stepped out onto P Street, the new wide-open road he had imagined unfolding in front of him seemed to narrow, shorten, and finally disappear into nothingness.

"Sorry about that," Ricky said as they walked toward a queue of taxis. "My friends can be real jerks when they drink."

"Hey, that's okay," Josh said. He zipped up his jacket over his new yellow shirt and pulled up the collar against the cool evening breeze. It felt too cold for May.

"But, I'm really glad you finally decided to call me, Josh" Ricky said. He reached out and gently rubbed the back of Josh's head. Ricky's thumb ring felt cold and tingled against the nape of Josh's neck.

"Yeah... I'm glad I did too," Josh answered. *Finally.*

The Last Fight

"Josh, when are you coming to see me?" the voice said. Each word was stretched out and soaked in thick phlegm. "I'm all dressed and waiting for you."

Josh cleared his throat out of sympathy. "We're on our way," he said. This was the third time his father had called that morning.

He closed his cell phone with a snap and slid it into the left inside breast pocket of his tweed jacket. The autumn foliage was at its height now, but you certainly wouldn't know it, Josh thought, as he stared out the car window at the dreary warehouses and office buildings that lined the highway. Here, in this corridor of tedium between Toronto and Hamilton, the season was always the same—gray.

"They should plant more trees along this stretch," Josh said. "It would make it a nicer drive." He rubbed away a smudge on the walnut trimmed armrest of the passenger door. He frowned. He wouldn't care about a little smudge like this in a cheaper car.

Beside him, in the driver's seat of their silver Lexus, Glenn rode with one hand resting on the steering wheel and the other on the leather and wood shift knob in the middle console. "You say that every time we drive to Hamilton," Glenn said. He glanced over at Josh and smiled without showing his teeth. Glen never showed his teeth when he smiled. It had been Glenn's smile, along with his intense brown eyes, cleft chin and strong Roman nose that first attracted Josh. Obviously, Josh thought with a small twinge of jealously, Glenn would be one of those men who actually became more handsome as they got older. Unlike many men his age, Glenn's dark hair hadn't yet started to thin or turn gray.

Josh fiddled with the buttons in front of him on the dashboard. Their new car had independent temperature controls for both the driver and the passenger. Josh never understood how they could create two different climates in such a small space, but like everything, if one paid enough, they could. Though why they had it he didn't know—to Josh it was just another silly expensive option that they didn't need. "I don't see why we need a car at all when your office is just down the street," Josh had said when Glenn took him to the Lexus dealership for the first time. "And my office is only a short subway ride away." But when Glenn had suggested that they buy the hybrid Josh acquiesced. It was, Glenn had said, good for the environment. *Yeah, sure.* Glenn took a quick glance over his shoulder and then accelerating, steered the car to the far left lane to pass a transport truck. Josh had to admit that, wearing his Hugo Boss chocolate brown sport coat and starched white shirt, Glenn looked damned good behind the wheel of the Lexus.

Inside his jacket pocket, Josh's cell phone rang again. He ignored it, pushed his glasses up the bridge of his nose, and leaning over slightly to the driver's side, rummaged through a stack of CDs in the middle console of the car. Christ, it *is* warmer on this side, he thought. He slid an Edith Piaf CD into the disk player in the dashboard and turned up the volume. Finally, his cell phone stopped ringing.

Glenn took his hand off the shift knob, reached over, and ran his hand through the back of Josh's short hair. Unlike Glenn, Josh's hair was turning gray. *Getting some silver 'mongst the gold.* Soon it'll be completely white, Josh thought, but since his bald spot at on the top of his head seemed to have stopped growing for the time being, he really didn't care what color it was—as long as he still had some. Glenn moved his hand from the back of Josh's head and caressed his cheek.

"You forgot to shave," Glenn said.

"Yeah," Josh said. He rubbed his face against Glenn's hand. It felt good.

"Hey," Glenn suddenly said, grinning. "Is that your shirt you're wearing or mine?"

Josh looked down at the lavender gingham shirt he wore beneath his tweed jacket. "It's mine… I think."

Josh and Glenn had been together six years. They had met at a Saturday night Alcoholics Anonymous meeting specifically for gay men in Toronto's gay village. At the time, Josh had only been sober for six months, and Glenn hadn't had a drink for two years. During the meeting, Josh was captivated by Glenn's dark features, never listening to what anyone said that night. After the meeting though, Josh hesitated for a few seconds before making his move. Over the preceding months he had been taken aside but a couple of other members who had heard gossip about Josh hooking up after the meetings. "You should be more mindful and considerate," one of them had said. "People come here vulnerable."

We're all vulnerable, Josh had thought as he maneuvered himself beside Glenn that first night. And after a few minutes of chat-chat while sipping on notoriously bad AA coffee, Josh asked Glenn if he was interested into heading over to Josh' apartment—"for a decent cup." Glenn accepted and an hour later the two men were having sex on Josh's leather sofa. "I used to use Australian Shiraz to lure men into bed," Josh had said as he held Glenn. "Now I'm using Folgers." Three months later, Josh had moved into Glenn's condominium near the lakeshore.

At first the match between Josh, the computer consultant, and Glenn, the banker had been unsteady. Josh had come out in his early thirties and, like many men who come out later in life, he had tried desperately to get back the years he missed. When Josh met Glenn, Josh was dressing like a college boy, sporting cargo pants and Abercrombie and Fitch T-shirts. He had been coloring his hair in those days too, though it never looked anything but fake in direct sunlight. And it wasn't until Josh and Glenn had been going out for over two months that Josh told Glenn his real age—he had been shaving off five years and thinking everyone was buying it. But Glenn was patient. He seemed to understand that Josh needed to go through this second adolescence, going so far as to looking the other way during a number of Josh's foolish indiscretions the first year the couple was together. Today Josh cringed when he thought about how stupid he looked and how idiotic he had acted back then. *Like an old fool.*

But now Josh believed that the two of them complemented one another. Glenn, a few years older than Josh, provided a grounding influence. Glenn had persuaded Josh into returning to university to finish his B.A. and supported him when Josh returned to complete a master's degree (though Josh had often wondered if it was to benefit him or so that Glenn wouldn't be embarrassed telling his friends that Josh was a community college dropout). And in turn, Josh accepted Glenn's life as a closeted senior investment manager. For although Glenn was out to his parents and siblings, he stayed tightly in the closet at the bank where he worked, even going so far as taking Carole, a lesbian friend of Josh and Glenn's, to his company Christmas party as his date. Maybe, Josh thought, Glenn's hiding has something to do with the fact that he never shows his teeth when he smiles. It was a shame too, because Glenn had beautiful teeth.

Josh and Glenn had been coming to Hamilton every other Sunday for the last two years, ever since Josh had put his father into the Albion Villa Nursing Home. At first, after Josh's mother had died, Josh had hoped that his father could continue living in the house he had shared in the east end of Hamilton with Josh's mother for thirty years. But one night, after not seeing his father for a couple of months, Josh received a phone call from his ex-wife, Allison. "I was just stopping by to see how your Dad was," she had said. "And he didn't know who I was... and even from the front porch the house smelled really bad... you'd better come down and look after this, Josh." The next morning Josh and Glenn had driven to Hamilton and, using a spare key his mother had given him years earlier, Josh let himself in. As he stepped through the back door, he was immediately struck with the stench of rotten food, sour milk, and urine. Apparently the only food his father had been eating was pork and beans out of a can and instant Cream of Wheat he was making with warm tap water. Around the house there were dozens of dirty cans, empty boxes, and other garbage. How could things have gotten so bad so quickly? And, to Josh's horror, at some point his father had started drinking again, and there were empty beer bottles strewn all over the floor. Josh had found his father naked in the front room, sitting in the front of the television. Somehow his right leg had been injured and a large gash, swelled and infected, ran down the back of his thigh. When Josh tried to dress him and take him to the hospital, his father had become combative, landing a hard punch to the side of Josh's head. "Don't touch me, you fucking cocksucker," his father had said. Finally, it had been Glenn who was able to convince Josh's father into putting on some clothes and going to the hospital. No one knew then that it would be the last time his father would ever see his house.

Glenn and Josh drove along the Queen Elizabeth Way toward Hamilton until the highway split and then they traveled to the left toward Niagara Falls. The familiar industrial scent of sulfur and slag crept into the Lexus. As they rode up the Skyway Bridge above the bay, Josh studied Glenn's face. He always did when they drove into Hamilton. Josh was looking for traces of a turned up nose or a curled lip at the smell of the city. He knew he shouldn't, but he would take it personally if Glenn showed any sign disgust in his face. Still, Josh thought, it doesn't seem to smell as bad as it did when he was young. Is it really any cleaner or has his memory become clouded with time? Or maybe his sense of smell isn't as good as it was when he was young. Josh turned and looked at the mills around the bay and tried to remember which one his father had worked at. One time his father had pointed it out to him.

"It's not such a bad view if you look past the steel mills," Glenn said at the top of the bridge.

"That's hard to do," Josh said as he stared across the bay.

The Lexus turned off the highway and soared down Woodlawn Avenue. Josh did not point out to Glenn the elementary school he went to when he was young. He had already done that a dozen other times on their bi-weekly Sunday drives to Albion Villa. He only did it to make conversation anyway.

They crossed the CN railroad tracks and then, passing an old peeling billboard for Five-Star rye, turned right onto Barton Street. Boarded up businesses, once a problem only of the downtown area of the city, had crept, like gangrene into the east end. No one ever walks down the streets in Hamilton, Josh thought, as he studied the deserted sidewalks. Maybe if they walked more, the businesses wouldn't be boarded up. Back in Toronto, people walked everywhere. No matter the time of day or night, there were always people on the streets. When you strolled down the crowded sidewalks of Toronto, you were never alone; there was always someone walking in front of you and there was always someone walking behind you. But here they drove for blocks and blocks without seeing a soul.

"There's a lot of blue conservative signs in the neighborhood," Glenn said. "For Hamilton, that is."

"Well there are a lot of old folks in this neighborhood," Josh replied. "They were probably all good union people once."

"I didn't think there were any conservatives in Hamilton. Except you that is. "

Josh winced. He had gone door to door canvassing this neighborhood back in 1988 for some conservative candidate whose name he, mercifully, couldn't remember. He must have had a thousand doors slammed in his face. "That was a long time ago."

"You are one of the few people who actually became more liberal as you grew older," Glenn said while turning a corner.

"Sometimes I wonder if that whole conservative thing was just another way of closeting myself."

Albion Villa was nestled between the mountain and the Canadian National railway tracks in the east end of the city. Here autumn had burst alive with the trees along the escarpment's ridge of rock and earth and covered it in deep reds, burnt oranges, and gold. Albion Villa was one of the newer buildings in the area, only about a decade old. It was a sprawling three-story brick building with green-tinted windows. In the front of the building was a well-kept lawn with a pathway that led to a bus shelter on the boulevard. At the back of the building, beside the parking lot, there was a large garden with a white cobblestone path lined with wooden benches which rambled through flowerbeds and foliage. The garden was surrounded by trees and nicely trimmed hedges.

There were two sides to Albion Villa, each with its own entrance. The south side housed the senior retirement residence. People who lived in the south side of Albion Villa were still mobile and cognizant. This lucky bunch lived in their own apartments, each with its own kitchen, bathroom and lock on the door. They had their own furniture, their own food, did their own shopping, and filled their days with group daytrips to Niagara Falls and the botanical gardens in chartered buses. South side people enjoyed a life of independence. On the north side of Albion Villa was the nursing home. This provided twenty-four hour care. In the north side were the dementia and Alzheimer's patients, the incontinent, and the terminally ill. There were no locks on any of the doors in the north side, no walking away, and no daytrips. Over time, if they were to live long enough, everyone eventually moved from the south side to the north side. But Josh's father never saw the south side of Albion Villa. He was put directly into the nursing facility the day he was released from the hospital.

As Edith Piaf sang one of her few happy songs to an accordion and a jingling piano, Glenn pulled the Lexus into Albion Villa's parking lot. He drove slowly over the many speed bumps and maneuvered the car backwards into a spot near the door with ease. He turned off the car, silencing Edith Piaf's cheerful French tune.

Glenn turned to Josh. "Ready?"

For a moment, Josh just sat in the passenger seat and let Glenn look at him. *Am I ready*? He exhaled.

"Yes, I'm ready" he finally said. He grabbed the plastic bag lying on the floor, stepped out of the car and shut the door. *Yes, I'm ready.*

Josh had thought about putting his father into a nursing home in Toronto, to have him closer. However, his father, not having yet deteriorated to the point at which he was now, had steadfastly refused to leave Hamilton. "I want to stay near my family and friends," he had said. What family and friends? Josh wanted to ask, but didn't. Both of Josh's half-brothers had moved to British Columbia years ago, and most of his father's family was dead. *Dead and gone.* They had all thought they would be raptured into heaven in a glorious white light by the hand of God. But instead they died like his Aunt Peggy, gagging on her own bile in the cancer ward of Hamilton General or, Uncle Andy, who they found face down on the cold bathroom tile when he tried to get off the toilet without an attendant. And then there was Aunt Sue, who didn't even know who God was when she wandered out of the nursing home on a rainy day. They found her, sitting with her legs crossed and her hands folded ladylike on her knee in a bus shelter on King Street the next morning dead, wearing only one slipper and a soiled nightgown.

Josh and Glenn entered the north side doors of Albion Villa and found Josh's father sitting alone on a bench in the hallway. He wore a faded blue U.N. peacekeepers beret and was leaning forward on his dark wooden cane. Below his beret, his white hair, which he had been refusing to cut, now hung in long thin strands over the shoulders of a heavy red plaid shirt. The navy blue suspenders he wore attached with silver clips to his pants, the trousers to his black suit, which were too large for him now. Josh wondered where his father found the gray slippers he wore.

"Hi Dad," Josh said.

His father looked up at him and scowled. "I've been waiting here for you all day," he said.

"I said we'd be here at noon," Josh said.

"I've been waiting all day."

"Where are your glasses, Dad?" Josh asked.

His father shrugged his shoulders. "What glasses?"

"Hello, Ted." Glenn said. "How are you doing?"

Josh's father looked up at Glenn, squinted, and then smiled. He always smiled when he saw Glenn. Josh wondered if Glenn reminded his father of someone from his past, his own father, or an old friend. Or maybe my boyfriend just reminds him of Henry Fonda or José Ferrer or Evil Kenevil—who the hell knows? Josh was done trying to figure out what was going on in his father's mind.

"Hello, there!" Josh's father said to Glenn.

Glenn held out his hand. Josh's father took Glenn's hand and attempted to rise from the bench as he shook it.

"No, Ted" Glenn said. "You don't need to get up."

Josh's father sat back down on the bench with a grunt, using Glenn's hand for support. "I've been dressed and waiting for you all day," he said.

"We bought you some new pants," Josh said. He held out the plastic shopping bag toward his father.

"I don't need pants," his father said ignoring the bag in front of him.

"Well you might need them some day," Josh said. He tossed the bag beside his father on the bench.

Josh's father sniffed, reached up and straightened his beret. The end of his nose had begun to droop over his upper lip and the weight loss had created extra skin that hung down around his mouth and off his neck. He looked older than his seventy-three years.

A nurse wearing a black leather bomber jacket over her uniform walked toward them holding a cigarette and a lighter in her fist. She stopped between Josh and Ted. She was about thirty years old, a short pretty Asian woman with a large lower belly and small breasts. Her long straight black hair was pulled back into a ponytail and she had bandages on three of her fingers. Josh had never seen this nurse before.

"Hello," she said. Her sing-song voice sounded too perky for the north side of Albion.

"Hi," Josh said. He smiled widely, trying to match her perkiness.

She looked down at Josh's father. "Are these your sons, Mr. Moore?" She raised her voice slightly.

Josh's father nodded.

"That's nice," she said rolling her cigarette in her hand. She had a strong Hamilton accent with its New York State influence. God, it took me years to get rid of that accent, Josh thought. *I'm go'n to the store to buy sam sacks... you know, sacks fer my feet.*

"We're just heading out for brunch," Glenn said.

"Oh, isn't that nice!" she said loudly.

"Yeah," Josh said. "But my Dad's hair is looking pretty long. The last time I was here I asked if someone could have it cut."

"Well, we did try our best but he wouldn't let us cut it. Would you Mr. Moore!"

"It makes him look like a lunatic," Josh said.

"Actually," the nurse said, "I don't think it looks that bad at all... and we keep it clean for him." She reached down and flipped a lock of Josh's father white hair behind his shoulder. "We keep it clean, don't we Mr. Moore!" He grimaced and swatted her hand away. "But if you really want it cut, I suppose we could use more force... but you'll have to speak to the director."

"We wouldn't want to force him," Glenn said.

"Well, we don't want him running around here like mad King George either," Josh said. "I'll speak with the director when we get back from brunch."

"Your father doesn't really like to be touched," the nurse said in a hushed tone.

"No, he never has," Josh said.

The nurse folded her thick arms across her chest. "Is it because of Vietnam?"

"Vietnam?"

"Your father told me he joined the American army and fought in Vietnam."

Josh looked down at his father. "Is that what you told the lady, Dad?" he asked as Glenn stifled a laugh. "No," Josh continued. "He never fought in Vietnam. He was a U.N. peacekeeper in Africa—for the Canadian army."

The nurse put her hands on her wide hips and chuckled. "Shame on you, Mr. Moore. Were you pulling my leg?"

Josh's father sat silently on the bench.

"You're the little trickster, aren't you, Mr. Moore!" she said.

"He sure is," Josh said.

"Anyway..." she said. "You have a nice lunch with your sons, Mr. Moore! And I'll see you when you get back, okay?" She turned, walked out the front doors, and lit her cigarette.

Shirts and Skins

"Come on, Dad," Josh said. "Let's get you ready."

His father leaned forward on his cane as Josh took him by the arm to help him to his feet. "The problem with this place," his father said as he stood up, "is all the fucking Orientals!"

◈

Outside Harry's Pancake House, Josh gently took his father's arm to help him from the car to the restaurant, but his father yanked away his arm, almost losing his balance as he pulled himself away.

"Alright, fine," Josh said putting his hands in the air.

His father adjusted his beret to the side of his head and walked unsteadily on his cane across the parking lot toward the restaurant where Glenn was patiently holding the door open.

As he walked closely behind the old man, Josh saw that the top of his father's adult diaper was sticking out the back of his pants. Josh always made sure that the nurses at Albion Villa put a diaper on his father when he and Glenn took him out (ever since his father had pissed in the backseat of their old Acura during a drive to the beach for fish and chips). Now, not caring that his father didn't like to be touched, Josh reached out and yanked up the back of his father's trousers, covering the white plastic diaper as he walked into the pancake house. *I'll be damned if I let the whole restaurant know he's in a fucking diaper.*

The restaurant smelled like morning, with an inviting scent of smoky bacon, grilling pancakes, and maple syrup. Josh, not hungry a minute ago, was suddenly famished and stood impatiently at the *Please Wait to Be Seated* sign.

The large dining room was packed with two or three generations of families crowed around each wooden table and hummed with voices shouting over the sound of clinking silverware. Josh surmised that since the restaurant was just around the corner from Albion Villa, many of the older folks were likely residents of the south side, taken out for Sunday brunch by their children and grandchildren. Residents of the north side weren't taken out too often.

A woman showed them a table at the back of the restaurant overlooking the parking lot. Josh helped his father sit down and, taking his father's cane, handed it to Glenn on the other side of the table. He didn't want his father taking a swing at the waitress if he got irritated.

"Just coming from church?" the young waitress asked as she hastily handed them menus.

"No," Josh said with a laugh.

"Is she's crazy?" his father asked.

"I'll be back in a minute to take your order," she said. She looked frazzled and had beads of sweat on her forehead and upper lip.

"It's their busy day," Josh said. "Church day." He opened the menu and frowned. His fingers stuck to syrup someone had spilled on the back.

"I think we were lucky to get a table," Glenn said.

Ignoring the chance to make a sarcastic joke, Josh leaned close to his father. "Do you know what you want, Dad?" he asked as he wiped his sticky fingers on his white paper napkin.

His father looked down at the menu and squinted. "What's that?" he asked pointing at a picture of a glass of orange juice on the menu."

"We have to find you your glasses when we get you back," Josh said.

"Do you want some pancakes, Ted?" Glenn asked, "Or how about some eggs and toast?"

"I want a corned beef sandwich..." his father said, "and a beer."

"They don't have that," Josh said. He closed his menu and placed it down in front of him on the table.

Ten minutes later the waitress came back, looking even more frazzled, to take their order. Josh ordered eggs over easy and toast for his father and pancakes and sausage for himself.

"And I'll have the French toast," Glenn said.

"Anything to drink?" the waitress asked.

"Three coffees," Josh said.

"I want beer," his father said.

"Two coffees and a beer," Josh said.

"What kind of beer? We have—"

"It doesn't matter," Josh said, cutting her off. "Just bring him a bottle of anything."

The waitress scribbled their order down on a pad and walked away. Josh took off his glasses and rubbed his eyes. "Dad, why did you start drinking again?"

"What?"

"You quit drinking over thirty years ago."

"You're fucking crazy," his father said. He looked across the table at Glenn, pointed his thumb at Josh and frowned. "He's crazy!"

Glenn stretched out his leg under the table and rested his foot up against Josh's shoe and stroked Josh's ankle. "I don't think one beer will do him any harm," Glenn said.

"No, not now," Josh said. He looked out over the tables through the large room and saw silver-haired grandmothers and bald grandfathers enjoying brunch with their families. They all looked so happy. *So perfectly happy.* Beside him, his father stared down at the silverware on the table.

Later, after the waitress had returned with their food, Josh's father sat chewing slowly on a piece of buttered toast and staring intently across the table at Glenn. If being stared at as he ate bothered Glenn, Josh thought, he didn't show it.

"Are you an Injun?" Josh's father finally asked Glenn.

"No," Glenn said. He swallowed his French toast and wiped his mouth with a napkin, "I'm not, Ted."

"You look Injun," his father said.

"Glenn is Irish, Dad," Josh said.

"My wife's Injun," Josh's father said. He dropped his toast on the tabletop and picked up his bottle of beer.

"Indian," Josh said. "Mom was Indian, not Injun." He cut a piece of sausage, slid it into a puddle of syrup and stuffed it into his mouth. "Eat your eggs, Dad."

"Where's she now?" his father asked.

Josh laid down his knife and fork on the side of his plate with a clank and picked up his mug of coffee.

"Where's Gloria?" His father turned his head from left to right, searching around him like he had just misplaced his umbrella.

"She's out shopping," Josh said. He looked out the window at their silver Lexus sitting in the parking lot, "with Aunt Doris."

"Doris! Shit," his father spat out. "All those two do when they're together is spend my money and bitch about me."

Josh gulped down the last of his coffee and frowned. It was bitter.

His father looked feebly across the table at Glenn. "Where's Gloria?" he asked.

Josh bit the inside of his lip. He had stopped telling his father that she was dead. It would just upset him—and then he would forget again.

"She's shopping," Glenn said. "She'll be back soon."

"Oh... okay," his father. He finished his beer and put the bottle down on the table beside Josh's left hand. He gasped. "What happened to your finger there?" he asked.

Josh sighed. "It was crushed in a machine a million years ago," he said.

"Oh no!" his father said.

"Yeah, well, what can you do?" Josh asked distantly. He made a fist with his left hand to hide his finger.

"Let me tell you something," his father said. He pointed his thin white index finger at Josh's chest. "The company will take everything a working man's got. First they'll take your fingers and then your hand... then your whole goddamn arm. They'll take *everything*—if you let them."

"Alright, Dad," Josh said. He looked over the crowd for their waitress. It was time to get the bill. "What do you think the chances are of that waitress ever coming back?"

"I don't care what they take from me, Josh," his father continued. "But they can't have my son." He stared out over the restaurant and began to sing softly to himself in an old rusty voice. "*Arise ye workers from your slumber... arise ye prisoners of want... something something... something... and at last ends the age of can't.*"

Josh grinned.

His father stopped singing and stared at Josh, as if searching for the words in his son's face. *"Away with all your superstitions..."* he continued, *"servile masses, arise, arise! We'll... change... the old condition, and.... and... and spurn the dust to win the prize!"*

How, Josh wondered, could his father remember that goddamn song when he didn't even remember that his own wife was dead? Somewhere in his father's brain a little path, bypassed all the Bible passages and years of dark seclusion, and opened to a long forgotten fragment of memory that had been hiding this old song. Josh looked into his father's eyes; they had suddenly become greener as an old wildness and clarity returned.

"What's that he's singing?" Glenn asked.

"It's *The Internationale.*" Josh said, never taking his eyes off his father.

"Is that a hymn?"

"No," Josh answered. "It's an old socialist song."

Josh watched his father, hoping his father would remember the rest. His father frowned, straining to grab one more handful of lyrics for the past. But the moment of clarity was fading. The little path closed.

"How does the rest go?" his father asked breathing heavily. "I can't remember it..." He shook his head and his face turned pink in frustration. He looked over at Josh, the wildness and clarity in his eyes now gone. He stared back down at the table.

Josh cleared his throat. *"So comrades come rally...and the last fight let us face..."* he sang.

"Yes," his father said. He smiled and nodded.

"The Internationale," Josh continued, *"unites the human race."*

"Yes! Yes!" His father laughed and rocked with enthusiasm in his seat.

And then together, in the middle Harry's Pancake House, Josh and his father sang together for the first time in thirty years. *"So comrades come rally for the last fight let us face! The Internationale unites... the human race!"* Josh began to tap the rhythm of the anthem on the side of the table with his fingers as they repeated the chorus again. *"So comrades come rally, and the last fight let us face! The Internationale unites... the human race!"*

Around the pancake house, families looked up from their plates of bacon and eggs and across the table, Glenn tapped his knife and fork on his plate and hummed along. Then, overcome with a feeling of affection, Josh reached over to his father, removed his old beret, and kissed the top of his head. The nurse was right, his long hair doesn't look half-bad, Josh thought.

An hour later, Josh and Glenn were driving their new silver Lexus back to Toronto as Edith Piaf sang about her broken heart.

"You two made quite the duet," Glenn said.

Josh smiled. "Just when I think there's no hope... the old son-of-a-bitch goes and surprises me."

"It was really sweet, actually," Glenn said.

"Hey... I don't *do* sweet," Josh said smiling.

"Liar," Glenn said.

Inside Josh's tweed jacket, his phone rang. He fished it out of his breast pocket and checked the phone number on the display. He hesitated and then flipped open the phone.

"Hello?" Josh said.

"Josh, when are you coming to see me? I'm all dressed... and I've been waiting for you all day...."

◈

That night after dinner, Josh and Glenn sat together on their sofa watching television in the dark. Another weekend was over.

"Do you have a busy week ahead?" Josh asked.

"Not too busy," Glenn said. He pulled Josh close to him. "What about you?"

"I've got a meeting with management tomorrow morning," Josh said. He yawned and laid his head on Glenn's chest. "Hey," Josh said looking up and smiling, "this is my shirt!" He tugged gently at the front of Glenn's white cotton shirt.

"Do you want it back?" Glenn asked as he tenderly caressed Josh's back with his fingertips.

"Maybe later," Josh said. He put his head back down and enjoyed the motion of Glenn's chest as he breathed. I really should do a load of laundry tonight, Josh thought, but for the moment, he was perfectly happy where he was.

"Remind me to go to the hardware store and pick up some furnace filters this week," Glenn said. "And light bulbs."

But Josh didn't hear him. He was already asleep.

Acknowledgments

Many people have helped in the creation of this book. First of all, thank you to Nino Ricci and Lauren B. Davis, my mentors at The Humber School for Writers, for their advice and guidance during the writing of *Shirts and Skins* and for continuing support of me and my novel long after the courses were finished. Thank you to writer Michael Rowe for taking the time to read the manuscript before publication and providing me feedback and inspiration. I would also like to thank the Toronto Arts Council for their financial support in the creation of *Shirts and Skins*. Finally, a big thank you to my husband Sean, without whose support, reassurance, patience and encouragement, this book would never have been written.

About the Author

Jeffrey Luscombe was born in Hamilton, Ontario, Canada. He holds a BA and MA in English from the University of Toronto. He attended The Humber College School for Writers where he was mentored by writers Nino Ricci and Lauren B. Davis. He has had fiction published in *Chelsea Station, Tupperware Sandpiper, Zeugma Literary Journal,* and *filling Station Magazine.* In 2010 he was shortlisted for the Prism International Fiction Prize. He was a contributor to the anthology *Truth or Dare* (Slash Books Inc. 2011). He lives in Toronto with his husband Sean. *Shirts and Skins* is his first novel.

319/P

9 781937 627003

CPSIA information can be ob
Printed in the USA
LVOW06s2359270814

401254LV00005B